FIGURE

— OF —

SPEECH

FIGURE

— OF —

SPEECH

Kasha Thompson

WEBSTER AVENUE PUBLISHING
LINCOLN, CA

FIGURE OF SPEECH

Paperback ISBN: 979-8-9862679-0-6

Copyright © 2022 by Kasha Thompson

All rights reserved. No part of this book may be reproduced in any form or by any electronic or mechanical means, including information storage and retrieval systems, without written permission from the author, except for the use of brief quotations in a book review.

This book is a work of fiction. Names, characters, places, and incidents are the product of the author's imagination or are used fictitiously. Any resemblances to actual events, or persons, living or dead, is strictly coincidental.

This edition published and arranged by Webster Avenue Publishing.

Printed in the United States of America. First Edition July 2022

Character Illustrations: Beka Giorgadze

Cover Design: Fiaz Ahmed Irfan AKA Dezinir99

Editing: Likely Write Editing

CONTENT NOTE

Please note Figure of Speech discusses topics which could potentially trigger certain audiences. Some readers may consider the following as spoilers.

- Coarse language: Moderate
- Sex: Several sexually explicit scenes
- Politics: Reference to politics and political parties
- Sexual Harassment: Briefly referenced

CHAPTER ONE

EVEN AFTER SPENDING THE ENTIRE WEEKEND CRAMMING FOR this interview, my stomach was rising and cresting like a storm-stricken sea. It made sense; it wasn't every day I was called for a job interview at the White House. After giving my name at the gate and going through the metal detector that flashed and buzzed upon entry, causing the Secret Service to fear a potential domestic terrorist threat, here I was sitting in the outer office just steps from the Oval, like my name was Olivia Pope.

Although my face appeared relaxed and unbothered, internally I was second-guessing my interview outfit choice. I'd settled on a monochromatic navy pant suit. Normally, subtle was not my style, I had a penchant for bold, bright colors with classic accent pieces, but this was an interview with the President of the United States, his chief of staff, and director of communications. I thought it best to save the fuchsia and orange for when I landed the job. Besides, I wanted my experience to stand out, not my impeccable fashion sense.

Mumbling softly under my breath, I practiced my interview notes for the two hundred sixty-fourth time, going over highlights from my resume I wanted to remember to mention. My education, my time working with prominent political figures, my strong relationships with dignitaries across the country. *Why is my knee bouncing up and down like this?*

A loud buzz from the desk of the personal secretary to the President, Abigail Monroe, interrupted the talking points swirling in my head. My hands were cold and clammy as if all the blood in my body seemed to make a b-line to my heart, causing it to kick into overdrive. Casting my eyes to the ceiling, with its centuries-old crown molding and raised fleur-de-lis, I said a quick prayer to God, Mother Earth, and Lady Karma, in hopes all would join forces like the Avengers to help me nail this interview.

Not only had I sacrificed sleep this past weekend brushing up on facts and statistics, but I had been preparing for this opportunity my entire career. Working in the White House had never been an if for me; it had always been a when. Even so, when I received the call a week ago asking me to interview for the newly vacant Press Secretary position, I was shocked. If you watched any of the news outlets, the abrupt exit of the former Press Secretary was all political talking heads were discussing. President Elmsworth hadn't been in office a month and he already had his first Washington scandal.

Abigail, the petite secretary, stood up with a friendly smile. "They're ready for you now, Ms. Bennett."

As I rose from the chair, I tried to inconspicuously wipe my sweaty palms on the side of my tailored pants. Satchel purse and wool camel coat in hand, I followed her through the open door.

"Good morning," Abigail addressed the room. "Clover Bennett is here for your ten a.m. appointment."

Inhaling courage, I walked forward, hand extended, ready to put on a show. After shaking hands with Chief of Staff Ross Gimble and Director of Communications Lisa Prince, I found myself in front of the newly elected President, Theodore Elmsworth. His handshake was what you would expect from the leader of the free world, firm grip, unwavering eye contact with a cool unaffected smile.

"Please, have a seat," Mr. Gimble said, pointing to one of the couches.

It was all I could do to not look like a fan as I took in the magnitude of the Oval Office. I'd done some cool things, back-packed through Europe, jumped out of a plane, sunbathed naked on the beaches of St. Barth, but this by far topped them all. This was the same office where John John hid under the desk from his father, President Kennedy. The same office where President Clinton had sexual relations with that woman. The same office where Malia and Sasha laughed with their dad, Barrack.

"Thank you for coming in on such short notice," Ross Gimble said.

"Not a problem." I smiled, silently reminding myself to make eye contact, be breezy, and continue to smile. For some reason, I always forgot to smile when I was nervous, which strangers took as me being angry or standoffish.

"So, can you tell us a little about yourself?" Director Lisa Prince asked, clicking her gold pen, ready to take notes.

"I have a bachelor's degree from Stanford University and a master's degree from Georgetown ..."

My mind shifted to autopilot as I rattled off my accomplishments and experience. As I talked, I sensed the President's steely eyes on me. His rich brown face wore a neutral, unmarked expression. If he liked what he heard, I couldn't tell. The questions were coming fast and furious. Questions about my experience turned to questions about my personal life and social media activity.

"Can you please explain your tweet from four years ago in which you said, and I quote, 'Breaking news. All men are trash. Your daddy, your pop-pop, your uncle Reggie. Hot, steaming piles of trash. Thank you for coming to my Ted Talk,'" Gimble asked, removing his reading glasses from the brim of his pointy nose.

A hard gulp jerked my chin, glancing at President Elmsworth, whose expression remained unchanged. "I meant exactly what I said. I don't believe the tweet requires an explanation. It's pretty self-explanatory and accurate."

With my eyes locked on Chief Gimble, I thought, *I said what I said. Men are trash, and that includes you.* To be fair, I wrote that tweet after a messy break-up that took months to officially end because I was stuck on stupid and kept taking him back.

Next, Gimble pulled up a series of photos and videos on his iPad from my social media pages. All of the photos were racy, me in low-cut, skin-tight outfits, me with three cups of brown liquor in my hand. A video of me twerking at a party in the Hamptons.

"What do you say to this?" Gimble asked.

Expelling a single-note laugh, I handed back the iPad. "If you're looking for a Press Secretary with no social media presence, then I'm not your candidate. If you want a Press Secretary who can field tough questions, pivot on her feet, and ensure the President's narrative is not only conveyed but trusted ... then I'm your woman."

The room fell silent as Gimble and Prince scribbled notes on their notepads. The President was reclining on the couch across from me, a passive voyeur, stroking his beard. He appeared completely unamused by the interview process. I was surprised when his secretary gave me the heads up that President Elmsworth would be in attendance. Surely, he had better things to do than participate in the interviewing process for the next Press Secretary.

"What can you tell me about the Honey Pot?" Director Prince asked.

Damn, they were more thorough than my gynecologist. President Elmsworth leaned forward in his seat.

"I worked at the Honey Pot in college. I was a bartender. Fully clothed. I made great tips and I'm proud to say I have no student loan debt." I smiled.

Most interviews didn't dig this deep. It had been over fourteen years since I worked at the Honey Pot. But I wasn't surprised; this was the White House, after all. No administration wanted to hire someone who could end up being a liability. The fact that they knew all my deepest darkest secrets and called me in for an interview anyway was a good sign. First rule to remember when interviewing for a government job is don't lie. If you lie, you're toast, because nine times out of ten, they already know and if they don't know, they will find out.

After a few additional hypothetical scenario questions, the interview was over. Air eked from my lungs, a wave of relief washing over me. Although I was the picture of composure, my underarms were like swimming pools.

"We have a few more interviews but we anticipate making a decision within the next couple of weeks," Director Prince instructed.

"Thank you so much for your consideration." Flashing one last pearly smile, I reached for my bag and coat.

"Gimble, can you clear the room? I'd like to have a word with Ms. Bennett." President Elmsworth lifted his hand, shooing the others away, all while never taking his magnetic brown eyes off me.

A forceful swallow worked my throat as I tried to maintain my poise, lowering myself back to the couch. Chief of Staff Gimble hissed out a breath, casting an irritated side eye in my direction before leaving the room with Director Prince shutting the door behind them.

Leaning forward on the cream brocade couch, the corners of the President's mouth ticked upward. "I'm sorry for all the formality. It kind of comes with the pomp and circumstance."

"No, it's completely fine, Mr. President." I crossed my legs, trying to pretend it was perfectly normal having a chat in the Oval with the commander in chief.

"It's weird to hear you call me that," he said, scrunching his chiseled face.

"Well, that's your name now." My nervous laughter sprinkled the air.

Elmsworth stood and my head inched upward. It was like

trying to register the grandeur of a sequoia tree. At six feet four inches, the task was daunting.

"Woman, come over here and give me a hug."

Scrambling to my feet, I walked into his massive arms, squeezing him tight. Briefly resting my head on his chest, I was surrounded by the scent of smoldering birch wood, rich and earthy like nature's incense.

"How's the fam? Ms. Sylvia?" he asked, capturing my hands in his strong, smooth grasp.

"My mom is doing well. She wants me to bring her back one of those little M&M boxes with the White House logo on it."

Pulling my hands from his, I took a step back, regaining my personal space. The President and I had a history, but it had been a few years since we last talked so I was pleasantly surprised by the warm reception.

"I think we can do better than that," he said with a wink. Walking over to the Resolute Desk, he opened the center drawer, pulling out an object. "How's this?" he asked, handing me a black and gold pen with the official White House seal emblazoned on the side.

"You know she's gonna post this on Facebook, right," I teased, impressed by the weight of the pen.

"Tell her to tag me." He gave my arm a gentle pat. "How have you been?"

"Good, you know me, working my ass off, but loving it." I tensed as his eyes dropped to scan my posterior. "I'd ask you the same question, but it's pretty clear that things are going really well for you."

The President flashed his signature smile. The type of smile that could win over votes, the type of smile that made you want to believe change was possible, the type of smile that made you want to push your panties to the side.

"I guess I'm just lucky."

"Don't try to be modest. You're not very good at it." I wagged my finger in his direction. "You and I both know you worked hard for this. You tapped into something that people were missing. Some kinda deep-seated desire—"

"Desire, that sounds interesting."

With a roll of my eyes, I hoped to push past his words and the streak of heat now traveling across my body. "You know what? I'm not doing this with you."

"No, I'll be good. Please continue." He sat on the edge of his desk.

With a tight-lipped huff, I resumed my thought. "People were disillusioned and had lost faith in government and were tired of fighting for a change that never seemed to materialize. You spoke to that and made people feel heard. So, it's no wonder you're standing in the Oval today."

"So basically, people voted for me off of vibes?" he teased.

"Umm, pretty much. Studies have shown that when it comes to voting for politicians, it's less about policies and more about personality."

"Yeah, well personality can only get you so far. Eventually, you have to produce. 'Cause those vibes can morph into vitriol real quick."

Gathering my coat and bag, I made my way to the door, not wanting to overstay my welcome. "Thank you for thinking of me for this position."

"Actually, that wasn't me, that was all Prince."

"Oh ... OK." It was silly to assume the President of the United States would recommend me for a job. I'm sure he had more pressing matters to attend to; minor staff shake-ups were the least of his worries.

"I meant your reputation precedes you. Your name was atop a very short list."

"Well, thank you again for taking the time to meet with me," I said, backing toward the door. "Oh, and congratulations on all this."

This was the first opportunity I'd had to commend Teddy since his resounding win. I'd followed his presidential run with rapt attention. From the primary election when his chances were slim to the general election where, oddly enough, people once again considered him a long shot.

But I recognized it from the moment he stepped on that stage in Prospect Park to announce his run, people were excited. Everything about him was refreshing. The way he talked, his less-than-privileged upbringing, the fact that he overcame some pretty daunting odds to make it to DC. Theodore "Teddy" Elmsworth was a game changer because he questioned every-thing, unwilling to blindly follow the rules.

"Thanks, Clover, it was good seeing you again."

CHAPTER TWO

"I WANT ALL THE DEETS," DAYSHA SAID, RUBBING HER HANDS together in anticipation of juicy gossip.

Daysha Foster was my best friend. We met five years ago at a nightclub, when she was shit-face drunk crying in the bathroom over some guy. I asked her if she was OK, at which point she told me her life story. We'd been friends ever since.

"There isn't much to tell," I said, carrying plates and napkins to my large upholstered ottoman coffee table.

Daysha threw her hands in the air. "Bitch, you went to the White House. *THE WHITE HOUSE.* There's a lot to tell. Spill everything."

Taking a long sip of my wine, I indulged in the moment. It was nice being the center of attention. Lately, my life had been endless deadlines and meetings. It was rare for me to have the opportunity to share a juicy story, so I was going to milk this cow for as long as I could.

"OK, where should I start?" I asked, sitting on my blue velvet sofa.

"Don't bury the lede. Start with the President." Daysha was an attorney, and if I didn't start talking soon, she would pepper me with questions.

"The President did sit in on my interview and we had a brief moment alone after."

"OK, you suck at telling stories, you're too ... rational. I need you to set the mood," Daysha said, pushing her auburn hair from her eyes. "What did he smell like?"

Ugh, I was losing her. I better turn up the wow factor. Closing my eyes, it was like being transported back into the room and his embrace. "He smelled like a forest, like fresh-cut wood and moss. Crisp and clean." Opening my eyes, it was obvious from the open-mouthed smile on her face that Day approved.

"So, you were alone with him? How'd that happen?"

"He asked his staffers to leave us alone." I jerked my shoulders into a shrug.

"And he remembered you?"

I gave her a pout. "How could he forget me? I mean..." I ran my hands over the space in front of my body for emphasis.

President Elmsworth and I had worked together ten years ago on his senatorial run. After he won the New York Senate seat, I stayed on as one of his many congressional staffers for a little over two years.

"It's just, you know how people like to act once they get a little taste of power." Daysha reached for a wedge of cheese from the overpriced Whole Foods charcuterie platter.

"A little? He's the leader of the free world. There's nothing little about that."

I was protective of Teddy; he really was one of those aspirational politicians that inspired others to make a difference. He went from the courthouse as a prosecutor to The Capitol as a senator and made it all the way to the White House. As a Black man, he was expected to be twice as good as his contemporaries, blah, blah, blah, you know the rest.

"What did you two talk about exactly?" Daysha asked, with a raised eyebrow.

"He asked about my mom." I grabbed a plate, loading it up with salami, cheese, and fruit.

"Your mom?"

"Yeah, he's met her once or twice," I said, popping a grape in my mouth.

"Hold up. Why do I get the impression that you haven't been fully honest about you and El Presidente?" Daysha said, jumping up from the white throw rug, grabbing the bottle of wine from the kitchen counter.

"Trust me, there's nothing to tell."

All there was between me and Teddy was some innocent flirting and a very brief drunken kiss. My phone pinged with an incoming message.

Seth: Hey.

Me: Hey!

Seth: Can I stop by tonight?

Me: I'd like that.

Seth: Excellent. See you around ten.

Me: See ya.

"Uh-uh, who's that? Who's got you cheesing at your phone like that?" Daysha's brash voice interrupted my vibe.

"Girl, it's just Seth." I chucked my phone back on the sofa cushion next to me.

"Seth? Hmph." Daysha frowned.

"Don't do Seth like that. He's a nice guy."

"He's corny," Daysha said, with a click of her tongue.

I scoffed out a laugh. She was right, he was a little goofy, but he made up for it in other ways. "He's not corny in the bedroom."

Daysha let out a sound of disgust. "I thought you were going to end ... whatever it is you two are doing?

"I am ... I mean, I plan to."

"But?"

"Look, you don't remove a player from the roster until you have a replacement."

"Oh, so you're just taking one for the team. Is that right?"

"I'm just making sure my next move is my best move."

Day shook her head with a pained expression. "Girl, you are gonna mess around and end up in a whole ass relationship with old boy."

"No, this isn't a relationship. This is sex. And Seth knows that."

"Whatever, if you like it, I love it." She waved her hand, dismissing all Seth talk. "Anyway, I'm your girl and I need you to be completely honest with me."

"OK ..."

"Have you fucked the President?" Daysha pointed her long, manicured fingernail at me.

"No, we were friendly acquaintances at best. Colleagues, really."

"I ain't never had an acquaintance meet my momma," Daysha said, tilting her head to the side and looking me in my eyes like she was sizing me up.

"OK, can we talk about the actual White House now?" I was ready to change the subject.

"Yes." Daysha snapped in the air. "Give me opulence, give me wealth, give me historical dynasty." She put on an exaggerated British accent.

"OK, I walked down this long hall and boom, a huge portrait of John Quincy Adams." I flared my arms for dramatic effect.

"Who? Girl, don't nobody care about no John Q. Where were the portraits of Michelle and dem?"

SITTING on the edge of my four-poster bed wrapped in a damp towel, I lathered my body in lotion. Seth was on his way and I wanted to provide an excuse for him to remove my clothes the moment he laid eyes on me. And my well-toned, moisturized legs were just the bait I needed.

I met Seth Wooten at a DC social event a few months back. He worked for the American News Broadcasting Station as an investigative journalist. The event was stuffy and boring, but Seth was down to earth and funny in a knock-knock joke kinda way, so I gave him my number.

We struck up a strictly platonic friendship, but eventually platonic turned sexual. We both agreed a friends with benefits arrangement could be mutually beneficial. He and I were both workaholics, which left us little time to cultivate romantic relationships. Seth was my friend, a friend who let me sit on his face every once in a while.

Unfortunately, Daysha was right. While I enjoyed our no-strings-attached arrangement, Seth was clearly interested in more. I, on the other hand, had my fill of romantic relationships. I'd wasted entirely too much time on men who didn't deserve my attention. And I can admit when I fall in love, I can be a little crazy.

Like, if I call and you don't answer your phone, I'm going to assume you want to see me in person. If I find another woman's number in your contact list and it's not work related, I may bleach your clothes. Yes, I have stalked a boyfriend's social media page and could tell you what pictures he was liking and who was liking his. It took a lot of work to maintain that type of energy, so eventually, I decided to hit pause on the relationship stuff and just pursue what was really important to me, and the one thing I could completely control, my career.

Standing in my modest walk-in closet, I scanned through the clothes searching for something that would send Seth into overdrive. I settled on a simple coral tank dress and smoothed it over my curves. The goal was to give an air of effortless beauty; meaning, I wanted to look like I'd done nothing when in fact I had done all the things right down to the no makeup, make-up look I mastered after watching several YouTube videos. The buzz of the doorbell caused my insides to leap, excited for the leg quivers that would surely follow.

Swinging the door open, I posed seductively, making sure Seth took in my curvaceous form. I didn't spend all that money on a personal trainer for nothing.

"Hey, beautiful," Seth said with that deep, sexy voice of his.

Forget Daysha, Seth was fine, in a nerdy, bookworm kinda way.

"Hello." I smiled back as he leaned in to kiss my lips. I was ready to drag him to the bedroom, but he raised a bottle in his hand. "What's this?"

"It's champagne. It's cheap champagne, but still." He raked his fingers through his messy brown hair.

I frowned. The cheap stuff gave me gas. Stepping aside so he could come in, I asked, "What are we celebrating?"

"This is because you had an interview at the White House and you're about to land the job," Seth said, tossing his parka on my side chair.

"Let's give those eggs a chance to hatch first, shall we?"

Seth's blue eyes sparkled as he planted kisses along my neck. "Last time I checked, you were the smartest, most qualified, and capable woman I have ever slept with."

"You forgot beautiful," I reminded him, tugging on the hair at the back of his neck.

"How could I forget beautiful, and sexy." Seth pulled me closer, trailing kisses along my jaw line before returning to my lips. "So, did you meet the big guy?"

"I did. He stayed the entire interview, even though I'm sure he had better things to do."

"I can't wait to tell people I have an informant in the White House." Seth's hand kneaded the tense muscles in my neck.

"I gotta get the job first," I muttered between kisses.

"Are you kidding? It was a lock the minute you walked into the room."

Smiling against his lips, I said, "We'll drink the champagne if I get the job."

"We will drink the champagne when you get the job," Seth whispered.

Grabbing my ass, he lifted me upward until my legs were securely wrapped around his waist. I nibbled on his earlobe as he walked toward my bedroom. Forget all the unnecessary pleasantries and Seth's interest in my career path, this was what I wanted. And if the bulge in Seth's jeans was any indication, he wanted it too.

CHAPTER THREE

"Good morning, Clover."

"Morning, Alan. How was your night?"

"Uneventful, per usual. Netflix and pill," Alan said, following me to my office.

Confusion shadowed my smile. "Netflix and pill?"

"Yeah, Netflix and my pillow." Alan cracked up.

I shed a laugh at Alan's joke. At twenty-six, my assistant was constantly teaching me new things. Helping me stay socially relevant.

"What did I miss yesterday?" I asked, setting my purse on my desk and removing my coat.

I'd been away from the office in meetings all day. Much of which was spent eagerly checking my phone. A practice that had become a habit since my White House interview a few weeks ago. Every time my phone dinged, chimed, or vibrated, I was hopeful it would be them, but so far it was radio silence. Maybe they'd decided to go in a different direction. I'd admit I was starting to worry, but I had to remind myself everything moves at a snail's pace in DC.

"Gurrl?" Alan raised an eyebrow and closed my office door.

"Uh oh, what?" I hung my wool coat on the coat rack.

There was always some kind of drama at McCaskill, Ford, and Huntington. As the company's public relations and communications officer, they kept me busy. Whether it was a partner being accused of sexual harassment or office staff losing their damn minds, I was always cleaning up some mess.

"Amanda." Alan tilted his head to the side.

"Yeah?"

"She quit."

"Shut up." I leaned back in my chair.

"Yes ma'am. She went all Jerry Maguire on their asses. Screamed at Cooper McCaskill Jr., telling him to go fuck himself." Alan seemed to delight in retelling the story.

"Damn, not quiet, mousey Amanda."

"Well, apparently, Miss Amanda was secretly having an affair with Coop," Alan said, examining his nails.

"Wow, that's crazy," I exclaimed, shaking my head.

I already knew that; it was part of my job to know what was happening before anyone else. A little over a month ago I had a sit-down intervention with Coop Jr. I told him he needed to cut things off with Amanda. Their relationship was a liability, but that arrogant fool didn't listen.

"I'ma need all the details at lunch."

"You better be prepared for some piping hot tea," Alan said, headed for the door.

"Just how I like it." I smiled as Alan exited my office, closing the door behind him.

A closed door didn't offer any privacy; the office building was made of glass. So, you had a bird's eye view of everyone. We called it the glass palace. I powered up my computer, hoping to tackle the emails that had accumulated in my inbox, when my cell phone rang from an unknown number. *This better not be a telemarketer*, I sighed.

"Hello?"

"Hi, can I speak to Clover Bennett?" the slightly familiar voice on the other end replied.

"This is she," I said tentatively, because these telemarketers stay trying it.

"Hello, Clover, this is Lisa Prince from the White House Communications Department."

I let out an audible gasp, unable to hide my surprise. "Yes, hello, Ms. Prince. How nice to hear from you again."

"Is this a good time to talk?" Lisa asked.

"Yes, of course." I stood, pacing around my office.

"Great, first I want to say we were all so impressed with your interview and your years of experience. So much so that we would like to move forward and offer you the position of Press Secretary at the White House. If you're still interested."

I dropped the phone from my ear and did an impromptu praise dance.

"Hello, Clover, are you still there?" Lisa called from the other end.

"Yes, I'm here. And still interested," I said, unable to suppress the huge smile on my face.

"Oh, thank God. I was afraid you may have changed your mind. So, let me give you some details."

As my new boss rattled off information about background checks, fingerprints, and White House access, all I could think about was Teddy. Had he pressed for this because of our past connection? Don't get me wrong, I knew my worth and when it came to public relations, I was a bad bitch through and through, but still, I wondered if I had President Theodore Elmsworth to thank for this.

"Mommy, where are you?" I yelled.

"In the back room," my mother's muffled voice called.

After work, I drove to my mother's house to deliver the good news. I wanted her to be the first to know.

"Aye, how are you?" I leaned in to kiss her on the cheek.

"Good, good," she said absentmindedly while rummaging through her file cabinet.

"What are you doing?" I asked, looking around the room where documents were scattered across the floor.

"You remember Mr. Johnson?"

I nodded my head, not certain who she was talking about.

"He passed a few months ago and Corina wants to see the funeral program. So, I'm looking for it," my mother said, pulling out a file folder.

I frowned. My mother collected funeral programs. She didn't even have to know the person that passed. If I attended a funeral, I better grab a program for her.

"Hmm, good luck with that."

"What are you doing over here on a Tuesday night?"

I smiled. "I have some news to share."

My mother slid her reading glasses to the tip of her nose. "Are you pregnant?"

"No, Mommy. Why would you ask that?"

My mother shrugged. "I'm just waiting for the day when you come home to me and tell me you are with child."

"Mommy, I'm thirty-five and very responsible."

"You are thirty-five and very single." My mother, the queen of shade.

"Don't even start." I shook my head.

"All I am saying is, maybe you could focus as much time on your personal life as you do your professional one. You are my only child. I would like to have a grandbaby while I am still young enough to play with her."

"Maybe kids aren't in the cards." I pursed my lips.

My mother kissed her teeth and looked at me like I was a slow learner. "You are a beautiful woman; you need to meet a man and start a family."

"So, anyway." I rolled my eyes. She was always begging for a grandchild. I didn't know much about kids, but I did know they required your undivided attention, something I couldn't spare.

"Like I was saying before you womb shamed me, I have exciting news."

"I'm listening," my mother said, flipping through her stack of funeral programs.

"You are looking at the new Press Secretary for the White House." I did a little razzle-dazzle with my hands at the end to really make it sing.

"You got the job?" My mother jumped up, wrapping her arms around me, giving me a tight squeeze as we swayed from side to side. "I am so proud of you. How much does it pay?"

I laughed. That's my mother, all about the Benjamins. "Around a hundred eighty thousand."

My mother turned her nose up. "Ahh, Miss Big Time."

"Oh, that reminds me." I opened my purse and pulled out the pen from Teddy, handing it to my mother. "I saw the President when I interviewed. He asked about you and wanted you to have this."

My mother turned the pen over in her hands. "Is this an official White House pen?" she marveled.

"Yep, and there is more where that came from. Now that I got this job, I'm gonna have you laced with all types of official White House merch.

"Ooo, I can't wait to tell Martha that my baby is working at the White House. Her son just started his residency and she's been rubbing that in my face for months now. But I think White House trumps Georgetown University Hospital."

THE REMAINDER of the evening was spent on the phone with Daysha, who during most of our conversation called me a Bad Ass Boss Bitch. Daysha was like a sister to me and aside from my mother, she was my biggest supporter and hype man. I was already pretty excited before talking to Day but after our conversation, I had to mind my head when walking through doorways because she had hyped me up so well.

As I lay in bed with my headscarf and under-eye mask on, I scrolled through the official Instagram page for the President of the United States, stopping at a photograph of President Elmsworth from the night he was elected. On election night my confidence wavered. I remember thinking there was no way America was going to elect another Black President. I was hopeful but realistic, mindful of what had happened to the world after we elected Obama.

The racism jumped out and showed its ass all up and through this great country of ours. Teddy won the election, but not much had changed. Opposition on the right was still calling him everything but a child of God. And like Obama, they questioned his citizenship and tried to otherize him because of his parents.

My scrolling was interrupted by an incoming call from an unfamiliar number.

"Hello?" I answered.

"Good evening, Lucky."

I'd recognize that cool, relaxed voice anywhere. It was Teddy. He was also the only person who called me Lucky. A nickname he created for me years ago. I cleared my throat, putting on a professional tone.

"Hello, Mr. President," I said, slipping off my headscarf even though he couldn't see me.

"Aht, aht. Don't get all formal with me."

"I'm not being formal, I'm just being respectful."

"Of?"

"Of the office. You're the President now and people need to put respect on your name."

"It's just you and me here, so you can drop the pretenses."

"OK," I said, taking a deep breath.

Before the presidency, Teddy and I used to rib one another all the time. He seemed to believe nothing between us had changed. But when one person was the President and the other was a staffer working for said President things were bound to change. But I was willing to test his theory.

"So, you just gonna ring my phone at booty call hours?" I teased.

"It's eleven o'clock at night. How is that booty call hours? I could see if it was like one in the morning."

"Well, for people who got jobs, eleven is definitely booty call hours."

I could hear him laugh on the other end. "OK, I'll keep that in mind for future calls. I heard you got the Press Secretary job and I wanted to congratulate you."

"Thank you, I appreciate that, Mr. Presi..." I bit my tongue. "Teddy."

"When do you start?"

"I need to give my employer the requisite two weeks' notice, and then there's the background check and live scan, so I would imagine sometime after that."

"Well, I'm looking forward to working with you again," he said.

"You mean *for* you."

We would not be colleagues; he would be my boss, and it would be wise for me to remember my place in the food chain.

"Yes ... for me. Not much has changed. I'm still a bit of an asshole to work for." Teddy's voice was so deep it seemed to vibrate in my ear.

"Trust me, I remember. We used to call you Teddy the Terrible when you were senator."

"Wait, who?"

I bit my lip. I thought he knew his staff coined that pet name for him. "Everybody."

Theodore Elmsworth was a perfectionist and his standards were extremely high. This was one of the things I liked the most about him. He motivated others to give 110 percent because he was also willing to exert the same effort.

"Working in the White House is a different type of animal

from our days at The Capitol. I'm talking early mornings and late nights for everybody. It is all consuming."

"I've never been afraid of a little hard work," I reminded him.

"I have to admit, it'll be nice having a familiar face walking the halls. It was important to me to hire staffers that represented America but more importantly, that repped the neighborhoods you and I grew up in. Politics should be accessible to everyone. Chad from Laguna Beach and Deshawn from Detroit."

"Representation matters," I chimed in.

"It damn sure does. And now little girls all across the country will get to see a Black woman stand up and command the press room every day."

A smile spread across my face. I hadn't even taken the time to consider my place in history or the impact I could have outside the press room.

"Anyway, congratulations. When Prince told me you accepted the offer, I was relieved."

"Why?"

"Because there's finally someone I can be real with. Someone who knows me and who won't judge me if I don't properly enunciate all of my words."

"I doubt anyone is judging you," I said, twirling the end of my braided ponytail.

"Are you kidding me? It's like a fishbowl, everyone watching, waiting for me to fuck up. Most of these assholes in Washington are still wondering how I got here."

"Sounds like buyer's remorse," I teased.

"Never, I'm the President of the United States. I get to write my own ticket." I could hear his love of the adulation in his voice.

"And you get to shape the future of the country, positively impacting the lives of millions of Americans and our partners around the world," I added.

Teddy bellowed with laughter. "Look at you, already spit shining my inarticulate words."

"That's what you pay me the big bucks for, boss."

"Welcome to the West Wing."

His words caused goose pimples to come alive on my flesh. Soon I would have a White House staff badge dangling from my neck. "Good night, Mr. President."

"Sweet dreams, Lucky."

CHAPTER FOUR

I lived fifteen minutes from the White House, so I opted to take the Metro into work on my first day, using the time to get abreast of the important news stories of the day. Locally there was the winter storm that had packed a wallop in Texas, leaving millions without water and power. Internationally it was all about North Korea and nuclear power. As the Press Secretary, it would be my job to speak to these issues and more.

After going through security, I headed to my office, which was a stone's throw away from the Oval Office.

"Good morning," I beamed as I entered my new working space.

"Good morning, Ms. Bennett, I'm Brittany Boyle, your assistant. It's so nice to meet you finally." Brittany was young, in her early twenties, with curly red hair and a face full of freckles.

"First thing's first, call me Clover. It's nice to meet you, Brittany." I looked at her desk stacked with file folders and binders and wondered when those items would find their way to my desk.

"Let me show you to your office."

Brittany walked me to the door at the right of her desk. Opening the office door, she stood back, allowing me to walk inside. The space was bare, just the essentials. Dropping my carryall on the curved desk, I walked over to the windows, pushing back the curtains to allow some light. My office at McCaskill, Ford, and Huntington was ten times nicer, but the proximity to power made up for the lack of visual aesthetic.

"I got you some black coffee from Bean There, Done That. I hope you drink coffee. If not, I can run back and get you something else," Brittany said, fidgeting with the multiple rings on her fingers.

I could understand her apprehension. She had a new boss and she didn't know if I was going to be tolerable or a total bitch. I had similar thoughts about my new boss, Director Prince.

I waved my hand. "Black coffee is fine. Just point me in the direction of the sugar and creamer and I'll be all set."

"Oh, I'll get that for you," Brittney said, hurrying out of the office, not giving me a chance to object.

Looking at my desk, I opened the folder that lay on top. Inside was a welcome packet with a map of the building along with first-day orientation type documents that needed my signature. Next to the packet was my company phone already set up with important contact numbers and emails, all I had to do was change the password.

"Good, you made it," Lisa Prince said, entering my office. "Where's your assistant? She wasn't at her desk."

"Oh, Brittany just ran off to get me some creamer for my coffee." I lifted the grandé cup.

"I know it's your first day, but did you have a chance to look over the day's itinerary?"

I had been here for less than thirty minutes, so that would be a no. I scanned my desk, hoping it was there. "I don't think I have that yet." I smiled.

"It's in your binder. Did Brittany not give you your binder?" Lisa sighed, heading to Brittany's vacant desk. I stood by my door watching her move folders and document stacks aside, hoisting a black binder in her hand. "This is your Bible. It will be updated every night with new information including your daily itinerary of meetings and events that require your attendance."

Taking the binder from Lisa, I ran my hand across the White House seal. The binder made everything seem that much more official.

"You'll be shadowing me for much of the day." I'll let you settle in for a bit. I'll be back in thirty minutes. We have a meeting with the President at nine."

"Understood." I stood in the doorway clutching the Holy Writ.

As Lisa exited my office, Brittany returned with three types of creamers and several sweetener options. "You really shouldn't leave your desk unmanned," Lisa said, with a cold smile before brushing past.

Brittany waited until Lisa was out of the outer office before speaking. "I'm sorry I was gone so long. It won't happen again."

"Oh, no worries. It's all good." I shifted my weight from side to side. "Is she always that ..."

"Yes," Brittany said, offering a knowing smile. Stacking the creamers and sugars on my desk, Brittany headed back to hers.

Plopping into my chair, I powered up the encrypted laptop on my desk. My cell phone dinged. Reaching for it, I could see I already had seventy-three unread emails. I opened my binder and right on top was my itinerary. Meeting with President Elmsworth at nine, introduction to the press shop at ten, meeting with Lisa at one, and a series of briefings to close out my afternoon. Air left my nostrils in a huff as I shut the binder. Maybe I could whittle down some of these emails before my nine o'clock.

"Welcome to the big leagues," I told myself.

Taking a seat next to Lisa, I pulled out my binder and a notepad. The meeting room was filling up quickly with cabinet members and various staffers. The atmosphere was loud and it was difficult to hear Lisa, who was whispering the names of the power players who entered the room. I pretended to listen, but I didn't need any introductions. I knew very well who everyone was and the role they played in the Elmsworth administration.

When President Elmsworth entered the room, the mood shifted. Gone was the idle chatter; the remaining members quickly found their seats. I looked at my phone, it was nine on the dot. Looks like Teddy ran a tight ship.

Unbuttoning his navy-blue suit jacket, Teddy took his seat in the designated chair reserved just for him. "Alright, where are we at with Texas?"

I listened intently as a small, elvish-looking man talked about the devastation across Texas and the people who had literally frozen to death in their homes because of the power outages.

Teddy groaned, "FEMA has been deployed, but the people of Texas are going to need a whole hell of a lot more than that. I'm interested in an emergency aid bill. Texas will need help long after the snow has melted and this storm has passed."

"It will be near impossible to get Republicans to sign off on an aid bill," Gimble, the President's chief of staff, said.

"Listen, I'm all for bipartisan action but if they don't want to move then, we'll do it ourselves. Gibbs, call the Speaker of the House and make sure she understands how important this is. We need every Democrat to fall in line on this one."

"Yes, Mr. President," Gimble said, frantically writing notes on his notepad.

"We will also need to make sure we get in front of this thing before the opposition can poison the well. Do you think you can handle that, Ms. Bennett?" President Elmsworth asked, leaning forward in his chair.

Clearing my throat, I nodded my head. "Yes, I can do that. My first press briefing is tomorrow morning. I will craft a statement outlining your position regarding financial assistance for Texas. That coupled with stories of the suffering of our fellow Americans will make it difficult for our colleagues on the other side of the aisle to reject this bill. Truthfully, they'll probably still vote against it but with the right messaging, we can make it cost them politically."

Teddy's mouth curled into a crooked smile. "That's what I like to hear." Pointing in my direction, he continued, "Everyone, this is Clover Bennett, the new Press Secretary. I think you can see why we hired her."

I gave a wave to the others in the room. This room was like a scene from *Animal Kingdom*. It was important I establish dominance quickly so others knew I was not one to be trifled with. It was all about bold ideas and speaking in a way that made it sound like you knew what you were doing even when you didn't. Never let them see you sweat because the minute you do, it's over and whatever is left of you is getting picked on by the vultures.

AFTER THE COMMUNICATION staff meeting in which I got to meet the rest of my team, Topher and Rebecca, I headed back to my office. I was grateful to have a team and had already assigned Topher, my press assistant, with the task of drafting the statement regarding aid for Texas.

Stopping at Brittany's desk, I asked, "Any messages while I was out?"

"No ... but ... ahh ..."

"Just spit it out," I insisted. If she was going to work for me, she needed to know I believed in getting to the point, no fluff, no stammering. Whatever it was, good or bad, just rip the Band-Aid right off.

"The President is in your office," she whispered.

"Ahh, I see. Great, thanks." Grabbing a Kleenex from the

box on Brittany's desk, I patted down my oily T-zone. With a twist of the brass gold doorknob with engraved foliage circling the edge, I opened my door to find Teddy standing at one of the windows.

"Mr. President. What brings you to my neck of the woods?" I asked, closing the door behind me.

"How's your first day going?" Teddy asked, still staring out the window.

"Busy. Lots of meetings, but that's to be expected."

"You really need to pop some artwork on the walls, brighten this place up." Teddy turned, pointing to my naked walls.

I tossed him the side eye. Did he really expect me to have my office fully decorated on my first day of work?

"You should contact Herschel with Staff Services. He can hook you up with some historical photographs and paintings. Whatever you need. He's great."

"I will keep that in mind, thank you," I said, dropping my binder and notepad on my desk. "How can I help you?"

"I'm taking you to lunch to celebrate your first day."

I gave my Movado wristwatch a quick glance, it was twelve thirty. I would be lucky if I could scarf down a sandwich from the White House mess hall before my one o'clock meeting.

"I can't. I have a meeting at one."

"Reschedule," Teddy said, so matter of fact, like it was just that simple.

"I can't reschedule, it's with Lisa. Kinda important." I shook my head while fending off a laugh at the audacity of this man.

Pulling his phone from his pocket, Teddy tapped on a number in his speed dial. "Hey, Lisa, can you push back your one o'clock meeting with Clover?" I watched as he walked back and forth in my office rubbing his beard. "No, there's no problem. I just wanted to have a quick meeting with her. Yeah ... How about two instead? Great. I'll let her know." Ending the call, Teddy smiled wider than a Cheshire cat. "Grab your bag, loser, we're going to lunch."

GOING to lunch with the President was no subtle feat. There's Secret Service, armored protected vehicles, and the mass of people that show up wherever he goes. As The Beast, the presidential Cadillac limo, rolled up to the local burger shack, there was already press outside waiting. Before exiting the car, I gulped down a steadying breath.

I wasn't a public figure and I didn't relish the attention like Teddy did. It took a certain type of personality to be President and a good part of it was narcissistic. Can you imagine the balls it takes to decide you have the wherewithal to run an entire country? Like many before him, Teddy had balls of steel. I think his mantra was, if not me then who?

Stepping out of The Beast, the mechanical whirring and clicking sound from a hundred camera shutters flicking away at a frantic pace did nothing to calm my nerves. Louder still were members of the press screaming out questions toward President Elmsworth about Texas, Iran, and the Green New Deal. All hoping to get him to say anything on record they could loop repeatedly on the twenty-four-hour news stations. Teddy ignored the fuss, holding the door open for me as I quickly escaped inside the restaurant, thankful to be out of the spotlight.

As the smell of day-old grease and fried cheese hit my nostrils, I was reminded that coffee was the only sustenance I'd had all day. The reeling sensation floating in my head caused by lightheadedness confirmed I was ready to eat a flip flop if it was fried hard enough.

Standing in line, all eyes were on us but Teddy didn't seem to notice. I grabbed one of the laminated menus, looking for the burger section. Teddy hovered behind me, leaning in to read my menu. I stiffened my back, clenching my butt cheeks so our bodies didn't make contact. After ordering at the window, we slid into a booth and waited for our order. We had arrived in the middle of the lunch rush, so any chance at a quiet meal was out of the question.

"Have you been here before?" Teddy asked, grabbing the ketchup bottle, shaking it to make sure it was full.

"I'm from DC, so yes."

"My bad, I forget you're a native. You always give off bougie California vibes."

A frown line appeared between my brows at the intended insult. "No. Chocolate City for life." I poured some sugar into my iced tea. "And I know you're not dumping on California when New York is just as bad."

"What are you talking about? New Yorkers are some of the realest people on the planet."

"Yeah, real rude, real elitist." I sent a stink eye in his direction. "Give a city a statue and they never shut up about it."

"Oh my God, that's it, you're fired." Teddy waved his hands, dismissing me.

"Just like that, huh?"

"Yep, slanderous New York talk will not be tolerated." He pinned his arms over his wide chest.

"Damn." I checked my watch. "Five hours in and I've already been fired."

He gave his shoulders a slight bob. "You had a good run."

The waitress came with our food and I reached for a fry, but Teddy slapped my hand. "Aye, we need to bless the food first."

Dropping the fry, I allowed Teddy to hold my hands as he offered up a quick prayer.

"Lord, thank you for your abundant blessings. Please keep the hands that prepared this food for the nourishment of our bodies. Also, God can you please teach Lucky some manners because she is on a dark path."

I snatched my hands from his. "Amen," I said.

"In Jesus's name, Amen," Teddy laughed.

I popped a fry in my mouth, huffing between chews because

it was piping hot. "So do you take all your new staffers out to lunch on their first day?"

"No, just the pretty ones." Teddy winked at me.

I savored a big bite of my bacon cheeseburger, washing it down with iced tea before responding, "I hope that was a joke."

Theodore Elmsworth was single. He was the first President in over one hundred years to enter the office as a bachelor. His single status made him fodder for tabloid media with endless speculation about his dating life. He had done a good job of flying under the radar when he ran for office, but Teddy was a ladies' man and it was just a matter of time before the press found what they were looking for.

"I wanted to make sure your first day was more than boring meetings and staffer introductions."

"White House meetings and boring? Not possible." The corner of my mouth sloped into a grin.

"You have a point. I was shocked when I received the debrief on space beings," Teddy said, squeezing ketchup over his fries.

"Wait ... come again." I leaned in closer.

"No. I've said too much already." His mouth twitched as he tried to stifle a laugh.

Grabbing three fries, I shoved them into my mouth.

"Be careful of your fingers," he teased.

"I'm starving," I mumbled, with a mouth full of food.

"I can see that."

Sitting back, I took a gulp of my iced tea. For the first time since our food arrived, I observed the tables surrounding us and noticed most patrons had their cameras out taking photos and video of the President while their food grew cold. DC residents were supposed to be jaded and unimpressed by the political power players. I guess an Elmsworth sighting was still pretty exciting seeing as he'd only been President for two months.

"How do you deal with this?" I asked.

Teddy looked up from his plate. "With what?"

"With this." I inconspicuously gestured toward the restaurant-goers. "The attention. The cameras. The lack of privacy."

Teddy shrugged. "It's just kinda part of the deal. No real use in complaining about something I signed up for."

"You're better than me, 'cause I couldn't do this."

"Oh, just wait until tomorrow. Shoot, wait for the evening news, your face is gonna be breaking news."

Light strains of laughter escaped my mouth. "For a work lunch?"

"Nah for … breaking news … President Elmsworth was seen dining with a mystery woman." Teddy gave an accurate imitation of a news anchor. "That's right, Jane, the President was seen eating greasy burgers and fries with a very attractive woman who we have identified as his new Press Secretary, Clover Bennett."

My heart rate accelerated. "OK, stop."

Did I just make myself the story?

In the world of politics, as a staffer, you never wanted to be the story. Pushing my plate away, I wiped my mouth, my appetite now gone. I should have trusted my instincts and stayed my ass in the office with a soggy tuna sandwich.

Glancing back at the restaurant's patrons and staff, I realized they weren't just taking pictures of the President, they were taking pictures of us … together in this cramped booth, knees touching as we exchanged furtive smiles. A quick scan of my watch confirmed what my gut was telling me, it was time to leave.

"It's getting late, can we please go?"

"Sure." Teddy stood, pulling out his wallet to leave a tip.

"Thank you for lunch."

"Anytime."

Back at the White House, I made it to Lisa's office with three minutes to spare. Sitting at her small conference table was reminiscent of being sixteen at Lindell High School and preparing to defend my actions to the principal. Lisa took a seat across from me, a cup of tea in hand.

"Thanks so much for rescheduling our meeting."

"Well, when the President calls asking you to reschedule a meeting, you reschedule a meeting. What did he want to discuss with you, if you don't mind me asking?"

"Actually, he took me out to lunch." Shame bruised my cheeks, embarrassed to admit it.

"Aha, I see." Lisa slid a stack of file folders in front of me. I opened the first folder, readying my pen to take notes. Lisa leaned back in her chair, studying my face. "Can I offer a word of advice?"

"Please."

"President Elmsworth is a charming man, he is often the smartest person in the room and he walks around here like he knows it. He has the opportunity to be a transformative President if he could just stop letting his penis make the decisions for him."

"Oh no, I'm sure that's not why he asked me to lunch," I objected.

Teddy had tried and failed on more than one occasion to add me to his long list of conquests. Each time I'd given him a firm no. I don't mix business with pleasure.

"I'm sure by now you've heard what happened to the last Press Secretary."

I nodded my head, even though I didn't have the slightest idea what she was talking about. But her tone made it sound like it was common knowledge, and I didn't want to look like I was behind the eight ball on my first day.

"So fair warning, the President is single and has decided that the White House staffers are part of the eligible dating pool. Don't let a fling with the President ruin your White House career before it starts. I hired you, even though Gimble wanted me to go with the male candidate, because you were qualified and blew everyone else out of the water. Don't make me regret that decision." Lisa gave me a stern look over her glasses.

"No, I would never. I live by the belief that you don't crap where you eat. And any dalliance with the President would bring a whole lot of crap," I said, hoping I'd reassured her.

"Well, good. Let's keep it that way. Because I can tell you right now, the President can be a hard man to turn down. And you are just his type." She scanned me with her eyes.

As Lisa went over the talking points for my press briefing tomorrow, I tried to look fully engaged but my mind was someplace else. I hadn't even been here a full day and I was already drawing negative attention to myself. Going to lunch with the President was a misstep on my part. It wouldn't happen again.

As I walked back to my office, my stomach churned. I didn't know if it was from the greasy food at lunch or the fact that there was now a scarlet letter on my chest.

"Welcome back. How were your meetings?" Brittany asked.

"Good ... uhh ... can I talk to you in my office for a minute?"

"Sure." Brittany grabbed her pad and a pen and entered my office. I closed the door behind us, not wanting to be overheard.

"What happened to the last Press Secretary?" I asked, in a hushed voice.

"What?" Her body appeared to freeze for a moment.

"You heard me."

"I don't know if I'm allowed to discuss that." Brittany's eyebrows mashed together in a strained smile.

"I'm allowing you. Go on."

"Well, I don't know the full story. I just know the President visited her a lot and they had tons of closed-door meetings. And one afternoon I heard shouting coming from her office and then the President stormed out and the next day, she was gone."

"Does everyone know about these rumors?"

"Pretty much. Look, I'm not saying anything inappropriate happened, but—"

I held up my hand, stopping her. "Yeah, I get it. Thank you."

A wave of relief washed over Brittany's face as she headed for the door.

So, President Elmsworth was probably sleeping with the last

Press Secretary and now he's taking the new Press Secretary out to lunch. Did this man have no shame or at the very least, a sense of the optics? Sitting at my desk, I Googled Nadia Pike, the former Press Secretary. She was beautiful, blonde haired and blue eyed.

I scrolled through pictures of her all smiles standing next to then-candidate Elmsworth. And watched videos from her first day in the briefing room singing the President's praises. Closing out the multiple browser windows that had me sliding down the rabbit hole like Alice, I opened my email inbox. They hired me to act as part of the communications team not to chase rumors.

Whatever happened before I got here wasn't my concern. It was my first day, but I had a lot of work to do to get ready for my debut as Press Secretary. I pulled up the email from Topher, my press aid, reviewing his draft. It was a good first attempt. It was almost six o'clock, and by the looks of this draft, I wasn't heading home anytime soon. Selecting a Mary J. Blige playlist from Tidal, I gathered my hair in a ponytail and got to work.

CHAPTER FIVE

STANDING OUTSIDE THE WHITE HOUSE BRIEFING ROOM, I thumbed through my press binder one last time. I knew the content so well I could recite it backward. I'd spent much of last night inserting tabs and color coding the binder so I could easily turn to a specific topic at a moment's notice. Between reading through my talking points and flipping through the news, it was an eventful night. Just like the President predicted, my face was all over the evening news. Daysha called me screaming in my ear about my date with the President. Not exactly how I wanted to start my first day at the White House.

Shutting my binder, I gave myself a once over in the full-length mirror set up in the holding area just outside of the press briefing room. I decided on a dark purple sheath dress with a nude mocha heel for the occasion. Sweeping my tongue over my teeth, I entered the briefing room with a big smile plastered on my face.

"Good morning, everyone," I exclaimed. Standing at the podium, I positioned myself in the center of two American flags and in front of the official White House seal. "Good to see you all. First, I want to quickly introduce myself. My name is Clover

Bennett, and as you all know, I am the new Press Secretary for the White House and I am thrilled to be here. The Elmsworth administration is committed to transparency, and that belief applies to the press shop as well.

"Looking out into the crowd, I see many familiar faces and some that I don't recognize but am excited to get to know. So let me tell you how this is going to work," I said, clasping my hands in front of me. My delivery was upbeat and self-assured as I provided the press with a rundown of my expectations for our briefings.

As I stood at the podium, I reminded myself not to let my nerves get the better of me. No big deal, I'm just briefing the nation on the activity in the White House. A smile painted my face when I remembered my mother had traded shifts with another nurse so she could watch my first press briefing live. I could imagine her now in front of the television offering silent words of encouragement.

Then there was Daysha, who was surely in her office at that swanky law firm with the volume turned all the way up so she didn't miss a single word. But the most important viewer was the President. I had no doubt he was watching, ready for me to put on a show. It was well known that press briefings, while for the public, were mostly to stroke the commander in chief's ego. Basically, it was an hour and a half of me ticking off the administration's many accomplishments and goals.

"OK, with that I'll take the first question. Jonathan, why don't you start us off." I pointed to a graying reporter from Newsweek.

"Thank you, Clover. There has been some concern about the large number of executive orders the President has signed in recent weeks. Is he overstepping his authority?"

I flashed a complementary grin. "Jonathan, you know as well as I do that the President has broad authority. The executive orders he has signed were essential to getting the country on the right track. President Elmsworth promised on day one he would hit the ground running and that is exactly what he has done. We also understand not everything can be done through executive order, and the President looks forward to reaching across the aisle to achieve some of our more ambitious goals." I nodded my head, never dropping eye contact and never letting my smile falter. "Karen with CNN."

For close to an hour, I fielded questions about the possibility of the President having a sit-down meeting with Russia, the administration's plans to reduce America's reliance on coal and gas, and one about a junior senator that had used some inflammatory language on Twitter. Having time for one last question, I decided to call on Chet from the conservative outlet American News Broadcasting Station, ANBS. The last thing I wanted to be accused of was playing favorites.

"Thanks, Clover, so can you tell me what you and the President discussed on your lunch date yesterday?" Chet scowled at me, notepad in hand.

My jaw tightened, but I anticipated this question. "As Press Secretary, I am expected to speak to the President's plans, his vision for our country, and the policies he will enact to improve the lives of every American. Unlike the President, however, I require food to fuel my body, so President Elmsworth graciously agreed to a working lunch. And if you're still curious, the President had the sunny side up burger and he said it was delicious."

There was an audible chuckle from the journalists in the room. I was hopeful any further talk about our lunchtime excursion would fade away. There were far more important things to talk about.

"Alright, that's it for today, guys. Let's do it again tomorrow." Closing my press binder, I exited the room.

BACK IN MY OFFICE, I breathed a sigh of relief, happy to have my first briefing in the books. Kicking off my shoes under my desk, I turned the television to MSNBC to see what people were saying. Sure enough, they were discussing my briefing. I cringed as they played a clip of me talking about the administration's stance on immigration. I could never get used to the sound of my professional work voice. I sounded like a radio broadcaster from back in the day. *Up next are the smooth stylings of Peabo Bryson with his latest top forty hit.*

Muting the television, I tried to make out the muffled voices coming from directly outside my office.

Brittany's normally pleasant voice was high pitched and stammering. "I ... I should really introduce you first, sir." Without notice, my door swung open and the President was making his way inside, Brittany close on his heels. "I'm sorry, Clover. I tried—"

"No, it's fine," I said, shooting Teddy an icy stare. "Please close the door. Thanks." Once the door shut behind Brittany, I jumped from my chair. "You're an asshole. Do you know that? She was just trying to do her job." I bit my tongue, realizing I'd just called the President of the United States an asshole, to his face.

Teddy didn't even bat an eye. "I'll apologize on the way out."

"You don't just get to barge into my office whenever you like."

His face wrinkled. "I'm the President. I can do anything I want."

"Not anything," I whispered.

"Why are you so bent outta shape? Your briefing was great. Which is what I came over here to tell you."

"You could've sent an email," I said, reaching for my shoes with my feet.

"Yeah, but if I sent an email, I wouldn't be able to see the huge frown on your face," Teddy joked.

I stared blankly at him. Oh, he thought this was a game.

Rounding the desk, I pointed to my small circular conference table. "You know what? I'm glad you're here, because I have a question for you." Grabbing two mini bottles of water from the tiny fridge in the corner, I took a seat next to him, sliding one of the cold bottles his way.

"Shoot. I'm an open book." He twisted the cap off, lifting the bottle to his thick lips.

"Did you sleep with your last Press Secretary?"

Teddy froze mid-sip, the bottle and his hand suspended in air. "Wait, who said that?"

"Everyone is saying it. Not loudly ... but there are rumors."

"Did Brittany tell you that?" Teddy asked, pointing toward the door. "Because if she did, I will fire her ass."

"No, it wasn't Brittany," I lied. "And you're not gonna fire my assistant." My eyes snapped at him.

"My personal life is none of your business, Clover." Teddy stood, his jaw tight, replacing his usual carefree expression.

"But wait, I thought you were an open book? And you made it my business the minute you took me out to lunch."

"No good deed, huh." There was a superior lift to his chin.

I jumped from my chair. "Good deed? Good deed? I would rather you have saved the fifteen dollars you spent on my meal and kept me out of your bullshit."

"Damnit, Lucky, people are gonna talk regardless."

"That may be true, but we certainly don't need to feed them the story."

"OK, you know what, from now on I'm just gonna keep it totally professional with you. Because obviously, we can't be friends."

"Great, I would actually prefer that." I presented a defiant snarl.

"Great." Teddy's shoulders twitched, a flat gaze in his eyes. Scooping up his water bottle, he headed toward the door.

"Don't forget to apologize to Brittany," I called just before he slammed the door behind him.

I SUCKED on a wedge of lime after downing the tequila shot Daysha ordered in celebration of my press briefing.

"So, things you did. That. You broke your entire leg up to the thigh meat in that press briefing. Do ... you ... hear ... me." She clapped in between each word for emphasis. "Who got a bestie badder than mine. WHO!" Day tilted her head and her slick bob shook back and forth like a bobblehead doll.

"OK, inside voice," I said, looking around the crowded restaurant. The music was loud but Day's voice was louder. "I ain't gonna lie, though, it felt good."

"They needed to play some gangsta rap as you left the room because, like, you ethered them," Daysha yelled, reaching for an avocado egg roll.

"I don't know about all that," I said, trying to be modest.

Daysha waved my modesty off. "They had questions and you were in that bitch with receipts. And not just any receipts, the kind from CVS that are a mile long."

I couldn't wipe the stupid smile off my face. "You right. I did answer the hell outta those questions."

Day dipped her egg roll in the sweet sauce. "What did your boss think?"

"Lisa was really impressed. She said—"

"No, not Lisa, fool. The President," Day protested with a mouth full of food.

"Umm, he stopped by my office to congratulate me."

I decided not to bring up the fight with Teddy. Daysha would just ask too many questions that would cause me to doubt myself. Maybe I had come at it in the wrong way. Shoot, if I was him, I'd be pissed too if someone brought up my private life at work.

My day started great. The fight with Teddy was definitely a hiccup, but I wasn't going to be pushed around. For me, respect was paramount in any relationship. It didn't matter if it was romantic or platonic, it all started with respect. I wasn't going to allow our familiar relationship to supersede common courtesy.

"Well, I'm so proud of you. And good choice on the purple dress, you looked amazing." She raised her glass in my direction, making me blush. "Did your boyfriend call and tell you what a great job you did?"

"He's not my boyfriend."

"Well, it's just hard to tell when he wants to pop bottles to celebrate your new job and is over there sending you flowers after your first day."

Yes, Seth sent me a beautiful arrangement of flowers that were waiting at my front door when I returned home from my first day at the White House. It was a nice gesture and I planned on thanking him accordingly. But that didn't make him my man.

"He was being nice."

"Booty calls don't be doing all that." She took a sip from her glass. "I'm telling you he is looking for a contract. He wants to get drafted by the Washington Clovers."

I laughed at the team name. "We are not extending his contract." I hissed out a protracted breath. "It sucks, really, because he's a good player. He has heart and he hustles for the winning score. He's got good ball handling and a lot of endurance."

If Seth would just stick to the assignment, we would be good, but he's looking to do extra credit, and ain't nobody asked for that.

"So, when are you gonna break it to him, Coach?"

"I will after I line up some draft picks."

"Oh, so you looking for some new dick to replace the old dick."

"Exactly. There are three things a woman should never be without. First, a good stylist who knows how to lay her edges. Second, a shade of red lipstick that complements her complexion, and lastly, access to quality penis. Good dick is like a quality-of-life issue. You know, water, air, good dick, reliable Wi-Fi."

"Bitch, you so stupid." We both cackled loudly with a clink of our glasses.

I RANG SETH'S DOORBELL, waiting for him to answer. I'd had two pomegranate martinis and a few too many tequila shots and I was ready to act up. Seth opened the door to his Victorian-style apartment in his pajamas.

"Hi," he said. He was expecting me. I'd texted him some raunchy messages from the backseat of my Uber.

"Hi," I giggled.

Seth grabbed my hand, pulling me into his apartment. Kicking off my shoes, I almost tripped on the area rug in the living room.

"Whoa, are you good?" Seth asked, reaching out to steady me.

"I'm a little drunk," I whispered.

"I can see that."

"You have my consent to do whatever you want to me." Draping my coat over the sofa, I headed toward his bedroom, turning back around to remind him. "Except butt stuff. I don't do butt stuff."

With a firm grip on the wall to stop me from falling on my face, I stumbled around the dimly lit bedroom, dropping my purse and unzipping my dress. Seth came in carrying a bottle of water, handing it to me.

"I don't want water, I want that dick," I said, dancing around to a beat only I could hear.

"I can help you with that." Seth removed his flannel night shirt.

"Take it off. Take it off. Take, take it off," I sang while rolling my body like a snake.

Seth grabbed my face, preventing me from talking. "Are you going to ramble on like this the entire night?"

I shrugged. "I don't know, maybe you could put something in my mouth to keep me occupied." I wrinkled my nose with a smile. "I just know, whatever it is, it's gonna have to be substantial."

Seth smiled. "I think I have just the thing."

CHAPTER SIX

It had not even been a month and I was off on my first official trip for the administration. As I walked up the steps to Air Force One, I was tempted to pinch myself. Here I was actively living the life I had worked so hard to obtain. Walking through the spacious aisle, I found a window seat and settled in, reviewing the two-day itinerary.

We were headed to Oregon, not exactly an international trip to Dubai but still just as important. When he was on the campaign trail, President Elmsworth promised to make the American dream a reality for every American. It's a great sound bite, but the implementation is a little more difficult.

Tightening my seat belt, I gazed out the window as we taxied the runway. After our spat my first week, Teddy and I hadn't spoken. I saw him in meetings or stepped aside as he passed me in the halls with an ever-present group of advisers following close behind.

Rationally, I understood he was busy and didn't have time to shoot the breeze with me, but it felt like his absence was deliberate and calculated. I was probably being paranoid, but the last thing I wanted to do was end up on Theodore Elmsworth's shit list. Rumor had it, the list was long and he was actively crossing off names.

As we reached cruising altitude, I opened my laptop and a bag of gourmet trail mix, tossing a handful of glazed pistachios in my mouth. Work never stopped even when flying on an elite private jet as part of the President's entourage. I was on this trip to help push the President's message of 'A Dream Realized,' an initiative to provide resources and funding to underprivileged communities with a focus on education. Our first stop would be to visit Grover Phillips Middle School. The President would tour the school and then meet with the staff and the pre-teen students. My job was to reinforce that message with the press core at each stop on our short trip.

"Do you mind if I sit with you?" Looking up, I found Gimble in rumpled trousers and a briefcase clutched tightly across his chest.

"Sure, knock yourself out."

Taking the seat directly opposite me, Gimble let out a relieved breath. "FYI, the President is on the warpath."

My fingers moved rapidly over my laptop keys. I was finalizing the talking points that would be distributed to the press. "Uh oh, what happened?"

"Minority Leader Trumbull is what's happening."

Minority Leader Trumbull was the Republican Party's leader in the Senate. He was not happy when the White House shifted from red to blue, and he'd vowed to oppose this administration until his dying breath. Which by my calculation should have happened years ago.

"Well, that's nothing new," I said.

"He's an obstructionist and racist if you ask me."

"Well, you know what they say. Everyone's a little bit racist."

"Who says that?"

Raising an eye from my laptop screen, I wanted to say everyone who isn't white says that, but I didn't want to engage in a conversation about allyship and white guilt. "There's more than one way to skin a cat. The President is going to have to figure out a way to work with Trumbull or push past him."

Gibbs removed his glasses, cleaning them thoughtfully. "It will definitely need to be pushing past him."

"Well then, Gibbs, I guess you better gas up the bulldozer." We shared a light chuckle.

Ross Gimble had been in DC for a long time. He was a power player in liberal circles and after running Teddy's campaign and helping to get him elected, some were calling him a kingmaker. Gimble had strong connections on both sides of the aisle but in an increasingly divisive political landscape, those connections no longer held the weight they once did. He was smart, an ivy leaguer who had a playbook for every conceivable situation.

In my humble opinion, his playbook was a bit outdated, but Teddy trusted him and valued his counsel. Gibbs would suggest a play and the President would run a variation of the play, making tweaks to account for the increasingly combative nature of politics. If you came to Washington to make the world a better place, you needed to be ready to get your hands bloody. And with three months under his belt, Teddy's hands were already dripping.

"How are things going with the new gig?"

I shut my laptop. It was clear I wasn't getting any work done with motormouth over here. "It's busy. But I'm weird, I thrive under pressure."

"Unlike me, who has mini freakouts throughout the day."

I whispered a laugh. "Well, you also have a ton more responsibility. If something fails, you're in the direct line of fire. I'm not sure I could handle all that."

He shrugged. "I drink, that seems to help." There was not a hint of humor in his face. "What was it like working for Elmsworth when he was senator?"

"It was different. He was new to politics. It was really a learn as you go experience for him. We were literally figuring out what worked on the fly."

"Well, you must have taught him well because he is fully versed now."

"We taught each other. One thing about Theodore Elmsworth, he's a fast learner."

Gimble unbuckled his seatbelt and shifted to the seat next to me. "Can I pick your brain for a minute?" His tone was hushed.

"Sure."

"Do you think it's weird that the President isn't dating anyone?"

I blinked rapidly, caught off guard by the question. "I honestly hadn't given it much thought."

"I only mention it because I've noticed you've gotten asked about his personal life on more than one occasion and people are always questioning me about it."

"People are nosy."

"Yes, but from a public relations aspect, could his dating life be a distraction, maybe even a liability?"

"He's the first single President in close to one hundred years so yes, who he dates is always going to be a topic for discussion, but it's my job to redirect the conversation."

I guess Gimble's playbook didn't have a page for a bachelor President. While almost every President before him came with a First Lady in tow, being married was not a prerequisite to hold the office.

"Hmm." He pursed his lips, his forehead wrinkling with concern.

I flashed a bright smile. "Don't worry, Gibbs. I'm really good at my job."

On our arrival at Grover Phillips Middle School, the President was greeted by the principal, Darius Fullerton. If he was in a bad mood, as Gibbs claimed, you wouldn't be able to tell by the way he engaged with the staff. He listened intently as he discussed supplies and resources with a group of teachers. One seventh-grade teacher recounted how she spent her own money to ensure her students had the tools they needed.

"How many of you are coming out of your own pockets to meet the needs of your students?" Teddy asked.

Each teacher raised their hands. "It seems like every other week I'm buying something," one of them said.

Teddy scoffed, "It's always been crazy to me the way we say our children are the future of this country and yet, we expect our teachers to make it work with outdated textbooks, two sticks of chalk, and a bum projector like they're MacGyver or something."

A grizzled teacher chimed in, "No child left behind my ass. Pardon my language, Mr. President."

"No need to apologize. This is a problem we've let go on for far too long."

"What exactly are you planning to do about it? Every election cycle you political types take a trip to the hood and make promises you ain't never gonna keep."

The group in the cafeteria mumbled in agreement as the press core shuffled to get a better camera angle of Teddy's face.

Clearing his throat, he answered, "Look, that's a valid question. Honestly, I don't have to be here. I don't need your vote, I just won an election. I'm here because I want to be here. I'm here because when I look at the students of Grover Phillips and thousands of students across this country, I see myself. I grew up in the hood, Crown Heights, in Brooklyn. My grandmother lived on Eastern Parkway for most of her life until she passed away a few months ago." Teddy grew silent for a moment, his features growing dark.

"Like most of you and the students you teach, I grew up with the odds stacked against me. My mother was a drug addict who was more interested in chasing her next high than raising a kid. My grandmother took me in and she busted her ass to provide for me and my uncles. And even with multiple jobs, it wasn't enough." Teddy clenched his jaw with a shake of his broad shoulders and softened his tone.

"Everyone deserves an opportunity, a chance to believe there's more to life than this. And it's my mission to make that a reality. No more talk, talk's gotten us nothing; it's time for action. Legislative action, community action, and funding from inside the government and beyond ..."

The room fell silent as he spoke. He had the staff's full attention. Teddy was good at selling dreams to people who had given up on dreaming long ago. But for Teddy, he actually believed the dream too. Some of his goals were ambitious, but he had a plan. He was an idealist and realist at the same time. He believed most people were good and were willing to work for a better life, but he also saw things as they really were and knew to get to the idea, you would have to defeat the doubters and naysayers.

After talking to the staff, we headed to the auditorium, providing the perfect photo op as he interacted with the kids. Flashing his kilowatt smile so the press could get the best shot. I tugged on my fleece-lined leather gloves; even though we were indoors, the school was noticeably chilly. One of the teachers informed me the heater was busted, so the kids wore their winter coats inside most days.

Principal Fullerton made his way to the middle of the auditorium and addressed the crowd of faculty, students, and reporters. As he talked about the school's history and its students, I observed the room. It was part of my job to read rooms, to make sure our message was connecting with the intended audience.

Most of the eyes in the room were firmly planted on President Elmsworth. He was the main attraction, a Harvard grad and lawyer, he was smart, charming, and had the looks of a movie star. The icing on the cake was his single status. If Principal Fullerton instructed the crowd to fight for Teddy's hand in marriage, this auditorium would turn into the 77th Hunger Games.

My gaze landed on Teddy standing in the corner pretending to listen to the speech. His arms crossed over his broad chest and his face thoughtful. A trick he'd perfected years ago while running for senator. His thoughts were probably a million miles away, but you would never be able to tell from his face.

Teddy caught me staring and took it as a sign he should head in my direction. My heart was a klutz and it tripped as he took long assured strides my way. He stopped right behind me, causing my temperature to rise even though this room felt like an icebox.

"How am I doing?" Teddy asked, leaning in from behind.

"Are you fishing for a compliment?" I whispered, surprised he was speaking to me after declaring our "friendship" over.

"No, I was just looking for an honest opinion."

"It's going well. But you already knew that." I tried to keep my resting bitch face at bay, plastering on a subtle smile.

Teddy sighed, his breath visible. "Is it just me or is it cold as hell in here?"

"The heaters are broken."

He sawed out a bitter laugh. "Of course, they are, because students don't need to be warm to learn."

"Apparently they don't need heat, books, computers—"

"Yeah, well this administration is gonna change all that." His tone was determined.

It was hard not to believe him, even for a pessimist like me.

AFTER TWO MORE STOPS TO a veteran's hospital and to meet victims of a recent mass shooting, I headed to my room at the Sentinel Hotel and settled in. Ordering room service, I chose to eat in my room alone instead of grabbing a bite with Gimble and the others at a nearby restaurant. I was at my limit for social interaction for the day, and if I had to engage in witty banter or listen to one more story about some old fart who did something and inevitably got a building named after him, I was going to scream. With a minor in public policy, I enjoyed talking about regulations, lobbying, and government gridlock, but that did not mean I wanted to have those conversations at eight o'clock at night.

After scarfing down a personal pizza and bottle of beer, I headed to the hotel pool, pleasantly surprised to find it empty. I'd loved the water for as long as I could remember and was on the swim team in high school. Being in the water was relaxing. It seemed less like a workout and more like a meditation session in which I could block out the world. Tucking my hair under my swim cap, I jumped in. My feet fluttered behind me as I advanced the length of the pool. Slapping the wall, I flipped and swam back the way I came as Kendrick Lamar rapped 'we gonna be alright' in my ears.

Based on the events of today, I kind of agreed. Good and politician were two words you rarely heard uttered together, but I think Teddy was one of the good ones. He wasn't perfect, but he cared about this country and more importantly, the people who lived in it. Teddy knew what it was like to go to bed hungry. He understood the hard choices millions had to make every day. Do you pay the light bill or buy groceries? And he learned early in life that hard work doesn't guarantee you the American Dream when the odds are always stacked against you.

As my head bobbed out of the water, I was greeted by men in familiar suits. The President's Secret Service agents were circling the pool. Agent Tally glared at me treading water in the center of the pool and said "all clear" to the agent on the other end. Minutes later, the President entered the room, an embroidered hotel towel slung over his shoulder. Agent Tally and his partner circled the pool one final time before taking their positions in opposite corners of the room.

Teddy moved past the pool, casting a glance in my direction as he headed to the hot tub. My eyes focused on his chest as he removed his T-shirt, tossing it on a nearby lounge chair.

A blush took over my face as I tried to inconspicuously examine every ripple and bulge along his toned physique. Plunging my head under the water, I attempted to remove the steamy thoughts that were clouding my judgment. Coming up for air, I wiped the water from my face to find Teddy staring at me.

"I thought I was gonna have to jump in there and save you," he yelled from across the room.

"I don't need saving. I can take care of myself."

"I have no doubts about that. But just because you can doesn't mean you have to." He slid his hand in the bubbling water, checking the temperature. I guess it was to his liking because he climbed in.

"I'm pretty much done here. I'll get out of your hair."

"You don't have to leave. In fact, I'd appreciate some company."

"I don't want to impose."

"Don't make me beg, Lucky."

Now that I would pay to see, the commander in chief graveling, preferably at my feet. With a side eye, I swam to the shallow end of the pool and climbed out. Grabbing my towel, I moved toward the jacuzzi tub.

"I highly doubt you have to beg to get the things you want."

He let out a slow, deep laugh. "You'd be surprised at all the things I want."

His eyes bounced over my body in my two-piece swimsuit, making me a bit self-conscious. I submerged myself in the hot water, hoping it provided some cover.

"So, do you actually have a plan?" I asked.

"For what exactly?

"For The Dream Realized initiative."

"Good old Lucky, always the workaholic."

"What, I'm curious."

"I don't wanna talk about work." He audibly breathed air through his nose.

That was fair. I could certainly understand. "OK, then what *do* you wanna talk about?"

Teddy shrugged. "I don't know. What do you do in your free time?"

"What free time? Do you have time for hobbies?"

He nodded his head. "Hell yeah. Don't tell anyone, but when I get stressed, I go to the Lincoln Bedroom and play *Call of Duty*."

"Why Lincoln's bedroom?"

"Because no one ever looks there." He offered a crooked smile.

I looked at him thoughtfully before revealing, "I like puzzles."

"Crossword, jigsaw, brain teasers?"

"Jigsaw. I always have one puzzle spread out on my dining table."

"Huh." The corners of his mouth pulled into a frown.

"What?"

"I didn't take you for the jigsaw puzzle type of gal. Do you have cats?"

I splashed a generous amount of water in his direction. "Go to hell, Teddy." My stomach sank after the words escaped my lips. I was talking to the President of the United States, he wasn't one of my little friends. "I'm sorry, that was inappropriate."

"Nah, don't worry about it. It's fine." He waved my concerns away.

"It's actually not. It won't happen again."

The smile vanished from his face. "Tell me this shit hasn't gotten to you too?"

"What?"

"Everyone treats me with such reverence. I'd hoped you'd be different."

"What do you want exactly?" I shifted my body so my back was tickled by the jets from the tub.

Teddy floated closer until he was seated beside me. "I just want you to be real with me."

"I thought you didn't wanna be friends anymore?" I searched his face, beaded with water, now inches from mine. My eyes dropped to his lips, the urge to kiss him noodling around my brain.

"When did I say that?"

"My second day on the job."

"That's not what I said. I said I wanted to be friends ... *more*." He gave a broad smirk.

I narrowed my eyes. Such a politician. "Wow. Did you just—"

"Yes, I did."

"Well, glad to see you're no longer mad at me."

Teddy palmed the water, letting it slip through his fingers. "I was never mad at you. I was just giving you time to cool off."

I wrinkled my nose, turning my head to the side. "Cool off? Like I was a car radiator or something?"

"No, cool off as in you were upset with me. I thought it best to give you some space."

"Huh..." I didn't want to start a fight. I should just let it go. But I was never one to hold my tongue. It was my best and worst quality. "You do know how difficult it is to be a woman in a male-dominated field, right? You do realize people make these asinine assumptions about my talent and ability? Not only am I a woman, I'm a Black woman, and the last thing I need is to be sexualized in the work place. The last thing I need is for my coworkers to think I'm flirting with the boss or that we are having some type of inappropriate sexual relationship."

"OK, what do you want me to say exactly?" His tone was flat, like my words fell on deaf ears.

"I don't know, Teddy. Maybe I want you to say you understand," I said, planting my feet on the base of the tub, ready to remove myself from this situation.

"You don't think I understand? I get it. I do. You don't think I experience some of the same things? All my life has been a series of people wondering who let the Black guy in the room. Harvard. The District Attorney's office. The Capitol. Hell, the White House. I hold the highest office in the land and I still have to prove myself every day. Look, maybe we shouldn't have gone to lunch, but I just wanted to celebrate my friend. I am genuinely happy to have you here. Is that so bad?"

I needed to learn when to pick my battles. Did I really want to die on this hill?

"I know you meant well. And I'm probably being sensitive, but I just want to prove myself based on my own merits. Not because I'm friends with the boss." I shook my head, maybe I had overreacted. "You know what? I'm tripping, it doesn't even matter."

Teddy twisted his body toward mine, hooking his thumb under my chin. "No, it matters to me because it matters to you. You got this job because you know your stuff. Truth be told, you were kinda overqualified. Clover, I don't give a fuck what everyone else is saying as long as we know what it is."

His knee brushed against mine, flooding my brain with flight or fight thoughts, or more appropriately, flight or fuck thoughts. His gaze wandered from my eyes to my mouth to my chest and back again. I was certain his brain was also performing the mental gymnastics trying to figure out the opportunity costs versus benefits of kissing me. It didn't take me long to determine the price was too high, shifting my body to the opposite side of the jacuzzi.

"I'll always be real with you," I offered.

"That's all I ask. Somebody's gotta let me know when I'm being an asshole."

"That I can definitely do." I smiled.

A laugh rumbled from the depths of his chest.

CHAPTER SEVEN

THE NEXT MORNING, I MADE MY WAY TO THE PRESIDENT'S suite to take part in the morning briefing. A rundown of everything that happened in the world overnight so we were prepared to speak intelligently on any subject if asked. The last thing a Press Secretary wanted was to be caught off guard. In the already crowded living quarters, I sought out the coffee station, pouring myself a generous cup.

I found a seat on one of the couches next to a senior aid and was handed a briefing portfolio from the President's travel assistant, Bruce. Pulling out a red pen, I scanned the briefing book, writing notes in the margins. The buzz of chatter died down when Teddy entered the room still working on the buttons on his crisp white shirt.

"Let's get this briefing over with," he said.

I shifted my eyes, watching his biceps flex as he pulled his purple patterned tie through the front loop.

Gibbs took to the center of the space, running through the important topics of the day. Teddy walked to the wall-to-ceiling windows, appearing more interested in the happenings down below. After Gibbs's briefing, Bruce ran down the itinerary for the day.

"Lastly, we have the museum event tonight," Bruce said. "The President will be in attendance and we thought it would be a good idea if a few of the staffers also attended, just to show that this administration supports the community and believes in the importance of the arts and its programs." Bruce flipped a page on his clipboard, continuing. "I randomly selected the names of who will attend. So, we have—"

"Hold up." Teddy whirled around. I guess he was listening. "I'm not going to attend an event with people I wouldn't grab a drink with." His statement was met with cold stares. "No offense." Walking over to Bruce, he held out his hand. "Let me see your list." He took a second to review the names. "Yeah, no." His gaze flitted about the room. "We're gonna go with Angelo, Scott, and ... Clover."

I winced. The last thing I wanted to do was go to some art event. I was swamped with work assignments. When they say you'll get to travel with the President it sounds exciting, but they fail to mention that your workload doesn't magically pause just because you're out of the office. Away trips equaled long hours. I didn't close my eyes until 1:30 a.m. last night and when I woke up at 5:00 a.m., my emails looked like I'd never made a dent.

Clearing my throat, I spoke up, "I have a ton of work to do. While I appreciate the invitation, I just don't have the bandwidth for an unproductive night."

A young staffer eagerly raised her hand. "I can take Ms. Bennett's place if you like."

The President didn't acknowledge her words, focusing on me. "So, making connections with Oregon residents and voters is considered unproductive?"

"For you as President it is very productive. But as the Press Secretary, I don't think I can offer much value to the event."

"So, you don't see yourself as a valuable part of this team?"

I plastered a smile on my face. "That's not what I meant, and I think you know that."

The room was silent. You could hear Gibbs in the corner

strangling his itinerary pages, most likely pretending it was my neck. All eyes were on me, the woman foolish enough to openly challenge the President.

Teddy screwed his face. "No, I don't know. Please enlighten me."

I shot Teddy a defiant stare. He was being an asshole, doing that thing where he leaned on his presidential power to force others into submission.

"You know what, it's fine. It is fine, I will make it work."

"Great." Teddy placed his hand over his heart. "Thanks so much. Let's roll out, people."

The suite hummed with activity as staffers gathered their belongings and discussed carpooling. Bruce, the travel assistant, approached me and whispered, "A little friendly piece of advice."

Crossing my arms over my chest, I tilted my head. "What?"

"Never question the President."

"That's funny, I thought this was a democracy."

"The country, yes. This administration, no."

Shoving my items into my tote, I resisted the urge to flash him the finger. I had a piece of advice for him also, mind your damn business.

THE EVENING'S event was held in one of the private exhibition rooms at the Portland Museum of Art. As I walked aimlessly through the art exhibits on display, it was just as I'd anticipated, my talents were being wasted. I should be in my hotel room eating a greasy burger and watching a movie on HBO but instead, I was eating stuffed mushroom caps and hoping to blend into the background. The President was across the room in an animated conversation with a group of people, including the mayor of Portland. This mini trip had been a success and it appeared Teddy would be able to add a few more names to the Theodore Elmsworth fan club.

Unlocking my phone, I responded to a few emails and reviewed a document saved onto the White House press shop's encrypted drive. We hadn't even been here an hour, but I was ready to go. Having to smile and make small talk all day had totally depleted my social battery. Which at 8:43 p.m. was already running pretty low.

"That piece is on loan from the Louvre." Teddy had made his way across the room and was now standing next to me.

"Very generous of them." Tossing my phone in my clutch, I leaned in for a closer look at the sculpture.

"That's the amazing thing about art, the way it can connect people from two different worlds." Teddy's gaze meandered over my features. Can't say I blame him. I looked stunning in my silk, fuchsia, halter top dress. Thank God I'd decided to pack something less nine to five. "Take a walk with me."

"What?" I frowned.

"I need to stretch my legs and quite honestly, all this chatter is giving me a headache."

I looked around for one of the other staffers. I wasn't interested in babysitting the President.

"Come on," he said, walking to the exhibit exit.

I had to walk briskly to catch up as we made our way through the main museum, his two Secret Service agents in tow. We walked in relative silence, stopping at the occasional art piece before moving on. Maybe he did just want a little company. From what I had gleamed from Agents Tally and Mulvaney, neither seemed to be witty conversationalists. Thinking on it, I don't think I'd ever seen either man smile.

Swinging my eyes in Teddy's direction, part of me felt a little sorry for him. I imagined being commander in chief was a lonely profession. He didn't have any family in Washington and he spent most nights tooling around that big house all alone. It was probably hard to maintain friendships, hence his desire to be treated like a regular guy. Power changes people, and not just the person who holds the power but the people around them.

Can you imagine having a best friend who is suddenly thrust into the spotlight as President or the Queen of England? Despite every attempt to maintain the relationship, things would change.

Teddy interrupted my thoughts with a compliment. "You look ... nice."

"You sound surprised."

"No, never a surprise. One thing you're always going to do is turn heads when you walk into a room."

I waved him off, raising a disbelieving eyebrow.

"Seriously, men pause when you enter a room. And then you speak and you make them all feel inadequate when they realize they wouldn't know how to handle you."

"I make men feel inadequate?"

"Not me." He pointed to his chest. "But most men, yeah."

"What makes you different?" A smile tickled my cheeks. I'd always enjoyed the back and forth between us. Flirting with Teddy was like playing tennis with Serena Williams. He was one of the greats.

"I know you."

"You know me professionally. Who people are, how they react in romantic situations, is a totally different beast."

"I've been a student of Clover Bennett for quite some time, and I know exactly what you want."

The sound of my laughter pinged across the walls with an echo. "I can't wait, do tell."

"OK." He smiled, rubbing his hands together. "You want a man who can take control."

I laughed, "So I want to be dominated."

"I didn't mean it like that. Although I'm sure you'd like a little of that too. But what I meant was someone you don't have to tell what to do or what you need because he knows."

"What else?"

"You want a straight shooter, because you believe in transparency and don't like playing games."

My eyes flickered. For someone who was just spit balling, he was actually pretty accurate with his guesses.

"Lastly, love. Someone who's not gonna just say the words, because any fool can do that, but someone who will make you feel it in every fiber of your being."

"I'm not really a love type of girl."

He pursed his lips and a quick no-jerked his head. "I don't believe that. Everyone is a love person. They're just either too hurt or too scared to admit it."

"Sounds like you have me all figured out." The muscle in my jaw flexed uncontrollably. I hadn't spoken to this man in years and he thought he had my ticket. Was I really that predictable?

"Nah, that's just the surface stuff. You are far more complex than that."

I was finding it difficult to meet his gaze, which was insane because this was Teddy. I'd witnessed him fall down the stairs at a state building that was slick from ice. Why was I nervous? "My turn. Let me guess what you want."

"Knock yourself out."

I took a moment, considering his face. "You want a big ass, slim waist, and a smile."

A ripple of laughter rose from his abdomen. "Come on, I'm gonna need a little substance to go with all that."

"Oh, the substance is whatever she's injecting into her ass."

Our laughter rang out across the empty exhibit hall.

"So close." He pinched his thumb and index finger together.

"I guess we don't know one another as well as we think we do."

"I'm willing to learn. Tell me everything." He was walking in circles around me like a shark closing in on its prey.

"Hmm, I wouldn't wanna bore you."

"Can't you see you have my undivided attention?" Teddy stopped, his gaze delved deep, our eyes entangled, tripping up my heart.

A series of uptempo palpitations flooded my chest. "Mr. President ..."

"Ms. Bennett." He mimicked my formal tone.

Turning on my heels, I examined a fabric portrait by Bisa Butler called Broom Jumpers. I needed a respite from his focused, intense gaze. Teddy stood directly behind me, leaning forward, his chest touching my bare back. I should have moved, distancing my body from his, but the warmth and hardness of his frame against mine keep my feet locked in place. If one of us shifted just slightly, I would be able to feel all of him against me. It was as if he was testing the boundaries of just how far I would let him go. This was no longer innocent flirting and felt more like a reconnaissance mission.

Teddy reached out, running his fingers across the cotton, wool, and velvet portrait.

"You're not supposed to touch the pieces."

Dropping his arm, he rested his hand on my shoulder. "Oh, so now you're the portrait patrol?" He stared down at me.

"No, I just—"

"Do you always follow the rules?"

"The important ones."

"I believe rules are meant to be broken."

Turning to face him, I said, "That's big talk from a man whose entire job is based on rules and protocol."

"When did you become a moral, upstanding citizen?"

"Since always." Walking to the next portrait, I sought some much-needed distance between us. Which allowed the naughty thoughts to vacate my head.

"I remember a time not so long ago when you were willing to ignore several rules. Breaking and entering, public indecency, theft." His eyes flashed bright. "Do you still have that garden gnome?"

A smirk pulled at the corner of my mouth. He was referring to a drunken night in Amarillo, Texas while he was senator. "No, it broke after I threw it at someone's head."

The then senator and I thought it would be funny to enter an unlocked backyard and go for a skinny dip. Looking back on it, we were lucky we didn't get arrested. A police record would have made running for President a whole lot harder.

"See, breaking rules can be fun."

"That was stupid. Even for you," I teased.

"I don't know, there's something about doing shit I shouldn't that just gets me going." He licked his lips. "So, tell me, Lucky, what kinda forbidden shit do you wanna do?"

Am I tripping or is the President laying it on super thick? I mean, there's flirting and then there's shooting your shot. Right now, it appeared Teddy was standing at the free throw line hoping for net. "We should head back."

"Or we could just keep walking down this path and find out how deep it goes."

"What?" I wasn't sure what he was talking about, but I was certain he was no longer speaking in past tense.

"*What?*" he said.

"I'm heading back."

"I'm right behind you."

I could feel his eyes on me as he walked a few paces behind me. I tried my best to minimize the wiggle in my hips and the jiggle in my ass. Turning left, I stopped short, Teddy's firm grip on my arm.

"Wrong way," he said, his hold sliding from my arm to my hand.

With my hand tucked into his, he pulled me gently in the opposite direction. As we walked back to the main hall, Teddy brushed his thumb back and forth across the inside of my wrist. His touch ignited my nerve endings, which in turn shot waves of electricity throughout my body, culminating in sparks emanating from my core. Steps from the main room, he released me, but the damage was already done. My heart rate had spiked and was erratic, my neck and chest were warm, and my thoughts were in shambles with not safe for work images playing in my mind.

"Thanks for the company, Lucky."

I wasn't able to respond as he was accosted by several people eagerly looking to bend his ear. Teddy was whisked away. The center of attention, he smiled and put on his listening face.

The President's time was valuable and the fact that he'd spend twenty minutes of it talking to me was noted. Having the ear of the President was a very valuable tool. That sounded nefarious, like I'm Brain from *Pinky and the Brain*, looking to take over the world. What I meant to say was, being trusted by the President was a big deal and I fully intended to use this to my professional advantage.

CHAPTER EIGHT

LONG CIRCULAR LINES ADORNED THE EDGE OF ONE OF MY binder pages as I doodled while Gibbs droned on about wind power and something having to do with migrant workers. My ears perked up when Lisa called my name.

"I'm sure Clover could speak to this at her next press briefing," Lisa said, pointing in my direction.

"Of course, I can. Just shoot me over the talking points and we should be good to go," I said, not even sure what I had just agreed to.

"Sounds like we're all set," Teddy said, standing to signify the meeting was over.

His mere presence made people's backs straighten. The White House was a weird vortex and for at least the next four years, Teddy was the energy center. Everyone and everything in the building was here for the purpose of serving him. From his closest advisers to the resident staff that ensured his pillows were fluffed, bed made, and everything was to his specifications. Teddy exited the room, allowing the imaginary valve to twist, releasing the pressure that had built up since the start of the meeting.

Collecting my things, I hurried to the mess hall to grab a

quick bite before my next meeting. I reviewed the sandwich board that listed today's specials. They had chicken pot pie on the menu. *Three of my favorite things*, I thought, laughing out loud at my corny joke.

"Hey, Clover," a familiar voice from behind called out.

I swiveled to find Chet from ANBS, tray in hand. "Hey, Chet." I turned back around, hoping the line would move faster and that would be the extent of our conversation.

"So, Clo, when can we..."

I flipped my head so fast Chet stopped mid-sentence. "That's not my name." I wagged my finger at him.

"My apologies." Chet lifted a hand like he meant no harm.

Maybe he didn't, but now he knew not to play with me. I hated when people tried to shorten my name. My name was Clover. It was short enough. His lazy ass could take the time to pronounce every syllable.

"When can we expect you to come on ANBS and answer some hard-hitting questions?"

"Impartial and objective, right?" I asked, narrowing my eyes.

"Of course."

"You know how this works. If you want me to appear on American News just reach out to my assistant, Brittany Boyle, and she can set something up."

"That would be great. It's nice to see that someone from this administration isn't afraid of a little honest news coverage."

"Are you implying that the President is afraid to appear on your news channel?" I asked innocently.

"He's been in office for over three months now. I thought he said he wanted to be the President of all Americans."

"He *is* the President of all Americans. Don't get all bent out of shape just because he hasn't appeared on your little news program."

"Now, Clover, you know that ANBS is watched by over fifty million people each day."

"What I do know is that two nights ago you aired a story comparing the President to a terrorist."

Chet threw his hands in the air. "Look, people are asking the question. I was just facilitating the conversation."

Grabbing a bowl of pot pie, I flashed Chet one of my signature fake smiles and walked away. Chet wasn't wrong. American News had a huge market share, and there was a whole swath of people who weren't receiving our messaging because they were solely relying on a network that openly admitted they were more entertainment than news. Maybe I should talk to the President about reconsidering his position on the deplorable news network.

While in my two o'clock meeting, I texted the President's personal secretary, Abigail.

Me: Hey girl, how's it going?

Abby: Ugh, is the day over yet?

Me: Oh no, what's up?

Abby: Just one of those days when a group of senators think they can treat me like Viola Davis from The Help.

Me: I swear these politicians think the world revolves around them.

Abby: Because most of the time it does. Anyway, what's up? Did you need something?

Me: I was just wondering if there was any room today on the President's calendar for me?

Abby: How long do you need?

Me: Fifteen minutes?

There was a pause. I imagine Abby was flipping through the pages of the President's sacred calendar. Yes, we were in the twenty-first century, but the administration still kept a paper calendar. That calendar tracked the President's every move and while it was also stored electronically, the leather-bound time tracker was viewed with great reverence.

Abby: I can give you ten at five twenty. Will that work?

Me: You're the best.

First rule of any DC job was to make friends with the gatekeeper. Abby was in control of the President's calendar, and if she didn't like you, it would take a cold day in hell before she penciled you in on that calendar. I'd spent the last few weeks cultivating a relationship with her. It didn't hurt she was cool as hell and the type of chick I would have drinks with after a long work week.

Now at five o'clock I was outside of the Oval waiting for an audience with the President. I didn't want to risk the chance of getting delayed by a wayward conversation in my office, so I would just pass the time chatting with Abby until the President was ready to see me.

"So, this fool had the nerve to tell me that he likes hanging out but he's not looking for anything serious," Abby said.

"Ahh, that sounds familiar. A brother wants you to cook for him, sleep with him, remind his ass about doctor's appointments but he ain't looking for more."

"Exactly, wants me to give everything while giving me nothing."

"How's the sex?" I whispered.

"Girl, that's the only reason I'm sticking around," Abby roared as we shared a high five.

"I know that's right." I laughed. Our girl talk was interrupted by the Oval door opening followed by the team of speech writers exiting the room like they'd just been told there was going to be six more weeks of winter.

"OK, Ms. Clover, it's all you," Abby said, turning her attention back to her computer screen.

Tucking my hair behind my ear, I stepped over the threshold of the Oval. Closing the door behind me, I hung back, not sure what mood he would be in. "Thank you for taking the time to meet with me."

"Yep, what do you need?" Teddy didn't even look up to acknowledge my presence.

I tried not to take it personally; he was the President of the free world and was most likely dealing with seven different crises at once. I'm sure he had things on his plate that would make my head explode if he shared it with me.

"I was thinking you should grant ANBS a sit-down interview," I said, swallowing hard. I knew this was going to be a tough sell considering the President's feelings in regard to that particular news station.

Teddy dropped his pen, looking up from the papers scattered across the Resolute Desk. "And why would I do that?"

"Because it's a missed opportunity," I said, approaching his desk. "I know the typical Elmsworth voter doesn't rely on ANBS for their news, but lots of Americans do. And day after day, those Americans listen to American News and believe their portrayal of you."

Teddy leaned back in his office chair, studying my face. Whatever was tumbling around in that head of his, at least I had his attention.

"So why not flip the script. Go on American News and answer their stupid and stilted questions. Show them who you are. You're not going to change every mind, but you can make inroads to chip away at the Borg mentality over at ANBS."

"That sounds like a huge waste of my time." Teddy furrowed his brow.

Since we'd returned from Oregon, Teddy had been all business. This meeting was probably the most we'd spoken in the past week. Which was fine, I'd barely even noticed I'd been so busy. OK, that's a lie, I noticed. I don't know what I expected, but it wasn't radio silence. Falling back into that once familiar friendship with Teddy was off the table.

When he was senator, it was different, the rules were ultimately made by us. It wasn't unusual for the then Senator Elmsworth and his staff to go out for drinks or for us to burn the midnight oil in preparation for an early morning hearing while sharing Chinese food and swapping dating stories. But he was the President now, and I could no longer poke my chopsticks in his moo goo gai pan. Besides, being friends with the President was more trouble than it was worth.

"Your opponents are on American News every day pushing their message. If this White House keeps ignoring what's going on over there, if we keep ignoring the very real fears and concerns of the Republican voter, then what?"

"ANBS is barely a news organization." Teddy shook his head, returning his attention to his papers.

"Last year ANBS made close to three point one billion, with a B, dollars. Their evening news line-up boasts millions of viewers every night. It may be one stone's throw away from the gossip rags when it comes to trustworthy news content, but American News is very much a contender."

"Hard pass." He stood, letting me know this conversation was over.

"So, you'll think about it?" I said in jest. The corners of his mouth curled, but I didn't get the full smile I was hoping for. Turning to leave the room, I called back over my shoulder. "Goodnight, Mr. President."

THERE WAS NEVER anything good in my mother's fridge. She had recently gotten hooked on a health kick, which was great, but now there was nothing in the fridge but bottled green juice smoothies, spinach, and cauliflower. Moving on to the pantry, I found a can of unsalted almonds and begrudgingly popped a few in my mouth. What was the point of having a Jamaican mother if there wasn't any ackee, pepper pot soup, or curry anywhere to be found?

"So, tell me about the job," my mom said as I re-entered the living room and plopped on her floral couch. I think this was the first couch my mother owned that wasn't covered in tacky yellowing plastic. "You've been so busy the past few weeks.

Neglecting your mother." It wasn't a conversation with my mother without a subtle guilt trip.

"I know. There's just so much to learn. And I want to put my stamp on the job, which means changing the things that don't work."

"Have you made any friends?" she asked, while nibbling on edamame.

"A few. There's Abby. She's the President's personal secretary and she's a hoot." There was also Edward, who was part of the White House legal team and made a point of visiting my office at least every other day. I think he was more interested in getting into my pants and less concerned with building a collaborative working relationship.

"Just remember what I always say. Don't be telling those white folks all your business."

"Abby's Black," I said with a shrug.

"Still, all skinfolk ain't kinfolk."

This was rich coming from the woman who started a phone tree calling everyone in her address book when I got my period at twelve. But she was right. I had perfected the art of fostering relationships in which I knew everything about the other person while they knew absolutely nothing about me.

"And Theodore, how are things going with him?" my mom asked, while casually flipping through the latest issue of *Essence* magazine.

"Fine, yeah, Teddy's fine," I said, pursing my lips.

Looking up from the magazine, my mother wrinkled her nose. "Why did you say it like that?"

My shoulder twitched. "It's just... we had a slight disagreement a few weeks back."

My mother tossed the magazine on the coffee table. "Oh Lord, what you done gone and did now?"

My mouth dropped open. "Why does it have to be my fault?"

"Because you talk too much."

I took a sip of my lukewarm green tea. "All I did was be

honest and lay out my expectations for our working relationship."

Ms. Sylvia kissed her teeth. "Strong men say they can handle a strong woman until they are actually confronted with one."

A quick no jerked my head in protest. "Teddy isn't like that."

"Hmm, so what are you going to do to fix it?"

"I'm gonna do my job," I said, staring at my mother like she had just grown a second head.

"OK, Clover, no need for that tone. Just don't get fired," she said, standing to search the couch cushions for the remote.

"It's already fixed. It was just a blip. We've moved on." Grabbing my mug, I headed to the kitchen, muttering under my breath, "I'm grown. Treating me like a child. I ain't fixing a damn thing." Placing my cup in the microwave, I pressed the digital display like I was dialing someone ready to cuss them out. But when it came time to close the microwave door, I was mindful not to slam it. Yes, I was thirty-five, but I could still get my ass beat and Ms. Sylvia had a heavy hand.

I don't even know why I mentioned it. So what Teddy had an affair with the last Press Secretary, that had nothing to do with me. I just didn't want to get wrapped up in any type of office drama. Work gossip can be just as bad as anything you'd see on one of those high school dramas, that I was entirely too old to watch but did with great enjoyment. Actually, work was worse because your money was tied up in that toxic environment. All I wanted to do was come to work, do my job, and stunt on a few hoes. Was that too much to ask?

"Hey, what are you doing next month on the seventeenth?" I asked, heading back into the living room, reheated tea in hand.

My mother reached for her phone, pulling up her calendar. "If the Lord spares my life, that's the weekend I'm going to Atlanta with Gladys for the women's conference at Life Church."

That's right, how could I forget she'd been talking about it for months and I had purchased her airfare as a Christmas present. My mother watched the church live stream every

Sunday and was looking forward to seeing the church in person.

"Yep, totally forgot."

"Why, what did you have planned?"

"Oh, nothing much, just the White House state dinner. I was hoping you'd be my plus one."

"You know I would if I could. I would love rubbing elbows with all those celebrities."

"No worries, there will be other opportunities and you will be at the top of the list. I'll just ask Daysha."

"Or you could actually bring a date to this dinner."

"That would require me actually dating." I shook my head. My mother didn't know about Seth. It didn't feel appropriate discussing my insignificant other with my mother.

She let out a labored sigh. "Clover, don't make the same mistake I did. What good is all this working, hum? All this money, yet you still go home each night to an empty bed."

"I like what I do and it fulfills me," I tried to explain, knowing she would never understand.

My mother was old school traditional, believing a woman couldn't be truly happy without a husband and kids. She was wrong. I'm not saying having someone wouldn't enhance my life. But having a boyfriend was just a cherry on top. You can still enjoy a sundae if the cherry's missing. Truth be told, I was loving my fifteen-hour workdays, drunken girl's nights out, and my standing dick appointment with Seth. Maybe in a few years I could slow down and focus on my personal life a bit more.

"Great, on your tombstone it will read, my work fulfilled me," Ms. Sylvia said, rolling her eyes and starting the Netflix movie.

CHAPTER NINE

It was a little past eight thirty, and I was rummaging through the breakroom fridge looking for something to eat. The West Wing was like a ghost town with people heading out early to enjoy the weekend. I pulled out a glass container filled with pasta. It smelled like it was still good, but you can't trust everyone's cooking. The last thing I needed was to have my stomach churning all night.

Pushing aside a bottle of apple juice, I found a roast beef sandwich still sealed in the packaging.

"It's my roast beef sandwich now, fool," I said aloud in my best Deebo from *Friday* voice.

"But my grandmomma gave me that sandwich," a deep familiar voice called out from behind me.

With an about face, I gave a coy smile. "You caught me." I raised my arms, sandwich still in hand.

"Ahh, so you're the refrigerator bandit," Teddy said, flashing his crooked smile.

It wasn't a flaw, this man was perfect. I tried not to stare at his well-toned upper body. Gone was his suit jacket and tie, the sleeves of his crisp white shirt rolled up to show off some of the tattoos that decorated the length of his right arm. God was not playing around when he created Theodore Elmsworth.

"Guilty as charged," I said, driving my lip between my teeth.

Teddy walked over to me, stopping just inches from my face. "Your secret's safe with me. But I think we can do better than a day-old sandwich. Don't you?" He flashed a moistening tongue over his upper lip.

Is he still talking about food?

"There was some pasta but it looked kinda sketch," I whispered, trying really hard to block out the naughty thoughts swirling around in my head.

Teddy stepped back, scanning my body from head to toe. My face grew hot under the glare of his chestnut eyes that were so hard to read. Shifting his weight, he stood directly in front of me. His broad frame blocking my view so that all I saw was him. "Clover?" he whispered.

"Yes," I said, looking up at the six-foot-four Adonis standing over me.

"What are you wearing on your feet?" he said, pointing to the floor.

Looking at my feet, I replied, "Crocs." Teddy raised his eyebrow, giving me a look making it clear he was seriously questioning my judgment. "What? They're comfortable," I protested.

I was sick and tired of having to defend my love of Crocs. While not visually appealing, they're functional and provide relief after wearing heels all day.

"They're ugly and look like something my grandmother wore," he teased.

"Plenty of young, fashionable people wear Crocs," I said confidently.

"Name one."

Swallowing hard, I thought for a minute. "Lakeith Stanfield," I said, my face brightening.

"Bullshit."

"No, he looks like the type of brother that would rock some

Crocs." I giggled at my rhyming skills. "Did you see what I just did there? Rock and Crocs."

"Whoa, so impressive you should've pursued a rap career instead of the political thing."

"Nah, the streets ain't ready," I said, swaying back and forth.

"Anyway, I came over here because I got some sushi from Nori..."

"Oh, I love that place." I sighed, pulling the roast beef sandwich up to my heart.

"I remember. Do you want ... would you like to split it with me?" Teddy shoved his hands in his pockets.

Was he nervous? No, it was wild that I even allowed myself to think I could make him nervous. This man had stared killers and war criminals in the eye. So, I don't think my presence would cause him to break a sweat.

"Sure," I said, tossing the sandwich back into the fridge. "Do I need to change my shoes, or are we good?"

"I'll allow it this one time." He raised a finger as a warning.

AFTER FOUR MAKI rolls and five California rolls, I was stuffed. This definitely beat that old roast beef sandwich. "This was delicious. Thank you," I said, licking the spicy sauce from my chopsticks. I could not believe I was eating sushi cross-legged on the floor of the Oval. How was this my life right now?

I took a sip of ginger ale before speaking. "Do you ever pinch yourself? I mean, over all this."

Teddy popped another roll in his mouth, chewing slowly. "No, I deserve all this. I worked hard. No pinching required, my hard work and dedication manifested this."

I wrinkled my nose, turning my head to the side. "I'm happy to see you haven't let all *this* go to your head," I teased.

"I'm just being honest. If my accomplishments sound like I'm bragging, I can't help it."

"Huh... I can remember a time when you weren't so confident."

Teddy smiled at our shared recollection. "And I remember a woman telling me that while I wasn't better than anyone else, the inverse was also true. No one was better than me. And that I needed to walk on to that debate stage like I belonged there because I did."

"Did I say all that?"

"You did. And you may not know it but those words, your words stuck with me. Even after all these years."

"Shut up." I rolled my eyes, ripping lines into the edge of my napkin.

"I'm serious. Other than my grandmother, you are the bravest woman I've ever met."

A string of laughter escaped my throat.

"You are balls to the wall. You walk into a room and your presence is felt. You demand respect and you don't apologize or water yourself down so that others can easily digest you. And that is the thing I love ... like the most about you." His eyes dropped to his lap.

"You do realize I only do that because this is a male-dominated field and I learned early on that I couldn't wait to be heard I had to speak loudly and often, with all the confidence and authority of an unqualified white man."

He shook his head in agreement. "Those underqualified, my daddy is so-and-so types really have none of the ability but all the bravado. It's insane."

We indulged in a moment of light-hearted laughter.

"I missed this," he said.

"What?"

"Talking to you." Teddy ran his hand over the tan carpet. "Why'd you never return any of my calls?"

All I could offer was a hitch of my shoulders.

After I left then Senator Elmsworth's administration for new opportunities, Teddy wanted to remain friends. And I wanted that too, but life just got hectic and the unanswered messages piled up and I didn't know how to fix it, so I just ignored it. After months of trying to connect, his text messages were reduced to special occasions wishing me Happy Birthday or a Happy New Year with a similar response from me and a promise to get together for drinks or dinner. Words we both knew were lies, but we kept telling them.

"Water under the bridge." Teddy scooted closer, placing his hand on my thigh. "You're here now and I'm not gonna let you go so easily this time. Time doesn't always ruin things, sometimes distance makes it better. It allows for things to ferment, like wine."

"Uh-huh," I said.

What the hell was he talking about? I was only able to catch every other word, probably because his hand was gently massaging my thigh, making it hard for me to focus on anything else other than ignoring my raging lady boner.

Teddy's hand slid from my thigh down my leg until my left foot was in his hands. Settling in on the floor in front of me, he slowly rubbed my foot. Using his thumbs, he stroked each one of my toes before shifting to the ball of my foot, moving his hand in a downward motion. His grip was firm, but he applied moderate pressure while working the arch of my foot.

Releasing a drawn-out breath, I closed my eyes in an attempt to keep my breathing even. With my lips clasped tightly, I tried to suppress the moan that was forming at the back of my throat. I don't know if he'd studied the art of reflexology, but I was certain he'd hit the pressure point that activated the pulsating throb of my clit. When I kicked him in the chest, Teddy went flying backward.

"Oh my God. Are you OK?" Those kickboxing classes were really paying off.

Regaining his balance, he smiled. "I'm fine. You OK, Lucky?"

No, I was not OK. I wanted to strip this man naked and fuck him atop the presidential seal.

"It's late, I should go." I tried to stand but my legs were wobbly. Leaning on the arm of a nearby couch, I steadied myself.

"Do you need help?" Teddy asked, jumping to his feet.

"No," I yelled, extending my hand.

The last thing I wanted was for this man to touch me again with his strong, knowing hands. Sliding my feet back into my Crocs, I headed gingerly toward the door, my legs still not at one hundred percent.

"Have a good night, Lucky." I could hear Teddy chuckle as I exited the room.

CHAPTER TEN

"Ugh, I ain't even gonna lie, I am so jealous of you right now," Daysha said, from outside my dressing room. "If it wasn't for this law firm retreat, I would've been so down."

"No worries, girl. You know there will be other events," I said, slipping the next dress off the hanger.

"I wanna meet the President," Daysha said. "You know I heard he's a freak."

Opening the dressing room door, I stuck my head out. "Who said that?"

"TMZ, the Shade Room, Bossip." Daysha shrugged.

"Ahh, so it must be true." Rolling my eyes, I closed the door.

"Is Seth excited?"

"He rented a tux." I smiled.

With my mother and Daysha both booked, I decided to ask Seth to be my plus one. I dreaded work-related social events and Seth would act as a familiar face who could help subdue my anxiety. Exiting the dressing room, I twirled around in a red off-the-shoulder gown.

"Bitch, who are you? Jessica Rabbit?" Daysha frowned. "Titties all out. Get back in that dressing room. This is a state dinner not Superbowl weekend in LA."

I looked down at my cleavage. "My breasts are not all out."

"Look, I don't know what to tell you. Maybe I'm just jealous 'cause I ain't got none. But it's a no for me, dawg," Daysha said, turning her attention back to her phone.

I sucked my teeth as I headed back to the dressing room.

"Is Bernie Sanders gonna be there?" Daysha asked.

"What?"

"Bernie Sanders?" she yelled louder, like we weren't in Nordstrom.

"I don't know," I said, stepping out of the red dress.

"I thought you and Seth weren't serious."

"We're not," I said, zipping up an emerald green dress.

"So, you really gonna bring your boner donor as your plus one?"

I stepped out of the dressing room with a frown. "No, I'm bringing Seth."

"OK, but when was the last time you and Seth went on a real date?"

My jaw fell slack as I tried to recall our last outing together. Clearing my throat, I offered, "A few months ago we went to Ikea because he was looking for shelves. We ate meatballs at the cafeteria."

"Ahh, yes, sounds like true love to me." Day crossed her arms.

Sitting next to her on the bench, I asked, "What would you have me do?"

"Quit playing games with his heart like the Backstreet Boys said." Day shrugged.

"I'm not. I've been very honest. He knows I'm not looking for a relationship."

"With him, you're not looking for a relationship with him."

"With anyone," I corrected her.

"OK, you may wanna act like Boo Boo the Fool, but Seth is in love with you."

I wagged my head with a frown. "That sounds like a him problem to me."

"Clover, I tell you white boy has his nose wide open and you don't even care?"

"I care. I just don't have the bandwidth to deal with it right now."

I don't know why Daysha was acting like I was some player who was leading Seth on. I'd made it very clear that I wasn't looking for a serious relationship. I carefully followed the friends with benefits playbook, no sleeping over, no leaving a toothbrush or change of clothes at my place, and absolutely no dates. Sure, accompanying me to the state dinner could be considered a date, but I didn't see it that way and Seth agreed to attend as my friend, nothing more. Plus, he was a reporter; it just made sense.

"OK," Daysha said, checking out her fingernails, her tone disapproving.

Last time I checked, I was single, like the ones in a stripper's G string, and if Seth was catching feelings, he could easily be replaced. I hissed out a long sigh. "I'll talk to Seth. After the state dinner."

Daysha's face brightened with an approving smile. "You're killing this green dress by the way," she said, squeezing my hand.

"WHAT'S your boss's name again?" Seth asked, fidgeting with his bow tie.

"Lisa Prince," I said, reaching for his tie to help him straighten it.

"Lisa Prince," Seth repeated. "I just don't want to embarrass you."

"You'll do great," I encouraged him. "You'll probably have our whole table rapt with questions about your investigative work."

Seth leaned in, planting a kiss on my cheek. "I doubt it."

As the driver pulled up to the White House, I gave myself one last once over. I had gone with the emerald green, form-

fitting, off-the-shoulder dress because I loved the way it comple-
mented my copper-hued skin. Squeezing Seth's hand, we exited
the town car.

Inside the White House we headed to the receiving line.
Giving our names to a staffer, we waited for our turn to greet the
President. The line was long but they tended to move quickly as
the President's time was precious. I knew Teddy was dreading
this. When he was senator, he told me he hated small talk. Fifty
percent of a politician's time was asking people about their
child's sports activities.

A military guard announced the next guests in line. "Congresswoman Elizabeth Joiner and Richard Joiner," The stoic
guard said.

As we inched closer, I could overhear Teddy's conversation.
"Now Congresswoman Joiner, the last time we talked you told
me your daughter Jenny had just gotten accepted into UCLA.
How has her first year been so far?" Teddy asked.

The congresswoman's face beamed in delight with the realization that the President of the United States had remembered
such an ordinary fact from a conversation they probably had
months ago. Even though he hated the schmoozing, this was
where Theodore Elmsworth shined. He remembered names and
prior interactions with individuals and would call back to those
conversations when he saw you again. He would ask about your
dog Fonzie who had cataract surgery, or if you'd had a chance to
perfect that banana bread recipe you'd been working on. *Hello,
Mr. Smith, how are your kids, George, Lilly, Sam, Rusty, Sue Ellen,
Brett, Tucker, and the little one who just turned two last month, Josie?* It
was a skill.

"Press Secretary Clover Bennett and Seth Wooten," the military guard's booming voice rang out.

When Teddy caught sight of me, a broad smile lit up his face.
As we walked forward, I could feel his eyes surveying my body.
His eyes were like heat-seeking missiles as they moved from my

eyes, to my mouth, to my Coke-bottle frame. I don't think he even noticed Seth until we were both standing in front of him.

"Hello, Mr. President. I wanted to introduce you to my friend, Seth Wooten."

Seth extended his hand and it was quickly engulfed within Teddy's large palm. "It's very nice to meet you, Mr. President."

"Seth works for American News as lead investigative journalist. You remember the political insider trading scheme? Seth broke that story."

I knew I sounded like a proud mother, but I just wanted to hype Seth up. He was good at his job and I wanted everyone to know it.

"I do remember that. I watched your segment. Good reporting," Teddy said, patting Seth on his shoulder.

"Thank you," Seth said, reaching for my hand.

Teddy blinked, his eyes traveling to my hand interlocked around Seth's. "Hope you have a good time tonight. Clover, always good to see you."

"Thank you, Mr. President." And just like that, it was over. Seth and I were ushered into the state dining room, which was already half full, to find our table.

As we walked to our assigned seating, Seth leaned in and whispered, "You know he wants to sleep with you, right?"

I didn't acknowledge Seth's words. Instead pretending to search for something in my gold clutch. At our table we were greeted by Lisa and her husband Frank.

"Ahh, you made it." Lisa smiled, standing to hug me. "You look amazing," Lisa whispered in my ear. "I want you to meet my husband, Frank. Frank, this is the one I have been telling you about, Clover Bennett." Lisa made room for Frank to stand next to her.

"You told me she was smart and a hard worker. But you didn't tell me she was drop dead gorgeous," Frank said, lifting my hand to his mouth for a quick peck.

"Ignore him, he was born in the sixties, he doesn't know any better."

"The *sexties*, now that was a good time."

"Frank, you were five," Lisa said, raising her hand to silence him. "I see you brought a guest." Lisa reached out her hand, giving Seth's a shake.

"Yes, this is Seth Wooten." I smiled, resting my hand on his chest.

Seth cupped Lisa's hand in his. "Nice to finally meet you. Clover has told me great things."

"Clover, I didn't know you had such a handsome boyfriend."

"No, he's my friend. We're just friends." I could sense Seth's body shift, his hand dropping from my back.

"I don't have friends as attractive as you. Must be hard, eh, Seth?" Frank leaned forward, he was a close talker.

"You have no idea." Seth winked. Turning to me, Seth whispered, "I'm gonna get us something to drink."

Nodding my head, I watched him walk away, imagining all the things I was going to do to him when we got home. I could sense Lisa on my left moving closer to me.

"I was worried about you. I thought all you did was work. He's cute," Lisa said.

"Thanks."

"Serious?"

"No, like I said, we're just friends."

Shoot, I could be engaged to Seth and expecting our first child and I wouldn't tell Lisa. I tried to keep a strict separation between my work and home life. I knew bringing Seth to this event was in total contradiction of that rule. But it was either bring Seth or go solo, and I would rather lick a seat on the Metro before I did that.

"Friends don't look at me the way he was looking at you," Lisa said, reaching for her water glass.

Mind your business, Lisa. There is nothing to see here, I thought.

"Uhh, work doesn't really allow for serious relationships."

This was true. I was out the door early each morning, and most nights I didn't return home until well after ten at night. That didn't leave much room for a social life. I was lucky if I saw Seth twice in one week.

"Frank and I have been married for eighteen years. But I understand that it's a different time. Word of advice: don't take these personal connections for granted. That's what separates us from the robots."

Giving her a curt smile, I picked up the menu, pretending to be totally fascinated by the four-course meal. That was enough sharing for the night. While Lisa and Frank turned their attention to the Energy Secretary and his wife, I used that opportunity to canvas the room.

At one table was a pop star who decided to don purple hair for the occasion. At another table was a basketball player and his wife who were still very much together after a public cheating incident at a nightclub. I eyed the guest of honor, the Prime Minister of Canada and her husband. The two made a striking couple. Canada was one of our closest allies and Teddy had built a solid relationship with Canadian leadership while he was a senator.

I found Teddy in a corner laughing with some dignitaries. He looked dashing in his white tuxedo jacket and black trousers tailored to expertly fit his solid frame. He knew how to dress and he took pride in his appearance, hairline always precise, not a stray hair on his goatee. His nails were always trimmed and clean. I don't know if he got manicures, but it wouldn't surprise me if he did. Standing next to him was a petite woman in a cream-colored dress, her long sun-kissed hair pulled into a slick ponytail.

The two looked grossly mismatched as Teddy towered over her. She wasn't his typical type with her slender frame and blink and you'd miss them curves. When I worked with Teddy back when he was senator, he didn't seem to discriminate. Black, White, Asian, Pacific Islander, it really didn't matter to him as long as they had something he could grab on to, if you know what I mean.

This was the handy work of Gibbs. He wanted to quell public opinion about the bachelor President. The opinion of the public was that President Elmsworth was a playboy, which was interesting because in the past few years, he'd done a good job of keeping that part of his life private. Teddy got around like Tupac. I saw it with my own eyes when he was senator. I was pretty confident he wasn't spending many nights in bed alone.

Seth returned to our table with two glasses and a huge smile on his face. "I just met Denzel Washington at the bar," he said, breathless, with a twinkle in his eye.

"Well then, your night's made."

"My night was made the minute you answered the door in that dress."

SETH SPUN ME AROUND, pulling me close to him. Wrapping my arm over his shoulder, I leaned my cheek against his. We swayed back and forth as Cynthia Erivo's melodic voice soared over the strings, drums, and piano.

"We should do this more often," Seth said.

"Dance?" I asked.

"Yes, but I meant spend more time together. Outside of the bedroom."

"I like our time in the bedroom," I joked, rubbing his back. I knew where this conversation was heading, and I wanted no parts.

"Me too. And I want more time with you." Seth pulled back so I could see his face.

"Umm ..."

This was not the time or the place for this conversation. Truthfully, there was no appropriate time for this conversation because I wasn't interested in changing our current arrangement.

They like to claim women are the ones who get all emotionally attached in relationships, but it wasn't true. The sex with Seth was great, but if he kept this up, I would delete and block him so fast his head would spin. After tonight, I was putting Seth on ice for a bit so he could cool off.

"Clover, I'm not asking you to marry me. I just wanna get to know you better."

"You know me. You know I like Junior Mints; you know my favorite color is plum. You know I like that thing you do with your fingers." I tried to lighten the mood.

"I don't know anything about your family or if you have siblings, even. We have been doing this for months—"

"Do you mind if I cut in?" Teddy seemed to appear from nowhere, tapping Seth on the shoulder.

I could tell Seth wanted to say no, but it was the President of the United States. What the President wants the President gets.

"Sure man. Just return her to me in one piece." Seth released me, stepping back.

I smiled weakly, hoping he wasn't too upset but thankful for the much-needed interruption. Teddy wrapped his hands around my waist, ushering me deeper into the crowded dance floor away from Seth's eyes.

With a hand on my back and one on my waist, Teddy and I swayed back and forth to the music. He took control, leading our feet to dance around in a small circle all the while never taking his eyes off me. This was the closest I'd been to Teddy since taking this job. I could feel my breasts rise and fall against his chest as his fingers tapped against my waist in beat to the music.

"You look amazing tonight," Teddy said, looking down at me with a smile.

"Thank you. So do you," I said, clearing my throat. "Very dapper, very debonair."

Teddy studied my face. As if he was analyzing every crease, every freckle, and every pore. "So, what's up with old boy?"

Teddy asked, twirling me gently before pulling my body next to his.

"Seth?"

"Yeah, Seth. Are you fucking him?" Teddy asked, with not a hint of shame.

Pulling back, I presented a defiant sneer. "Oh, so you're just gonna ask me a question like that?"

"We've grown." Teddy's shoulders bounced nonchalantly. "So, are... you... fucking... him?"

"That's none of your business," I countered.

Shaking his head knowingly, he said, "Got it. You're fucking."

"Do you sleep with every woman you're seen with?" I whispered, not wanting others on the dance floor to overhear our conversation.

"Pretty much, yeah," Teddy said, arching his eyebrow.

"Oh," I said, unable to suppress a laugh. *At least he was being honest.*

"So, he's not your boyfriend. A point you made very clear." Teddy pressed his hand on the small of my back, attempting to push me closer to him.

"No, he's just a friend." Why was everyone so interested in my relationship status?

"Good to know."

I grimaced. "What?"

Teddy made room between our bodies so he could get a better view of my face. "Lucky, how much longer are we gonna do this?"

"Do what?" I asked, my head flinching back.

"Play this game?" Teddy brushed my hair off my shoulder, his hand caressing my neck briefly before returning to my waist.

Teddy was handsome, and confident, and capable. If he wasn't such a slut he would have bagged me years ago. The presidency only seemed to heighten my desire. Power was an intoxicating drug.

"A little longer," I whispered. My eyes were drawn to his

mouth and thoughts of his lips devouring me. My body uncongealed against his.

If anyone was watching, and who was I kidding, they were all watching, they were getting a show. We were way too close and our gaze far too intense for tongues not to wag. It took all of my mental faculties not to pull his head toward my trembling mouth.

His tongue ran a slow trail between his lips. "I can wait. You're worth it."

Releasing me, he left me standing alone on the dance floor with my mouth and other things watering.

Did I just tell the President of the United States I was down to fuck?

CHAPTER ELEVEN

In the bathroom I used a face wipe to remove my makeup, wiping away my rose gold eye shadow and matte brown lipstick. I chuckled out loud reminiscing on the conversation I had with Representative Maxine Waters. She was a wealth of wisdom and always so supportive of those coming up behind her.

I reached for my face cleanser, pumping a generous amount into my hand, rubbing it all over my face. Normally I had a whole nighttime face routine but since Seth was waiting in the living room, I washed my face and then slathered it in moisturizer. Tossing my strapless bra in the hamper, I pulled a white tank top over my head.

"What are you watching?" I asked, lumbering into the living room.

"News."

"Ahh, of course. Can't we just turn off work for one night?"

"Clover, we literally just came from one of your work events."

I grabbed two beers from the fridge, lifting one to make sure Seth wanted it before popping the tops. "All the more reason," I said, handing him a beer and straddling his lap.

Turning off the television, Seth rested his beer on my thigh.

"Cold," I squealed, poking him in the ribs.

"It was a fun date. I can't believe I met Denzel Washington and Bruce Springsteen."

The dreaded "D" word made my body tense. "It was a fun night, but this wasn't a date." I wagged my finger at him.

He let out a labored sigh. "Would it really be so bad if it was?"

"No, but that isn't what it was. That isn't what we are." I climbed off his lap. I just wanted to have sex and go to sleep, but I couldn't encourage this behavior.

"God, Clover, not this again. You'd think you'd be ..." Seth stopped short, shaking his head.

"What? Finish your statement."

"Never mind."

"No, finish, please."

He shifted to look me in the eye. "You'd think you'd be happy a guy like me was interested in more."

I let out a mirthless laugh. "A guy like you? What is that supposed to mean?"

"Women are always talking about wanting a good man. Well, here I am, Clover, a damn good man."

Seth was a good man, I just didn't want him.

"So, I should just get on my hands and knees and thank God that you find me worthy to date?"

"No, that's not what I said. You're taking it too far."

Hello, my name is Clover Bennett and I take stuff too far. We'd passed our exit long ago, but here I am still tooling down this highway. "This isn't a relationship."

"Yeah, you've made that abundantly clear, thanks."

"Because you keep trying to make this a thing. There is no us. There's Seth and Clover." I spread my hands wide to drive my point home. "Separate and independent of one another."

"OK, so if you don't need me, why am I here?"

"Because you have a dick, Seth," I yelled.

He winced, giving me the clue that my tone was a bit harsher than I intended. But we needed to keep it all the way real. I wasn't here for the witty banter and mediocre cooking.

"Wow, is that how it is?"

"This is how it's always been. You're the only one who's spinning this into something more."

"I knew you were cutthroat at work, but damn."

"I'm not trying to be mean. I just don't want to lead you on."

"So, taking me to your work event, introducing me to your coworkers, dancing with me, rubbing my knee under the table, making out with me in the car on the way home ... what was all that?"

I gave him a perplexed shrug. "I was being nice, you did me a solid by coming with me. I was just showing my appreciation."

"Wow—"

"You've said that word a lot. Are you really surprised?"

Grabbing his shoes, he slipped his feet in. "I guess not."

"You don't have to go." Maybe I could still turn this night around. Popping up from the couch, I wrapped my arms around his neck, hoping I could convince him to stay. "Let me make it up to you."

"No, I think it's best I leave. I don't want to keep confusing this for something that it's not."

Dropping my arms to my sides, I stepped back, watching him collect his jacket. "Seth ..."

"Goodnight, Clover, when you figure out what you want, give me a call." He opened the door and headed down the stairs, never once looking back.

"MR. PRESIDENT, I hear you, but increasing the minimum wage is a touchy subject," Gibbs said, chewing on his pen cap.

"Do you know why people hate us?" Teddy paused for a response he knew wasn't going to come. "People hate us because we don't keep our promises."

"Look, no one would love to raise the wage more than me. But Dupont just did it a few years back," Gibbs protested.

"Yeah, and when he raised it to fifteen dollars an hour it was still too little too late. People deserve a living wage."

One of his advisers chimed in, "With all due respect, sir, don't you think you're being a little too ..."

"A little too what? Empathetic? Compassionate?" Teddy scratched his head. "Damn, this is what I hate about Washington. Since arriving in this White House all I hear is what I can't do."

"Sir, we want to move your agenda, but stuff like this takes time," Gibbs said, rubbing his hands on his pants.

"No, it doesn't. It's not time that we need. What we need is a back bone." Teddy shook his head. "I don't know, is it just me? Clover, what do you think?" Teddy and everyone in the Oval turned to look at me.

"Honestly, I think you're right. But if you take this to the Hill you will lose. There is not an appetite to tackle another wage increase. Most on The Capitol are still patting themselves on the back for the Dupont increase." I could see Gibbs breathe a sigh of relief because my statement aligned with his. "But you made a promise. It may have been a stupid promise, but you made it."

"First, it got people to the polls, and second, this isn't outrageous. We're talking about a dollar and fifty cents. It's not like I'm suggesting that every American should get a cost of living check each month."

"I understand, but the Senate is never going to pass another increase," I said.

"So, what do I do? Just back down?" Teddy asked, chewing on his bottom lip.

"No, you fight for it. You hit the trail telling anyone who will listen the benefits of this increase. We hire some economists to outline the positive impact, then you turn it over to The Capitol. At that point, the onus is on them to pass it. All the while giving you cover. You can claim, promise made, promise kept."

"That still doesn't get me what I want."

"Or you could play the long game and look to the next two years. You flip the Senate and then you can have whatever you want."

The room fell silent. I wasn't a political adviser but in the past few weeks, the President seemed to rely on my counsel. A fact I know pissed more than a few people in the room off. Teddy stood in the middle of his office with his hands in his pockets, deep in thought.

"Gibbs, you get the last word," Teddy said, leaning on the Resolute Desk with his arms crossed.

"Clover's two-year plan isn't a bad one," Gibbs said. I think it took all his strength to agree with me.

"Or we could just do both," Teddy said. "I hit the trail and make the rounds on the news channels. Pushing sixteen fifty. It goes to the Hill, fails in the Senate, and then we look to midterm elections and the importance of getting out and voting for people who are willing to make substantive changes."

"Understood, Mr. President." Gibbs rattled off assignments for each of us based on the President's directive.

I was assigned lining up interviews for him on all the major news networks. I would also throw in some fringe networks, podcasts, and social media outlets to cast a wide net.

As we were all heading out of his office, the President called, "Clover, can you hang back for a minute?"

Topher, my press assistant, gave me a look as he passed by. The type students would give when someone got called to the principal's office in the middle of the school day.

With the room empty, Teddy spoke, "I thought about what you said."

"What did I say? I mean, I'm sure it was brilliant," I joked, still lingering near the closed door.

"ANBS. I think you're right, and I want you to set up an interview."

"OK, yeah, sure. I can do that," I said, surprised by the one eighty. "What made you change your mind?"

"You. You've got good instincts. How does that saying go? If you want to build something that's never been built, you have to do things that have never been done."

I nodded my head, my mind collating a list of all the things I needed to do to successfully pull this interview off.

"One other thing, I have the *Meet the Press* interview coming up next week. I was hoping you could help me with some talking points."

"Sure, what do you need?"

"Maybe we could have a discussion this Friday, have a working dinner."

My laughter billowed across the room as I narrowed my eyes. Fool me once, shame on you. Fool me twice, shame on me. We were not doing any more working lunches, dinners, or breakfast.

"Don't worry, we won't leave the White House." Teddy held up his three middle fingers. "Scout's honor."

"You weren't a Boy Scout," I said, turning for the door.

"No, but I respect the creed. So, was that a yes?"

"I live to serve." Giving him a thumbs up, I walked out the door.

FINDING time to spend with Daysha was often difficult with our busy schedules. We decided to calendar a standing date once every two weeks so we could have some much-needed face time. Leaving work early, which really meant not staying until ten o'clock at night, I headed to Daysha's house.

"Hey girl, hey," Daysha greeted me at the door.

"Hi," I said, leaning in to give her a hug. Following her inside,

I set my bag and coat on the bench in the entryway, stepping out of my heels.

"Wine?"

"Duh," I giggled.

"True, that was a stupid question," Day said.

Looking around the living room, I asked, "Where's Nate?" Nate was Daysha's husband; they had been married for almost three years now.

"He's upstairs in the bedroom watching the game. He wants no parts of girls' night." She handed me a generous glass of wine. "So, what up, big baller, shot caller? Girl, you are all over the news stations sounding real professional."

"It's been insane. I knew I would be busy but damn, I hardly have any time to myself. I would love an uninterrupted weekend of nothingness," I said, taking a long sip of my pinot. Plopping on Daysha's overstuffed, extra-large couch, I tucked my right foot under my left leg.

"You can sleep when you're dead," Day said, joining me on the couch.

"I don't think this is the life our ancestors envisioned for us."

"Bitch, you love it. Your ass thrives when you have multiple balls in the air. Stop talking like you're shopping for retirement homes," Daysha scolded me.

She was right. If I had free time, I wouldn't know what to do with it. No one forced me to work on the weekends but at five months in, I had gotten to the point where I would come into the office for half the day on Saturdays. When I was younger, I thought my Saturdays would be filled with brunches, shopping, and pedicures, not emails, work memos, and interviews on *Face the Nation*.

"Have you heard from Seth?"

I let out an annoyed sigh, taking another gulp of wine. "No. I thought about reaching out once or twice in moments of weakness but decided better of it." I knew I was the one who said we weren't a couple, but I missed the companionship, as infrequent as it may have been.

"So, what's it been, a month now?"

I nodded my head, looking at my freshly manicured nails.

"Any viable replacements?" Daysha gave me a mischievous smile.

A vagrant laugh ripped through me. "There is one." A sudden heat crept over my cheeks.

"Is he someone from your bench or a new recruit?" Day leaned forward, readying herself for some juicy gossip.

"It's Teddy," I said with a grimace.

"Who the hell is Teddy?" Daysha asked, furrowing her brow.

"Oh, sorry, the President."

Daysha's mouth dropped open, and she popped up from the couch, pointing at me. "Bitch, you call the President of these United States ... Teddy?"

I scrunched my shoulders against my ears with a half-smile.

Daysha grabbed a throw pillow from the couch and hit me with it several times.

Raising my hands to protect myself, I screamed out, "Stop, could you chill."

Daysha dropped the pillow, breathing heavy from her forceful swings. "Clo, I don't know you," she claimed, pointing her slender finger in my face. "I knew you weren't being one hundred with me when you said there was nothing between you and him."

"There isn't."

Daysha shook her head, refusing to listen to my convoluted logic. "Didn't you just say you're fixing to sleep with the President?" Daysha clasped her hands. "Oh, excuse me, Teddy."

"I never said I was fixing to do anything. All I said is that Teddy is applying some serious pressure."

"Are you gonna do it?" Daysha asked, picking up the wine bottle to top me off.

"No, I'm not. I'm just ... look, I haven't had sex in over a month. I would probably seriously consider bumping uglies with Bert and Ernie at this point," I joked.

"I'd let Snuffleupagus hit." Daysha shook her head, her face mirthless.

"Is this something that you've thought about?" I asked, scratching the back of my neck.

"I mean, have you seen his trunk? And the way he be slinging it around when he talks." Day moved her arm from side to side to illustrate.

I pretended to gag so she understood how repulsed I was. "That's just a no for me."

"Don't you judge me when you're over there having triples with Bert and Ernie." Daysha wagged her finger.

"You know what, you're right. Let she who has not thought about sex with a Muppet cast the first stone."

"Do you want my advice?" Daysha asked, her voice gentle.

"Yes."

"Well, the way I see it, you have two options. You can give him a firm no and make it clear you don't get down like that."

"And option two?"

"Option two, you ride him like a cowgirl. Like some Howdy Doody, rodeo round-up, heehaw type sex. You have the chance to sleep with the President of the United States, not many people can say that."

A smirk played at the corners of my mouth. I wasn't so sure that was true in Teddy's case.

"I don't know, but for me it's a simple choice." Daysha slapped my thigh like the case was closed.

"He's my boss." I cringed, wondered if she'd even taken that fact into consideration.

"OK, and? My argument still stands. One good romp isn't gonna hurt anything. Do it for the culture if nothing else."

I was shocked. I was really expecting more of a con reaction from Daysha. Sleeping with your boss was never a good idea under any circumstance. Teddy was my friend and my boss, and no matter how much people tried to pretend otherwise, sex had a way of complicating things. Look at Seth and me.

My first job was as a sandwich artist at Subway when I was fifteen, and in those twenty years since being gainfully employed, I had never entertained the thought of sleeping with my boss. Granted, none of my bosses looked like Theodore Elmsworth. Teddy was the type of brother that had been fine all his life.

I remember when he was running for President, CNN aired a special of him and his rise to the top. They shared a picture of him from high school and he was just fine for no reason. If Teddy had attended Paul Laurence Dunbar High School, I wouldn't have graduated with my virginity intact.

"This is something you could tell your grandkids one day."

"Yeah, no. I don't think sleeping with the President is the type of thing you share with the grandbabies." Taking a long drink from my glass, I pressed her. "You don't think sleeping with a boss could lead to problems? Like, reputation ruining kind of problems?"

"*Teddy* has just as much to lose as you."

She was right to a point. If I did sleep with him and it got out, he would take a hit and have to endure a few off-color jokes, but he'd bounce back. I, on the other hand, would be branded a whore and be summarily knocked from my comfortable perch.

"I feel like you're ignoring all the reasons not to do this. This could end up being a dumpster fire."

"Sure, it could, but you're smart. You'd never let that happen to you."

Day was my best friend but when it came to me and men, she didn't know what she was talking about. Once, I drove ten hours to confront the woman who was sleeping with my boyfriend. I ended up beating her ass, slashing his tires, and catching a charge, which was later expunged due to a Black female judge that took pity on me. Sex with Teddy could only end one way ... badly.

CHAPTER TWELVE

By Friday afternoon I had compiled an array of talking points for the President's upcoming interview on *Meet the Press*. I was excited to go over them with him and get his take. If he didn't like what I prepared he would be brutally honest, but I was confident he would be pleased.

"Here are the documents you asked for," Brittany said, entering my office. "They were all out of black folders so I went with blue. I hope that's OK."

Taking the folders from her extended hand, I flipped through the first one to make sure it was compiled per my instructions. This was going to be seen by the President, and sloppy work could be an indication of a sloppy work ethic. I knew Teddy and I were cool, but that didn't give me the green light to slack when it came to my work product.

"This looks great. Thank you." I smiled up at Brittany whose mass of curly red hair was in a messy bun.

"Do you need anything else from me?" she asked, tapping her foot on the carpet.

Looking at my watch, I considered her question. Truth be told, I had a ton of things she could work on, but it was approaching six o'clock and it was a Friday. Just because I didn't have a life at the moment didn't mean she was in the same boat.

"No, why don't you head out and enjoy your weekend."

The look on Brittany's face said it all: she was dying to get out of this place. "Do you have any exciting plans?" she asked, leaning on one of the guest chairs in front of my desk.

One day she would learn to stop asking me that question. This weekend's plans were like last weekend's plans. I would work, run some errands, and maybe catch up on my much-neglected Netflix list.

"Ah, you know, dinner with friends, some shopping, maybe brunch," I lied. It was better than saying I had nothing special planned like I'd said the past few weeks.

"Sounds like fun. OK, I'm gonna head out. Lil' XYZ Baby is playing at The Jewel tonight."

"Wow, awesome. Have a great weekend," I said, waving as she left the room.

I scratched my head, wondering who the hell Lil' XYZ Baby was. Sitting back in my chair, I closed my eyes. My meeting with the President was in less than an hour and my stomach was churning. I wasn't nervous about the work conversation, that I could handle; it was the other stuff I wasn't prepared for. What if he went all Robert Redford on me and made an indecent proposal? I knew Daysha was all for this little entanglement, but I wasn't so sure.

Gathering my things, I prepared to head to the Oval. Since it was Friday and I had no forward-facing meetings with the press, I opted for a casual T-shirt with jeans and a red blazer with gold buttons. I had Brittany make two copies of the talking points, one for the President and one for me. We also created note cards condensing the same information for easy reference. Stuffing all my belongings into my carryall, I made a quick pit stop at the bathroom.

In the mirror, I looked myself over, tugging at my bra. I adjusted the girls so they were sitting just right. Rummaging through my purse, I pulled out my makeup bag, retouching my face. Finally, I spritzed my hair with hair mist so if the President got close, he would smell warm, fruity florals like gardenia, pear, and white nectarine.

What the hell am I doing? "This is a working dinner," I said aloud, tapping my reflection in the mirror. "You're gonna go over your notes and then you're gonna go home to that unfinished pint of Ben & Jerry's Milk and Cookies ice cream that you've been thinking about all day."

IT LOOKED like Abby had gone home for the night, the outer office to the Oval was dim, the only light coming from the open door. As I approached the door, I could see the President at his desk intently reviewing documents, the sound of The Roots playing softly in the background. Taking a deep breath, I knocked on the open door.

"Hey, there you are," Teddy said, dropping his pen and standing.

"Yes, I am." I stepped into his office and began setting my things on one of the couches.

"Whoa, don't get too comfortable, we're heading upstairs," Teddy said, shuffling the papers on his desk into a drawer.

"Upstairs?"

"Yeah, to the residence." He scooped up his cell phone, giving it a quick glance before shoving it in his pocket.

I had never been to the President's private residence. It was a space few White House staffers had access to. I was glad I'd missed lunch because the way my stomach was bubbling, I was fearful the sparse contents were looking for a way out.

"We can just meet right here. I'm not fussy," I protested.

"If we did that, how would I make good on my promise of dinner?" Turning off the office light, Teddy exited the Oval. "You coming?" he called from the exterior waiting area.

Grabbing my bags and files, I ran to catch up. I struggled to match his long strides as we made our way to the elevator that would take us to the second floor and the residence. With bedrooms, a living room, dining room, and kitchen, the second floor acted as the President's main living space.

"Hey, Barney," Teddy said, greeting the elevator steward.

Smiling sheepishly in Barney's direction, I entered the elevator standing next to Teddy to leave room for two of the ever-present Secret Service personnel, Tally and Mulvaney. As the elevator rattled upward, Teddy and Barney engaged in small talk.

"Good day, Mr. President?" Barney asked.

"Every day is a good day if you try hard enough." He winked in Barney's direction. The elevator came to a jittery stop on the second floor. "Have a good night. Tell Sally I said hello," Teddy said, patting Barney on the shoulder before exiting the lift.

"Good night, Mr. President. Ma'am." Barney tipped his head with a smile before the door closed.

Standing in the central hall, Agent Mulvaney walked to the east end of the hall. I tried to act unimpressed by this new space, but my head stayed on a swivel, taking in the paintings and tapestries that lined the walls. Teddy opened the door to the west sitting room, and standing aside, he allowed me to enter. Agent Tally remained in the hall outside the resident suite. The sound of the door creaking closed made my heart jump. We were all alone.

"Make yourself at home," Teddy said.

I stood completely still in a corner near the door. I didn't want to disturb anything. The residence looked nothing like I expected. There were three large floor-to-ceiling windows draped in elaborate curtains. In the center of the room was a crystal chandelier that seemed to twinkle in the dimly lit space. It was similar to a time capsule honoring the past. The only real modern touch was the art on the wall all from artists of color.

New and the old both competing for a place in this living museum.

Normally when a new first family moved in, they would update the living quarters to match their style aesthetic. I guess he had more pressing matters to attend to and couldn't be bothered with decor and wall paint. Approaching me, Teddy reached for my bag strap, removing it from my shoulder, setting it on one of three couches in the room. I suddenly realized I was clutching my file folders against my chest like I was holding on to a treasure map. Walking forward, I placed the files next to my bag.

"Do you mind if I change?" Teddy asked, already undoing the buttons on his shirt to reveal his muscular chest.

Averting my eyes, I coughed out, "Uh-huh."

"Feel free to make yourself a drink." Teddy pointed to a bar cart before disappearing into the master suite.

Perusing the bar cart, I was impressed Teddy had a mix of top-notch liquor and spirits. Grabbing the bourbon, I decided to put my four years of bartending at the Honey Pot to use. Taking a sip from my glass of whiskey sour, I smacked my lips. It was the perfect mix if I did say so myself. With glass in hand, I examined the space.

On the coffee table was a copy of a *Men's Health* magazine with Theodore Elmsworth on the cover. My attention was drawn to a framed picture on a side table of young Teddy with his grandmother. He was wearing a cap and gown, so it must be his college graduation.

"Are you done snooping?" Teddy's booming voice called from behind me.

I almost dropped the frame and my glass. Turning, my eyes danced across his body. He had changed into Dockers and a black polo shirt that hugged his muscular physique perfectly. It was weird to see him outside of his nine-to-five uniforms of suits and ties. I tried my best not to stare at his right arm that was an intricately woven piece of art, one tattoo connecting to the next to tell an elaborate story I had never gotten close enough to fully make out.

"I wasn't snooping." Lifting the frame, I asked, "College graduation?"

"Harvard Law," Teddy said, leaning in behind me. The scent of his cologne danced on the edge of my nose, drawing me in like a siren call. He took the picture from me, tapping at the glass. "It's funny how something can feel like it happened yesterday and a lifetime ago in the same moment."

"From the smile on her face, she seemed pretty excited," I observed.

"I wasn't the first in my family to go to college, but I was the first to go to an Ivy League college. It made her pretty proud."

Looking at his face, his expression was distant. His grandmother had passed away a month before he won the primaries, making him the democratic nominee for President. I remember there being talk of him potentially pulling out of the race because he was so broken up about her loss.

"I'm sure that wasn't the first or the last time you made her proud."

Teddy stepped back and studied the photograph in silence for a moment before replacing it on the side table.

Walking over to the bar cart, I reached for the second whiskey sour glass. "Drink?" I asked.

"Thank you." Taking a slow sip, a smile spread across his thick lips. "Are you hungry?"

"I could eat," I said, knowing good and well I was starving.

Extending his hand in my direction, we stood in complete silence. Narrowing my eyes, I examined his face. It was always difficult to decipher what Teddy was thinking. I guess as a politician having a keen poker face was a useful skill but in moments like this, it was frustrating. Slipping my hand into his, I let him lead me into the kitchen.

I LOOKED around for the take-out bags or containers, but the room was cold and empty. There was no food to be found here. Walking to the fridge, Teddy pulled out groceries.

"What are you doing?" I asked, as he moved from the fridge to the counter to the cabinets.

"Cooking," Teddy said, reaching for the extra virgin olive oil.

"When you said 'working dinner' I thought you meant take-out," I said, pushing my hair from my face.

"Ugh." Teddy wrinkled his nose. "Aren't you sick of takeout? When was the last time you had a home-cooked meal?"

"Does frozen chicken alfredo count?" I asked, tugging on my blazer.

"No," Teddy chuckled, slicing lemons on a cutting board.

"Do you need help?" I looked at the vegetables and spices scattered across the marble counter.

"Can you handle seasoning the salmon?"

"Yes." I smiled, happy to have a task I could manage.

"If you only use a pinch of salt and pepper I want to know now before I fall too deep."

Fall too deep into what? Does he mean with me? I could feel my face getting hot thinking of how deep he could go.

"My mother's from Jamaica, remember? Trust me, I know seasoning." Washing my hands, I sprinkled lemon pepper over the meat. "I didn't know you cooked," I said, looking for the smoked paprika.

"There's a lot you don't know about me." He smirked.

"Like?"

"I don't think you're ready for that conversation."

"OK, man of mystery," I teased, patting down the meat to ensure the seasonings stuck.

"Nah, I'm public domain. Any secrets I did have were all aired out during the campaign."

Teddy wasn't lying. The presidential campaign had been a brutal one. First during the primary election when he took friendly fire from his fellow democrats who were all vying for the top spot. Then again during the general election when the GOP slung mud from every direction hoping something would stick. They brought up some of his questionable votes while a senator. They brought up his affiliation with a childhood friend, now activist, who was calling for the police to be abolished. Then there were the personal attacks about his dating life and sexual activity.

"For someone who's in the public domain, you're still quite the enigma," I said. There was a lot of chatter and rumors about Teddy but very little facts.

He cut the ends off the freshly washed asparagus. "Ask me anything."

"OK," I said, pausing for a moment to consider.

I had the chance to ask the President of the United States anything I wanted, so I better make it good. Should I ask him why he picked James Conrad as his vice President? Conrad was nice enough but a safe pick not bound to ruffle many feathers. Or I could ask him about his controversial ideas when it came to climate change.

Drying my wet hands on a dish towel, I blurted out, "What happened, with you and Mariah?"

Teddy froze, the knife he was holding suspended in midair. I had clearly caught him off guard. "The same thing that happens to most marriages in America," he offered.

"Enlighten me," I said, downing the last of my whiskey sour.

Setting the sharp blade down, Teddy turned to me. "Well, Clover," Teddy said, his voice condescending like I was a child. "Sometimes when a man and woman love one another, that love isn't enough to sustain their relationship."

"You could have just told me to mind my business instead of being a complete asshole." I scowled.

Teddy's tone softened. "Being married to a public figure isn't easy. And truthfully, I can be a difficult man to love. It didn't work. Nobody's fault. Just the luck of the draw."

I nodded my head at his words, having nothing of value to add.

Teddy and Mariah were married for roughly three years. I didn't know her personally, but I was still surprised when they released a joint statement saying that while they still loved one another very much they had decided to continue the next part of life's journey alone.

"I almost got married once," I revealed, twirling my crescent necklace between my fingers.

Teddy raised his eyebrows. "Oh yeah, what happened?"

"I sobered up. We were in Vegas."

Teddy shook his head in a swift arch. "Clover the great adventurer. Backpacking through foreign countries, jumping out of planes, almost jumping the broom in Vegas."

My shoulders hopped. "Not so much anymore. Work kind of has me grounded."

You know that saying, be careful what you wish for. I wanted this job and I loved what I did, but it was severely impacting my social calendar. I knew this job had an expiration date. Most press secretaries were lucky if they last three years. I was willing to make the sacrifice, even if it meant my social life atrophied.

"It's all about perspective. There's still tons of adventure to be had. You're working in the White House helping to shape the future of our country. After this gig, the world is your oyster." Teddy smiled, while arranging the salmon, asparagus, onions, and lemon slices on a sheet pan, popping it into the oven. "So, what's the plan, Lucky? Where are you trying to go?"

My face brightened; I definitely had a plan. I wasn't working this hard for the hell of it. "I'm looking to break the glass ceiling and increase my net worth."

The ultimate goal was to start my own PR firm. I'd shared this with Teddy long ago, although I doubted he still remembered. When we worked together the first time, we shared a lot, our big audacious dreams included. Teddy wanted to be President and I wanted to own a public relations firm.

It would be kind of a one-stop boutique with speech writers who could craft the perfect mea culpa and lawyers who would say things like 'My client has no comment at this time,' while charging five hundred dollars an hour. We'd have brand consultants and social media gurus. Whatever a politician, athlete, entertainer, or six-figure earner needed.

"Ahh, so this is not just about public service."

"Public service is cool and all, but you know what's better? Generational wealth."

"I'm sure you have a plan, and if anyone can execute it, you can. There's just one thing missing."

"Oh yeah, what's that?"

"Someone to share it with."

"Why is it that when a man works hard, never settling down, no one bats an eye. But when a woman does the same, it's all biological clocks and having something more than work that gives you a purpose."

"I don't know. Maybe because women are different than men. You guys are nurturers."

"I can nurture my bank account, my 401K, and my stock options."

"OK, Ms. I Don't Need a Man."

My smile turned bitter. "Don't do that. Don't pull out that old trope. You're better than that."

"OK, you're right, Ms. I close myself off to others and wrap myself in work because I am afraid of being vulnerable and truly experiencing love because most of the men I've dated have been careless with my heart. So, it's just easier to throw myself into work and ignore the fact that I'm achingly lonely." Teddy took a drink from his glass. "Was that better?"

"That was much better, Mr. I overcompensate in every area of my life because people always underestimate me, and even though I currently hold the highest office in the land, I'm really just a scared little boy with mommy issues."

Any trace of a smile vanished from his face. "What the hell is wrong with you? That was ... mean. Accurate, but mean."

Throwing my hands in the air, I said in a sing-songy tone, "You go low, I burrow a hole into the center of the earth, or whatever it was Michelle said."

"Damn, you haven't changed a bit. In fact, I think you've gotten worse."

"Thank you." I took a deep bow, even though I didn't think he intended it as a compliment. Shifting my weight from one foot to the other, I looked around the kitchen. "What do we do now?"

Teddy's face lit up with a mischievous grin. "Now I give you the penny tour."

DURING DINNER, Teddy was eager to review the talking points I'd put together. He asked questions, questions I had anticipated and was ready to answer between bites of the expertly seasoned fish.

Grabbing a red pen, he scribbled notes over several pages of text before handing the file back to me. "Good job. I can see you put a lot of thought into this, which I appreciate."

Pursing my lips, I nodded. It wasn't a resounding success, but I could handle a few redlined pages. At least he didn't chuck the whole thing in the trash like he had done to Matt, one of the young speech writers. Resting my knife and fork on my plate, I wiped my mouth with my napkin, my stomach the perfect amount of full, making me content.

"What?" I asked.

"Nothing." Teddy shook his head, taking a swig of beer.

"You keep staring at me."

"Maybe I like the view," Teddy said, leaning back in his chair.

His legs were wide open like the men on the Metro taking up space. My heart beat loudly in my ears, drowning all other sounds out. Teddy's lips continued to move, but I couldn't quite make out the words.

"I thought you didn't wanna play games," I said, crossing my arms across my chest.

"I don't. Honestly, I'm just following your lead. I planned everything up to and including the dinner. What happens now is totally up to you."

"And if I wanna go home?" I asked, my arms still firmly resting over my chest like a shield.

"I'd have one of the drivers take you." Teddy shrugged.

"And if I choose to stay?" I whispered breathlessly, trying to quell the heat that was simmering deep inside me.

"I'd like that."

A nervous chuckle escaped my lips. Reaching for my wine, I tilted the glass back, pouring the contents of the glass down my throat. Teddy placed his hand on my knee. I jerked forward, escaping from my chair, crossing the kitchen to provide some much-needed distance between us.

Looking at his face, I could tell even though the ball was entirely in my court, he already knew I wasn't going anywhere. My poker face was not as practiced as his.

"Ground rules." My voice cracked as I clung to the island. Teddy stood at my words like a wolf ready to strike. "This is a one and done type of deal. What happens here tonight stays here. And we never talk about it again."

When it came to sex, I had always found it best to be upfront with my expectations. I wanted Teddy to know this was going to be purely physical. A business transaction in which we both got something we wanted. Teddy slowly walked toward me, causing my body to tense.

"And no kissing on the lips," I blurted out.

Teddy stopped, leaning on the other side of the kitchen island. Although it was made of wood and marble and he was a mere man, I got the distinct feeling if he really wanted to, he could fling it aside like a card table.

"Yes, to everything but the kissing," Teddy said. I opened my mouth to protest but Teddy stopped me. "It's nonnegotiable," he said assertively, like he was hammering out the details of a cease fire agreement.

"OK," I whispered meekly.

I knew once he was close it would be difficult for me to adhere to the no kissing rule, so it was useless to protest.

"OK," Teddy said, circling the island, never taking his eyes off me.

I took a few steps back as he advanced forward. Normally I was pretty aggressive when it came to sex, but Teddy's confidence had me all turned around. He was acting like a man who knew exactly how to handle me. Men like that were dangerous. Men like that tended to cloud my head and impair my judgment. I tried to avoid men like that.

Stopping just short of making contact, his mouth turned upward into a smug smile. "Do you wanna shake on it?" he asked, arm extended.

"No, I do not." I batted his arm away. Teddy raised his arm again, this time tucking my hair behind my ear. His finger ran down the length of my face until his right hand was wrapped around the side of my neck. Heat rose from the tip of my toes, rolling and bubbling up through my body like a tea kettle ready to whistle. Parting my mouth, I let out a soft sigh, trying to release some of the pressure.

Teddy's lips inched closer as my heartbeat took on a disorganized rhythm, erratic and unpredictable. Parting my lips with his, the warmth of his tongue washed over me like a summer wave. Teddy's right hand still caressed my neck while his left hand was busy grabbing my waist, pushing me closer to him. It was like the room disappeared and all I could hear was his soft anxious breath as his lips devoured mine. All I could taste was the bitter, spicy aftertaste from the beer that lingered on his tongue. All I could feel was a burning desire to lose myself deeply in Teddy's embrace.

I couldn't tell you how we made it from the kitchen to the presidential bedroom. All I remember was the sense that I was levitating, all the while my lips kissing, licking, and biting at Teddy's. I could feel his hands loosening their grip. He stepped back, his face looked as disoriented as mine did. His breathing labored, he gingerly removed his shoes and wrist watch.

I sensed he needed a minute to catch his breath. Following his lead, I removed my heels, chucking them in the corner of the room. Our timeout didn't last long before Teddy was looming over me. He made me feel small and delicate as he towered over my five-foot-eight frame. His hands tugged at my blazer, and then those same hands lifted my shirt over my head.

Teddy buried his face in my neck, planting kisses along my neck and shoulder blade. I grabbed his face, running my finger over his beard. Standing on my tip toes, I found his mouth, drinking him in. Teddy scooped me up like I was a rag doll so I didn't have to teeter on wobbly toes to reach him.

As I wrapped my legs around his waist, his hands roamed over my backside. Without warning, Teddy dropped me on to the bed. I gasped loudly from the unexpected change in position. I gave him a sly smile, letting him know I was ready to tussle. Undoing my jeans, I lifted my hips as he pulled them off. Teddy looked down at me, admiring my curves.

Lifting my leg, he rubbed my foot like he had in the Oval months ago. This time I didn't stifle any moans. Leaning in, his mouth traveled up the length of my leg, stopping at my thick thigh. I did my best to regulate my breathing. We had a long night ahead of us. I didn't want to short circuit before the main event. Teddy's kisses finally found their way to my sweet spot. He teased me with his tongue, leaving me eager for more.

Teddy was unlocking the beast mode in me. The type of shit that was only reserved for special select partners. You know the stuff you pretend you don't do because you're a good girl. Pushing him away, I dropped to my knees, pulling his pants and boxer briefs off, ready to put on a show. My eyes locked on to his as I licked his tip with my tongue. Teddy seeped in a drag of breath as my warm, wet tongue connected with his firm member. Now that I had his attention, I intended to keep it.

I took as much of him as I could manage into my mouth. Gripping the base with my hands, I moved my hands and mouth in unison, wanting to please him and show him how much I appreciated what he was bringing to the table. I also loved having the power to drive him wild and send him to ecstasy.

This was my one night with the President. This man wasn't getting any sleep tonight. Teddy gasped, his body tensed. Grabbing me, he threw me on the bed, flipping me over on my stomach. He used his tongue to show he didn't only like to receive, he liked to give. He gave every nook and cranny on my body a taste with his long tongue. I had to bite down on the pillow to stop myself from screaming out.

"Please," I moaned.

Right now, I was T-Boz, Chilli, and Left Eye because I wasn't too proud to beg. *Bump this foreplay*. I needed all of his inches inside of me immediately. Teddy could sense I was ready to boil over. When he flipped me around again, I waited anxiously as he rolled a condom into place. All the while licking his lips, still wet from my juices. With confident hands, I guided him in like a plane coming in for a landing.

My eyes fluttered closed as I inhaled deeply. Teddy was a lot to take in but I was up for the challenge. As he slid in and out, guttural moans escaped from deep inside of me. Grabbing at him, I pulled him on top of me. I needed to taste his mouth. His kisses were deliberate and searching, his tongue fluttering against mine like he was making love to every part of me. The firm weight of him hovering just above me was like a security blanket. Cradled between his strong arms seemed familiar, like I always belonged here. Right here beneath his love.

I bit at the inside of his arm, I needed to mark my territory. So he would remember I was here. Teddy returned the favor, but he was far gentler with a sweet love bite to my collarbone. His arms swooped me up, taking us to a seated position with me on top, my legs wrapped around him. I held him close, moaning over his lips as he moved in and out. Teddy's strong hands slid down my back, cupping my ass to help me maneuver over the length of him.

His deep, baritone voice echoed in my ear, his tone primal and raw. "You feel so good," he grunted out.

Teddy buried his face in my chest, rolling his tongue over my erect nipples. My moans filled the silence, each one louder and filled with ravenous ecstasy. Shivers rolled through my body as the waves crested inside of me. I grabbed his shoulder with one arm and dug my nails into his back with the other. Leaning back, I rode his wave all the way to the shore. Sinking into the bed, I looked up at him dazed and confused.

Standing back up, Teddy looked down at me and commanded, "Turn around."

I was exhausted and hungry for more at the same time, so like a good soldier, I obeyed. Turning around, I arched my back and waited. Slapping my ass with his strong hand, Teddy did not disappoint.

CHAPTER THIRTEEN

THE SUN CREPT IN THROUGH THE PARTIALLY DRAWN BLINDS. Squinting my eyes against the glare, I stretched in search of Teddy but his side of the bed was vacant. I canvased the room while rubbing the sleep from my eyes. On a chair in the corner my clothes had been neatly folded alongside my purse. Teddy's clothes, which I had eagerly removed last night, were gone.

His bedroom aesthetic was dark, with heavy masculine energy. I could tell from the bedding and furniture this was the one room in the residence Teddy had taken an interest in decorating. Every inch of the space was modern and contemporary. Perhaps that was because he had a bevy of women in and out of his bed.

His king-sized bed was plush. I burrowed deeper in the mattress, my eyes fluttering closed. Last night I'd had the best sleep I'd had in months; I would have to ask what kind of mattress this was. I tried unsuccessfully to stifle a smile that was tugging at the corners of my mouth as I remembered the events of the prior evening. A shiver licked up my spine at the thought of him, and I could still feel him filling me to capacity. What had I done to deserve all that he had given me last night? Lost in my thoughts, I didn't hear Teddy enter the room.

"I had the chef make us breakfast."

His deep voice invaded my ruminations. It was difficult to meet his eyes after the nasty things we did to each other just a few hours before.

"Uhh, I should..." I cleared my throat. My voice sounded raspy, and my mouth was drier than an Arizona summer. "I should probably head out." Gathering the crisp white sheet around me, I scooted to the edge of the bed.

His face flipped to a frown. Walking into the closet, he returned with one of his T-shirts. "Don't be rude, Lucky." He chucked the T-shirt at my head before exiting the room.

Pulling his oversized shirt over my head, I stood slowly, making my way to the master bathroom. My body was sore and a bit bruised from last night. At one of the two sinks, I swished some mouthwash in my mouth while scanning the smeared makeup on my face. Teddy's bottle of facewash was my only option. I scanned the back, checking over the ingredients making sure it wouldn't irritate my sensitive skin. With a shrug, I pumped a generous amount into the palm of my hand.

Wiggling my toes over the tiled marble floor, I realized the bathroom floor was warm underneath my feet. I padded back and forth in front of the sink and determined the floor was heated. The White House was notorious for being poorly ventilated. Rooms within the house were either too hot or too cold. I wondered if the heated floors were Teddy's idea or a renovation from one of the other former residents. Splashing my face with water, I returned to the bedroom, rummaging through my purse for a hair tie. Finger combing my hair, I secured it into a low ponytail.

Upon exiting the master suite, I was directed to the private dining room by one of the residence staff butlers. That was where I found Teddy, his face concealed by a newspaper. Next to his plate of eggs, sausage, and rye toast was a stack of newspapers waiting to be read. Dropping to the empty chair next to him, I coughed to announce my presence. Teddy didn't move, *The Washington Post* had his full attention.

"Can I get you something to drink, ma'am?" a middle-aged lady who was part of the residence wait staff asked with a kind smile.

"I will take black tea if you have it." I gave her a bashful smile in return, now painfully aware I was sitting next to the President in his personal residence with nothing but a T-shirt on.

I'm sure tongues were wagging among the residence staff. Pulling the shirt upward, I tried to partially cover my face, hoping to conceal my identity. Teddy didn't seem the least bit concerned as he sat beside me taking bites out of his toast.

The last thing I wanted was for our escapade to get back to the West Wing or worse, the rabid media. If someone from the residence staff was so inclined, they could make a pretty penny with a story about the President's late-night rendezvous with his Press Secretary. I wanted my name to go down in history, not infamy like other women who were romantic with sitting presidents.

The one thing I had going for me was the residence staff tended to be ferociously protective of the presidents they serviced. Mostly because they worked so closely with the presidents and got to see them in a way no one else did. Unlike staffers in the West Wing, the residence staff were known for their discretion.

I suppose their jobs depended on a level of discreet sensibility. If tea was to be spilled about in-residence activity, it could easily be tracked back to a handful of people. Sitting in the armless dining room chair, I was mentally keeping a list of everyone who saw me enter the President's residence. From Barney the steward to the nice lady pouring my tea. If I went down, they were all coming with me.

"How did you sleep?" Teddy asked, folding the newspaper and setting it on top of the pile.

"Very well, thank you."

I don't know why I was being so formal but the moment and the room, with its chandelier and striped blue and white wallpaper, seemed to call for it.

"Last night was fun."

"Uh-huh," I murmured, stuffing half a sausage link into my mouth.

"We should do it again," Teddy offered.

I covered my mouth, letting out a laugh that seemed to echo off the walls. "We agreed. One night only." Raising my cup to my mouth, I took a big slurp of tea.

"Who are you, Jennifer Holiday?" Teddy asked, leaning forward.

Ignoring his comment, I asked, "So what other staffers have you slept with in the White House?" Narrowing my eyes, I waited for his response, hoping I could determine the truth in his words.

"I've only slept with you." Teddy returned my gaze unblinking.

I knew BS when I heard it. Maybe he hadn't slept with any other current staffers, but he had definitely slept with the last Press Secretary and now me, so that was a disturbing pattern.

"Well, me and Nadia," I reminded him.

Teddy's warm expression turned sour. "I never slept with Nadia."

Rolling my eyes, I said, "Really? Because Brittany..." I pursed my lips. Damnit, I didn't mean to throw Brittany under the bus.

Teddy's eyes widened at the realization it was in fact Brittany who'd provided me with the intel months ago. "Oh, so it was Brittany. Yeah, well Brittany doesn't know what she's talking about."

"OK. So, what *did* happen between you two?"

I tried to keep my tone as nonchalant as possible. Not that it mattered, but there was a part of me that wondered if I was just one in a long line of post-election conquest or something different. Rubbing his eyes, Teddy let out a labored sigh. I could tell the gears in his head were spinning trying to decide where to start and how much to reveal.

"Nadia was a staffer on my presidential campaign. She was smart and funny. Just an all-around cool person. We hung out together with other people. Always with other people. After a long day, me and some of the staffers would go out for drinks or grab a bite to eat, Nadia among them. You know how it is on the trail." Teddy pointed in my direction. "Being around the same people every day for over a year ... you grow close. So, when I won, I offered her the Press Secretary position because she was loyal and she performed so well on the trail."

I was so engaged in his story I didn't realize my mouth was hanging open like a dullard. Stabbing my eggs with my fork, I shoved them into my mouth.

"When we got to the White House it was like someone flipped a switch. She started acting weird and clingy, kinda obsessed. It was like she thought she was entitled to my time and attention." He shook his head, rubbing his full beard with his hands.

It appeared he was still in disbelief regarding the whole situation. Teddy was an attractive man. I found it hard to believe this was the first time a woman had gotten too attached.

"At first I tried to ignore it, but she would send me emails laced with inappropriate comments or she'd slip a photo of herself in lingerie, and eventually completely naked, into a stack of documents for my review."

"What did you do to give her the impression that she could do all that?" I asked.

Teddy threw up his hands. "Why do you think I did something? I was friendly, that's it."

"You were friendly with me," I said, shaking my head. Teddy was a known lothario.

"I was flirting with you." Teddy's typically even tone was raised. "Being nice to someone and overtly flirting are two different things."

I bumped a shrug, continuing. "I don't know. I'm just saying, it's easy to conflate the two. She was a beautiful woman." Grabbing some fruit from a platter, I decided to let him finish.

"Yeah, she was," Teddy said, furrowing his brow. "I just wasn't interested. It was my first month in office. I had a lot on my plate and getting laid wasn't one of them."

"Why didn't you just report her?"

Once the words left my mouth, I regretted it. If Teddy were a woman, I wouldn't be treating his story so cavalierly. And I certainly wouldn't victim shame. It was a little hard to believe the most powerful man in the world could be sexually harassed, but it wasn't beyond belief.

"I ain't no snitch. Look, I asked her to stop. She wouldn't. I threatened to report her. She didn't seem to care. I just kinda hoped she'd stop when she didn't get the attention she was seeking. Also, she was really unpredictable. I didn't want to have this blow up in my face."

I started to speak but stopped short when one of the butlers returned to refresh Teddy's coffee cup. My leg bounced anxiously, eager to finish our conversation. As the butler left, I whispered, "That's a reasonable concern. If she was doing all that, why were you always in her office?" I hoped my tone came off as more curious than accusatory.

"I'd come to her office asking her to stop, begging her to stop. Threatening her so she'd stop."

"You threatened her?"

"It wasn't my finest moment but yeah, I did. She was getting all fatal attraction, single white female on me." Teddy cleared his throat, shifting in his chair.

Clearly this topic was uncomfortable for him.

"Our last conversation, the one Brittany overheard, I'd had enough and I told her I was gonna have to tell Gibbs. She started crying and pleading with me. At that point I was fed up and didn't wanna hear her crocodile tears anymore. I yelled at her and called her some choice words. The next day she handed in her resignation, claiming a family emergency."

"Was that Gibbs's doing?"

Teddy shrugged, taking a sip of his coffee. "I don't know, but I never told him what happened. When she quit I was just relieved it was over."

"I'm sorry that happened to you," I said, reaching for his hand.

Teddy pulled his hand away. "Don't be sorry. Next time don't accuse me of some dumb shit when you don't have all the facts."

I thrust out a stiff breath. "Fair point. But let's not act like that behavior is out of character for you."

"What do you mean?" Teddy asked, staring at me.

"It's like a revolving door with you."

Teddy wagged his finger at me. "See, there you go assuming once again."

I took another big gulp of tea.

"The last time we spent any considerable amount of time together before you started working here was years ago, so you don't really get to speak about my character."

I raised my hand in surrender. "You're right. That's fair. We don't really know each other anymore."

All I know is that Senator Elmsworth was the definition of a fuckboy. President Elmsworth seemed a bit more refined, or maybe he was just better at hiding it. I worked for him years ago and people change. I know I had, so I was willing to give him the benefit of the doubt.

Teddy let out an exasperated sigh. We sat in silence for a long moment, just the sound of our forks scraping the plates. I had this sinking feeling I'd overstayed my welcome. Raising my tea cup, I took another sip.

"You know you slurp your tea when you drink?" he said.

"Oh, sorry." I wiped at the corners of my mouth.

"No, I like it. It reminds me of last night."

My head pitched back. "We are not talking about that."

Images of Teddy in all his glory flashed in my head. My body tingled as I recalled the way he responded to my touch. The look in his eyes as I drove him to the heights of ecstasy.

"What do you have planned for the rest of the day?" I asked, trying to wipe the stupid look off my face.

"Well, that kinda depends on you." Teddy smiled.

"Me? How so?" I asked, tugging at the neckline of my T-shirt.

"I was hoping we could squeeze in round two before you leave."

"Uhh ... we already had round two, remember?"

Teddy had woken me in the middle of the night, fired up and ready to go. And go we did.

Teddy's brown eyes sparked with recognition. "Yeah, I remember." He smiled wide, not looking me in the eye.

I chewed at my lip between my teeth, proud of myself for making the President of the United States blush. "Anyway, I really think I should go."

"Now wait a minute," Teddy protested. "If this is really a one-time thing, shouldn't we get our money's worth?" He reached for my thigh, kneading it with his oversized hand. Even though my mind was ready to leave, my body very much wanted to stay.

"Teddy," I whispered. "The waitstaff is just in the other room. We shouldn't."

Teddy's hand stopped its slow incline up my thigh. Standing, he walked through the swinging door to the kitchen. His intense full-toned voice commanded the room. "I think we're good on breakfast. Could you guys come back later? Thank you, every-thing was great."

Back in the dining room, he smiled mischievously, clearing the plates, platters, and cups to the other end of the table. Teddy pulled me out of my seat. His hands finding my waist, he led me to the edge of the dining table. Taking a seat in front of me at the head of the table, parting my legs, he kissed and licked the sensitive flesh in between my thighs with his tongue. My mind went blank as I stared straight ahead at the striped wallpaper that for some reason seemed to wave and vibrate against the wall. His tongue found my sweet spot, sending me collapsing back onto the table.

This can never happen again, I thought as I clutched the side of the table. Parting my lips, I screamed, "Mr. President."

CHAPTER FOURTEEN

Returning to my apartment, I hopped in the shower and changed into sweats. My emails were in the hundreds and my missed calls were in the double digits on both my work and personal cell phones. I had essentially been MIA for the past seventeen hours. My personal cell phone was manageable; I had a missed call from my mother and a few friends. This didn't include the missed calls and text messages from Daysha that escalated in violent undertones with each message. The final text reading, '*Bitch, if you ain't dead I'm gonna kill you when I see you next.*'

My work cell was worse with calls and emails from my staff and a smattering of reporters. I also had four messages from CNN asking me to appear on *Inside Politics* tomorrow morning. Tackling CNN first, I returned their call, agreeing to appear and asking them to provide a rundown of the topics they wanted to discuss. After CNN I called Topher and Rebecca, asking them to email me some talking points on Bolivia and France. Next, I decided to tackle the hundred or so work emails that had accumulated over the night.

"But first, coffee," I said to myself, shuffling toward the kitchen in my fuzzy socks.

Dropping a K-cup in the machine, I selected a large cup. As I swayed side to side waiting for my hot cup of jo, my mind wandered back to the events of last night and this morning. Although it felt good in the moment, hella good, sleeping with Teddy was a mistake. I knew it, he knew it, even if he wanted to pretend otherwise. Sleeping with your boss was always a no-no. But sleeping with your boss who was also the President of the United States was a hell nah.

My mug was close to overflowing. I gingerly took a sip from my cup, indulging in the nutty aroma. Back in the living room, I open my laptop, pulling up the endless work emails. Letting out a loud sigh, I opened the first email and got to work. I confirmed our need for the Secretary of Defense's presence at a Wednesday press briefing to discuss the situation in Afghanistan. I RSVPed my attendance at a Women in Washington symposium. I sent Brittany an email with a list of to dos for next week. I'm sure she hated that I worked on the weekends and that on Mondays she was already behind trying to accomplish the tasks I'd assigned her over the two days that were supposed to be dedicated to rest and relaxation.

Loud, aggressive rapping emanated from the other side of my front door. Glancing at the clock, I stood with a big stretch. I'd been working through these emails for the last hour and a half. Opening the door, there stood Daysha with a sore look on her face.

"I thought you were dead. The news this morning said they found a female body in the park and you walk sometimes and I thought it could've been you." Daysha pushed past me, looking around my apartment like she was surprised to find me alone. "So, what do I do? I call you to make sure you're not the one lying in a ditch bleeding out. And what do you do? You ignore my calls and text messages. I was about to tie a note to a pigeon's ankle and hope that it found its way to you."

"Sorry, I was working," I said, pointing to my laptop. "I was gonna call you later."

"See, you ain't my friend." She shook her head. "Friends don't leave friends on read while they're having dinner with the President."

My eyes rolled to the back of my head. Daysha was so dramatic, if she hadn't gone to law school, she could have been an actress because right now she was giving Regina King a run for her money.

"I didn't leave you on read. I was busy."

"I bet you were." Daysha clapped her hands, breaking out into a snake like dance.

"I thought you were worried about my safety?"

"I was, that's why I'm over here checking on you," Daysha said, dropping her purse on the ottoman. "So, are you good? You straight?" She opened my kitchen cabinets looking for something to eat, kissing her teeth when all she found were saltine crackers and some canned soup. Work was keeping me busy and my cupboards bare.

"I'm well, thank you. I do have this slight crick in my neck. I think I may have slept on it wrong or something." I tried my best not to smile, knowing she did not care a wit about what ailed me.

"OK, so you really gonna make me say it?" Day sauntered over to me.

"What?" I creased my brow, playing coy.

"So how can I say this delicately? Is the commander in chief a grower or a shower?" Daysha said, her hands sliding back and forth to estimate length.

"Is it possible to be both?" I asked, clicking my tongue.

"Oh my God. Oh my God," Daysha screamed, circling the living room couch. "This is happening." She let out a giddy giggle. Grabbing my face, she said, "I want to know *everything*. Do you understand me? I don't want you skipping or skimming a damn part." Releasing my face, she looked back toward the kitchen. "I'ma need some food for this."

While we devoured a large pizza, I told Day how Teddy

devoured me. I know she wanted the full story, but I decided to leave the naughtier parts out.

"So, on a scale of one to ten where does he fall?

I shrugged. "He was good."

Day rolled her eyes. "Scale ... one ... through ... ten."

"OK, damn, he was a fifteen. Now can you please stop badgering the witness?" I asked, taking a bite out of my third slice of meat lovers pizza.

Daysha was my girl, but I was over story time. I wanted to keep a piece of my time with Teddy just between him and I.

"So, are you gonna..." Day inserted a finger through a hole in her hand. "Again?"

"No, nope, absolutely not.

"You wanted to see me?"

"Yes, Clover. Please close the door." Teddy looked up from his desk, waving me in. He stood, walking around to the front of his desk before leaning on it. "I've been thinking."

I opened my notepad, ready to jot down directives. Teddy's legs were spread wide, taking up all the room. His presence was undeniable and even though I was a good foot away, I could feel him invading my space. I tried my best not to look at his crotch, but I kept stealing peeks when I thought he wasn't looking.

"I would like to see you again." His piercing eyes stared into mine.

Closing my notepad, I chuckled. "No. Please tell me you didn't call me down here for that."

"Can we talk about it before you just shut me down?"

"We already talked about this and agreed." My eyes flashed to his large hands that just a few nights prior were all over me.

"You know as well as I do that agreements can be revised."

"Yes, but both parties have to agree to the changes."

"I just think our agreement as it stands now is way too prohibitive."

"OK, so what would you suggest?" The words flowed from my mouth before my brain had a chance to process the next steps. His face lit up with a smile. He thought he'd won. "That last statement was more of a rhetorical one," I said, hoping to clarify my position.

Teddy stood, advancing toward me. I clenched my notepad across my chest as if it could protect me from his wiles. My body seemed to pulsate in anticipation of his touch.

"I want you, Lucky," Teddy said, just inches from my face. He didn't touch me. I was both relieved and disappointed.

"I know you're used to getting what you want, but that's not how things work with me."

"What *I* want? Please don't act like you don't want it too."

"I don't." My voice was a whisper, my tone unconvincing.

"You know you're a bad liar, right?" Teddy asked, reaching out to brush a loose tendril of hair from my eye.

His touch caused me to swoon, producing a noticeable shiver. "You don't have to believe me," I said, taking astep back.

"Do *you* believe you?" Teddy asked, with a tilt of his head. He turned, walking back to his desk. "I would love it if you'd join me tonight to watch a movie. I'll be in the movie theater at seven. Hopefully, I won't be alone." Teddy's eyes searched mine. A knock on the door pulled his attention away. "Come in," he yelled.

Chief of Staff Gimble entered the office, stopping in his tracks when he caught sight of me. "Sorry, am I interrupting something?"

"No, Clover was just updating me on the ANBS interview. We're having some scheduling issues. My calendar is kind of full." Teddy turned to me. "But we'll figure it out. Won't we, Clover?"

Was he still talking about the interview?

"Yes, Mr. President, we will definitely figure it out," I said, heading toward the door as fast as I could without running.

***

MY TEAM WAS surprised when I let them leave at six. Normally on a Monday I'd have Brittany, Topher, and Rebecca work until eight or nine. I needed to think and if I did decide to meet Teddy, I wanted as few witnesses as possible. There really wasn't anything to think about, I knew what I should do. What I should have done was pack up my bag and head home but here I was at six forty-five, still at my desk, weighing the pros and cons.

The cons were many and could ultimately end in my termination. If it got out that I was having a sexual relationship with the President, he would walk away bruised but I would end up battered, broken, and blacklisted. Powering down my laptop, I stuffed it into my carryall.

"You're smarter than this, Clover. Go home."

As I walked through the White House, I had every intention of heading to the exit, but my feet had other plans. I found myself heading toward the East Wing. I moved past the suite of offices reserved for the First Lady, which remained vacant since Teddy was unmarried. All social events that would normally be handled by the First Lady's office were being managed by a team of event planners.

I did my best to blend in with the striped wallpaper as I walked past the military office.

"Can I help you?" an unfamiliar voice called from behind.

I turned to find a military officer in full uniform eyeing me suspiciously. Which made sense, as press secretaries didn't normally frequent the East Wing.

Smiling brightly, I replied, "Umm, I'm looking for the President. Abby told me he was in the theater." I raised the folder I held in my hand. "Work never stops."

The officer smiled back. "Tell me about it. I've been trying to get out of here for the last hour now."

"Get a job at the White House, they said. It'll be fun, they said." I arched an eyebrow and leaned in, whispering. "When exactly does the fun start?"

The officer and I shared a laugh before he said, "I saw President Elmsworth head to the theater about fifteen minutes ago."

I glanced at his name badge. "Thank you, Officer Wrice.

"Call me Jace," he said, his eyes traveling over my curves in a sheath tangerine-colored dress.

"Good night, Jace," I said, continuing to walk toward the direction of the theater. "I hope you have better luck at leaving this place than I'm having," I called over my shoulder before turning a corner and disappearing from view.

With the exception of Officer Wrice, I'd been able to make it to the theater unseen. Hopefully all he'd remember was the curve of my ass in this dress.

Entering the dimly lit theater, it took a bit for my eyes to adjust. Once they did, I was greeted by a fully stocked concession stand. The White House was like a small town all its own, with every conceivable amenity, one hundred thirty-two rooms, thirty-five bathrooms, five full-time chefs, a tennis court, the bowling alley, and this movie theater just to name a few.

Running my hand over the glass concession case, there was a vast selection of sweet treats. Behind the counter was a freezer case filled with ice cream. The kind I would chase the ice cream truck for when I was a kid with bomb pops and choco tacos, and the old school Italian icees in the little cups that came with the tiny wooden spoons. A large popcorn maker stood beside the freezer filling the air with a buttery aroma.

"It's not Magic Johnson theaters, but it can still satisfy any craving you may have," Teddy said, appearing from the seating area.

He was casually dressed in jeans and a T-shirt that allowed me to ogle the muscles in his arm. I knew my face lit up when I saw him and I silently cursed myself in my head. The last thing I wanted was for Teddy to think he had the power to affect my emotions. Once men knew that, they tended to wield it like a tool they could use against you. I examined the case, looking at the full-size candy bars and boxes of sugary sweet treats.

"If you don't see anything you like, I could always have the kitchen bring us something," he offered.

I saw several things that piqued my interest. This was the exact moment I realized I was in trouble. One and done my ass.

"I'll take the Junior Mints," I said.

Teddy wrinkled his nose. "Gross, but OK." He brushed his hand across my back as he made his way to the case to retrieve the candy. "Anything else? There's drinks inside."

"Nope, I'm good." I shook the candy box in my hand. "What are we watching?"

He walked from behind the counter, reaching for my bag and file folder, placing it in the corner. "I was thinking of a Black cinema classic ... *Love Jones*."

My face lit up. "That's one of my favorite movies. Did you know that?"

"You may have mentioned it once." Teddy shrugged.

Searching my memory, I tried to recall the last time we discussed something as trivial as movies in recent months; I came up empty. Had he remembered that obscure fact about me from years ago? While my mind did cartwheels, Teddy leaned in and kissed me. My body tensed but as he pulled me close, I gave in, exploring his mouth with mine. His hands rested gently on the side of my face as I inched closer, wanting to lose myself in him. He smiled against my mouth, slowly pulling away to my dissatisfaction.

"Are you ready to start the movie?" Teddy asked, wiping my lipstick from his mouth.

"Yes." I pouted slightly.

I was suddenly less interested in the movie and more interested in getting up close and personal with Teddy. With my hand in his, he led me into the theater. We took our seats in the front row in plush red recliner chairs. Teddy pulled out his phone, typing a code into an app, and a minute later the lights went dark and the curtains pulled back on the large projection screen starting the movie.

By the time Dionne Farris's "Hopeless" ended, Teddy's hand was inching its way up my thigh. I parted my legs, giving him full access. My hands clutched the armrest as his finger slid inside while his thumb massaged my bud. Teddy's eyes were locked on my face, getting a kick out of my physical response to his mastery of my body.

I always thought I was hard to please, oftentimes having to provide detailed instructions. Yes, I could be a bit controlling, but if you made it to the final level you needed to bring it. Because what I'm not doing is faking an orgasm to boost your confidence. With Teddy, the only words that needed to be spoken were 'Yes, just like that' and 'Please don't stop.' It was like he had downloaded the Clover Bennet user manual and read it cover to cover. He had me squirming in my seat, screaming obscenities. I begged him to stop and keep going in the same breath.

Once he finally released me, I stood, stepping out of my panties and hiking my dress over my thighs. Teddy was already pulling down his jeans, opening the condom wrapper with his teeth. I straddled him, teasing him with my tongue. I felt satisfaction when I heard the soft whisper of his breath as he exhaled from the sensation of my mouth nibbling on his ear. I'd clearly found his spot. Teddy's hands coasted up and down my back, squeezing me close.

I was ready to ride but he stopped me, whispering, "Take your clothes off."

A tightness gripped my chest as I swallowed down a dry patch in my throat. Anyone could walk in and find us. At least if I was clothed, I had a chance to recover. Teddy didn't repeat himself, he just waited for me to comply. I wondered if he knew

I was trying to quickly analyze the statistical probability of us being caught in the act.

Did he lock the theater doors? If someone came in through the concession area, I may be able to crawl into a dark corner and hide. But if someone entered from the door to our right it was game over. Who was I kidding, Teddy was half naked and erect. I didn't have the will power to object.

Turning, I let him unzip my dress before removing it. I quickly tossed my bra to the floor, climbing back on top to the nicest surprise. Pulling his shirt over his head, I gave his mouth one last kiss before leaning back and riding the length of his manhood. Teddy's arms were draped over the armrest, allowing me full control. I floated my hips back and forth over his lap, slowly at first, needing to adjust to the power of his width. Bracing my hands on his knees, I increased my pace, sliding up and down with ease. With every downward thrust I moaned louder.

"Lucky, what are you doing to me?" Teddy asked breathlessly.

I smiled, leaning forward to find his lips. "Do you want me to stop?" I teased.

"I didn't say that." Teddy's large hands found my ass, helping me maneuver back and forth.

Fondling my breast with his mouth, he tickled my nipple with his tongue. My eyes fluttered closed as a deep moan broke free from my throat. I couldn't believe I seriously considered never having this man touch me again. Teddy wrapped his arm around my waist. Standing, he managed to get us to the floor with little effort. I was no longer in control. Laying on the red carpet, my eyes rolled to the back of my head with each thrust.

"Teddy," I cried out in a stutter.

I need something in my mouth. Since what I really wanted was busy driving me out of my mind, I settled for his thumb. Sliding it in my mouth, I worked my tongue over it. Teddy caressed the side of my face while I sucked. All I could do was try my best to return his expert strokes as he explored me, each stroke deeper than the last. My pleasure only heightened by the recklessness of our actions. Should I be worried about someone catching us? Yes, I should. But at this point, I wished a mother-fucker would.

I clawed at his back, as shivers overtook my body. His thumb fell from my mouth as I screamed, letting Teddy know that what he was doing was working and I was about to boil over.

Teddy lowered his body on top of mine, our hips still moving in a kinetic rhythm. "Don't hold back, baby. Get it all out."

Always one to follow directions, I moaned, cursed, and screamed my way to nirvana. My body was still firing as Teddy indulged in a few final strokes before growling low and primal in my ear, then growing still on top of me. I caressed the back of his neck, not quite ready to let him go. Teddy ran his mouth over my shoulder before kissing my cheek. He looked me in the eye with a cocky smile.

"This changes nothing," I said.

His fingers found my soft spot, causing me to contort like a puppet on a string.

"Are you sure?"

"I hate you," I groaned against his lips.

CHAPTER FIFTEEN

"Hey, boss lady," Alan yelled from the park bench.

I practically ran up to him, giving him a Herculean hug. "I missed you so much."

Since leaving McCaskill, Ford, and Huntington, Alan and I had not been able to chop it up like we once used to over morning coffee and a sweet pastry. To work in the White House, I was willing to sacrifice most things, but my friendship with Alan wasn't one of them.

"You look good. Give me a twirl." I spun around slowly, allowing him to catch the fashion I was dishing out. "Love the hair."

"Thanks, I decided to go a little longer this time." I ran my fingers through my newly installed weave.

Sitting on the bench in Lafayette Square Park, I reached into my reusable tote, pulling out two large salads from Don't Fork with Me.

"I'm starving." He spread a generous amount of ranch dressing all over his tri-tip salad.

"You do realize that totally defeats the purpose of eating healthy?"

"Baby steps. Salad drenched in ranch today, veggie burger

tomorrow."

We both laughed out loud at that blatant lie.

"So how are things over at 1600 Pennsylvania Avenue?"

"*Things* seem to never stop. It's like you can't catch your breath before something new pops up."

The corners of his mouth curled. "You love that kinda mess."

I wrinkled my nose. "I know I do. What's wrong with me?"

"There are several things wrong with you, like the fact that you don't like dogs. But that overachiever workaholic ideology is a generational defect."

He was right. I'd missed the lesson on work-life balance operating under the motto that you get what you work for not what you wish for. So, if that meant that I missed parties, and had very little downtime, so be it. I was working toward the future, and that future required a plates always spinning, multiple balls bouncing type of mentality.

"For the record, I like dogs, they're just a lot of work. And if I was a dog mom my dog would be disappointed because I'm hardly ever home. I don't need that kinda pressure."

Alan shoved a forkful of leafy greens into his mouth. "So, tell me more about your fine ass boss," he said, in between chews.

I clenched my jaw, trying to suppress a smile. "He's demanding, but fair."

"I'd sure like for him to give me some demands. That man has gotta be the hottest President of all time."

"You know Dwight Eisenhower was quite the looker back in his day."

"Yeah, well it sounds like Elmsworth is more like Kennedy than Eisenhower."

"How so?"

"Girl, do you ever watch anything other than CSPAN?"

I shook my head, waiting for Alan to continue.

"The gossip sites are claiming that your boss is dating that model who only has one name."

"Which one?" I hoped my tone reflected how unbothered I was by this bit of news.

"You know the one with the cheekbones who used to mess with ole boy, the football player."

"Dominique?" I mumbled through a mouthful of spinach, tomatoes, and grilled chicken.

Alan snapped his fingers, pointing in my direction. "Yep, that's her."

The industry would classify Dominique as plus size but in the Black community, homegirl was slim-thick. She had curves in all the right places. Why was this the first I was hearing about this? If he was, in fact, spending time with this model that was none of my concern. I was with Teddy for the sex, and I wasn't going to let rumors get me all worked up. Dominique may be a meal, but *I* was a family reunion spread with all the fixings, the kind of feast that required you to unbuckle your belt and left you knocked out in a recliner in front of the television with your hands down your pants.

"Like I tell the press every day, the President's personal life is none of our business."

"You're not even a little bit curious about who this brother is bumping and grinding with?"

I didn't need to wonder about a question I already had the answer to. I shook my head, careful to avoid eye contact.

"Well, I know that tall swallow of iced tea is not spending his nights alone. I'm surprised he hasn't hit on you." Alan nudged me with his elbow.

"That's ridiculous."

"Don't get all modest on me. You're a bad bitch, and them squats you've been doing have got your ass sitting."

My face brightened from the compliment. "Really? See, I thought they were working but I wasn't sure."

Alan made a popping sound with his mouth. "Like a Georgia peach. And I know good and well that your boss has taken notice of that wagon you're dragging."

"He's been nothing but professional. I assure you."

"Boring. You could at least brush by him and accidentally on purpose find out what he's working with."

"So, sexually harass him. You want me to sexually harass the President of the United States."

"Well, when you put it that way it kinda takes the fun out of it." Alan took a sip of his raspberry lemonade. "I just know it's big," he said, shaking his head wistfully.

"I ... don't know. I would not ... know that." I turned my attention to a pigeon who was pecking at a crust of pizza. Gathering our trash, I threw it into a nearby trash receptacle. "I'm so glad we did this."

"I'm just glad you still remember the little people."

"Shut up, I could never forget you. Anyway, enough about me, tell me about what's happening at the office. How do you like my replacement?" I hooked my arm in his.

As we strolled through the park, Alan filled me in on all the drama transpiring at my old firm. The White House had drama but nothing like McCaskill, Ford, and Huntington. As we made our way through the park, I vowed we wouldn't go three months between visits. Besides, if it wasn't for Alan and Black Twitter, I wouldn't know what was going on in the world.

I LICKED MY SPOON, releasing a slow moan. Teddy and I were sitting on the kitchen floor of the residence next to the refrigerator eating ice cream in our underwear. Despite my best efforts, I was still in deep with Teddy, seeing him several nights a week.

"What's your favorite ice cream flavor? I'll have the steward order some."

"You don't have to do that," I said, dipping my spoon in for another scoop of the black cherry chocolate chunk.

"I know I don't *have* to, I *want* to, that's why I asked."

"I don't *want* you going to the trouble."

"What trouble?"

I shrugged.

He had already bought me a toothbrush and miniatures of my favorite face wash and toner. He even placed a satin-lined pillowcase on the side of the bed reserved for me. He was going to a lot of trouble for a casual fling, and I didn't want to encourage him.

"Why is everything a fight with you? Can you just tell me what kind of ice cream you like, damn?"

"Mint chocolate chip," I said plainly.

"Thank you, was that so difficult?"

I skewered him with an agitated gaze. "No, I just don't want you to—"

"What?"

"I don't want you to get comfortable."

Teddy smirked, slipping his hands between my thighs. "I'm very comfortable right where I'm at."

Balling my fist, I exhaled a shaky breath. "I'm serious."

"Don't worry, Lucky, you have made it perfectly clear what this is." Teddy removed his hand. Standing, he tossed his spoon in the sink.

"What's that supposed to mean?" I scrambled up from the cold floor.

"It means that you appreciate what I can do to your body, but you're not interested in anything else."

"You have my body. My mind and my heart, however, are off limits." I smiled sweetly.

"What if I want more?"

I let out a nervous chuckle. "Then you'll end up disappointed." I set my hands firmly on my hips.

Teddy was trying to move the goal post. This hook-up was purely physical, nothing more.

Teddy scrubbed his face with his hand. "Is the idea of being open to the possibilities really that bad?"

"You're the President and I work for you. There are no possibilities." I narrowed my gaze.

"So, we have this amazing connection and you just wanna ignore it."

"Leg-quivering sex doesn't equate a deep connection."

Teddy's head jerked back. "It's more than that and you know it."

"You can't really be this naive. Our current situation doesn't support anything more. You can be cavalier about this because it's not your career and reputation that would ultimately take the hit."

"So, you're saying that my interest in more than a booty call is selfish?" His six-foot-four frame was rigid, his once fluid posture stiffening. "I gotta tell you, Lucky, that's a new one for me."

"I'm saying this isn't a relationship. This is convenient and when it's no longer that, it's over." My extremities were twitchy with the urge to flee. Flee this conversation, this room, the White House. "If you're looking for a relationship, maybe one of the other women you're sleeping with can give that to you."

I eyed him closely looking for a hint, a twitch, a glimmer of guilt. Per usual, Teddy's face was a blank slate. If he was seeing Dominique or someone else, he wasn't taking the bait.

He rolled his massive shoulders before giving me a crooked grin. "Are you staying the night?"

"Do you still want me to?"

He let out an aspirated sigh. "What I want is for you to want to be here. But if you'd rather go home, that's cool."

I didn't want to go home. I wanted to stay in the residence with him cuddled up in the embrace of his firm, strong arms. I wanted him to wake me up in the middle of the night, his hands all over me like he'd dreamt about me and awoke to find that I was real. I wanted to taste him on my lips and run my fingers across his back. In the morning, I wanted him to share the shower with me, lifting me off my feet and pinning me to the shower wall, ensuring I had a great start to my day.

"I've slept over for the past few nights. I should probably go." I knew my tone was unconvincing, and part of me was hoping he'd ask me again.

Teddy's jaw tensed; he wasn't going to beg. "I'll ask Agent Tally to take you home."

It was the Fourth of July and the White House was hosting a celebration on the south lawn. There were musical performances, food, and activities for young and old. I was eyeing the face painting booth and planned to circle back and get some paint on my hand. The weather was perfect and the turnout was better than expected with residents from the neighboring area and out of town visitors.

"Here you go." I handed my mother and Aunt Edwina bottles of water.

"When is John Legend taking the stage?" Aunt Ed asked, twisting the cap off her ice-cold bottle.

"He'll be out a little later." He was the headliner, so he wouldn't be out until the sun went down.

My mother's face lit up at the sight of Teddy approaching our table. His booming voice greeted us. "I hope you beautiful ladies are having a good time."

Momma jumped up, extending her hand to shake Teddy's. He refused, pulling her into a hug.

"We're practically family, and family means hugs." He enveloped my mother in a warm embrace.

"I'm Clover's auntie, do I get a hug too?" Aunt Edwina asked.

I pursed my lips. The women in my family were not shy. If we wanted something, we were never afraid to speak up.

"Mr. President, this is my Aunt Edwina."

Teddy gave my aunt a wink, opening his arms wide. "I'm ready when you are, Auntie."

Aunt Ed took full advantage of her audience with the President, giving the muscles in his arm a quick squeeze before pulling away.

"Thank you for the invite, Theodore," Ms. Sylvia said.

"Mommy, you should really call him Mr. President or President Elmsworth." I cringed as I corrected her.

He waved me off. "It's OK, Lucky. Ms. Sylvia and I go way back."

My mother beamed. "Like four tires on a Cadillac."

"Like a La-Z-Boy," he said.

"Like Stevie Wonder's hairline."

Teddy and my mother laughed together like old friends. He'd always been kind to my mother. Always respectful and helpful. If my mother mentioned in a random conversation that she liked pineapples, a few days later she'd receive a delivery of pineapples from Hawaii. On one occasion they had a heated discussion over which city had the best hot dogs, New York versus DC. The next day my mother called me saying a man had delivered hot dogs from Gray's Papaya's in New York and they were fresh and hot. That was Teddy, always going the extra mile.

As they reminisced, I surveyed the crowd. I spied Lisa with her husband Frank, who was fanning himself with a Fourth of July itinerary program in the ninety-plus weather. Abby wasn't far from them. She had also brought her mother, who I had the most entertaining conversation with about a one-night stand she had with an infamous football player back in the day.

My eyes did a double take when I spotted Seth among the crowd. *What is he doing here?* I was pulled from my thoughts when Teddy's hand rubbed the small of my back, causing my entire body, right down to my toes, to tense. He must have sensed his misstep, quickly shoving his hands in the pockets of his Dockers. I suspect he forgot where he was, confusing this for a backyard

BBQ with my mother and auntie and not a public event with reporters and cameras all around us.

We locked eyes and he mouthed the word "sorry" before turning back to my mother and aunt.

"I'll be back, Mom, I'm gonna say hi to a friend."

I didn't wait for a response. I needed to put some distance between Teddy and myself. I felt it too, how easy it was being with him. Teddy was comfortable and when we were together, we could be our authentic selves. Maybe that was why I was working so hard to assert my boundaries. Crossing the grass, I scanned the crowd in search of Seth. I found him in one of the several tents that were erected across the lawn to provide cover from the heat.

Tapping him on the shoulder, I said, "Seth?"

He turned to face me. He looked good. His face had a bit of stubble on it and he was casually dressed in a polo shirt and jeans.

"I thought that was you," I said.

"Hey, Clover, how are you?" Leaning forward, he offered an awkward hug.

"I'm good. I didn't know you were attending this event."

"Yeah, ANBS was given a couple of tickets and I was able to snag one."

"That's great." I clasped and unclasped my hands.

"You look pretty."

I smoothed down my rainbow gingham dress. "Thank you. So do you." I screwed up my face. *Awkward much?* I thought. "You look pretty good."

"Glad to know I'm not the only one who's uncomfortable."

"No, I'm not uncomfortable. I was just happy to see you." The back of my neck prickled. Why was I acting like a self-conscious high schooler in front of her crush?

"Look, Clover, I'm sorry I didn't call. Standing in front of you now, that feels like a mistake." Seth's eyes traveled over my curves.

"I hate the way we left things. I had hoped we could still be friends."

He shoved his hands into his jean pockets. "Sorry, I'm not really interested in being your friend."

"Yeah ... no ... I totally get that."

We started out as friends, so wanting to maintain some semblance of friendship wasn't all that far-fetched. DC was small, and even though I could swim I tried to avoid burning bridges. You never know when the person you stepped on to advance could end up being the gatekeeper to another opportunity.

Seth fidgeted with his phone, flipping it over in his hands. "For the record, my feelings for you haven't changed. So, agreeing to a friendship when you and I both know I want more would be disingenuous."

"I get it and appreciate the honesty."

Who was I kidding? I hadn't trekked over here looking to make amends. I'd been meaning to give him a call for weeks now but didn't want to give the impression I was interested in anything other than business.

"So, I'm working on lining up an interview for President Elmsworth with ANBS."

"Sorry, I think I misheard you. The President is going to do a sit-down interview with ANBS?"

"Yep ... you interested?"

"In interviewing the President of the United States. No, not at all." The corners of Seth's mouth curled. "Decisions like that are made by the network, not me."

"What if I told you that ANBS has agreed to let us pick the interviewer from their *talented* pool of journalists."

ANBS journalists were talented. Talented at lying, talented at spinning the facts, talented at getting senior citizens all riled up. Seth was one of their better reporters, even though his time at ANBS was slowly rotting his brain. His questions would be fair and would allow Teddy the opportunity to make his pitch. I'd rather go with Seth than one of the other American News reporters who had nothing to lose.

"I'm listening."

"The interview would take place in prime time at the White House. You would have access to the President for three hours."

"Are you sure about this? I'm not going to go easy on him as some type of favor to you."

"I wouldn't ask you to. Ted ... the President can handle your questions. All that I ask is that you allow him to answer without interruption."

Seth eyed me suspiciously, like he was trying to figure out the catch. I smiled sweetly, letting my offer ruminate in his head.

Extending his hand, he said, "Shake on it."

I slipped my hand in his, sealing our deal.

He caressed my hand before letting it go. "It was good seeing you again."

AFTER CHECKING in on Auntie Ed and my mother, I made my way into the White House looking to escape the crowd, the noise, and the heat. Hiding out in the library on the ground floor, I admired the hardcover first editions that lined the shelves.

"Did you know this room used to be a laundry room? They didn't make it into a library until 1935." Teddy's all too familiar voice rang out behind me as he and Agent Tally entered the room, closing the door.

"Why is it that you're just full of useless facts?" I teased.

"Useless? Woman, if you're ever a contestant on *Who Wants to Be a Millionaire*, you're gonna want me as your phone a friend." Teddy leaned against an armchair.

This house was huge with over one hundred rooms and hidden, unmapped hiding places; there was no way he just happened upon me in the library.

"Are you following me?"

"No, I have an agent responsible for keeping tabs on you," he said with a serious face.

"How romantic."

"I like keeping track of the things that are important to me."

"Wow, you're giving off strong 1900s vibes right now."

"You OK?" Teddy moved forward cautiously. Like he wasn't certain which Clover he was gonna get. The Clover who couldn't keep her hands off of him or the one that kept him at a distance, warning him against catching feelings.

"Yeah, I just needed to get out of the heat for a bit."

"I really like your aunt. She didn't hold back."

I covered my face with my hand. "Oh God, I apologize if she said anything out of line."

"No, quite the opposite. She told me all about you and what a stubborn kid you were. And how you never allowed no to be the final answer, even when you were five. She said you have always been politically active and when you were in high school, you got over five hundred signatures to protest the school's sexist dress code. She also mentioned your work at that woman's shelter.

"OK, you didn't come in here to talk about charity work."

"Actually, I did. I wanna hear all about it and everything else you're passionate about."

I shrugged. "It's just a mentoring thing I do a couple of times a month to help women who've been displaced due to domestic violence or addiction."

"You help them find jobs?"

"Find jobs, help with resumes and mock interviews. The charity offers interview clothes and gives women a chance at a new start."

An uncontrollable heat washed over my face. I'd attempted to keep things shallow with Teddy, not wanting to venture too deep, mostly because I feared I'd drown in him if I didn't have my feet planted firmly underneath me. Hale House was doing great work and I was just honored to play a part in that in some small way.

"It's boring, I know."

"Not boring. It's nice to know you have a soft side." Teddy reached for my hand, pulling me closer.

I ran my fingers across his beard, giving his chin a tug. The room seemed to go quiet even though there was a swirl of activity just a stone's throw away. He ran his fingertips across my forearm, leaving a trail of goosebumps. Knotting my hands behind his neck, I inched closer. Teddy glanced toward the door where Agent Tally stood guard, his back to us. He slowly brought his lips down on mine, his kiss gentle and intimate, like he wanted to savor me and this moment.

"Your mother invited me over for dinner," he whispered between kisses.

"That is never going to happen." I gently bit at the palm of his hand.

"It's already set. I told her I'd bring a green bean casserole."

I threw my head back in laughter at the thought of Teddy in the kitchen trying to make a dish to impress my mother. He rested his arms around my waist.

"Happy Fourth, Lucky."

"Happy Fourth of July, Mr. President."

CHAPTER SIXTEEN

I PICKED UP A PLANTER THAT READ PLANT LIFE ON THE FRONT. "Maybe I should get a plant?" I said aloud more to myself than anyone else.

"How are you going to manage that?" my mom asked. "You're barely home and plants need sunlight, love, and attention."

Ignoring my mother, I placed the medium-sized pot in our cart. For the last few weeks, my mother complained that I was neglecting her, in spite of my taking her to the Fourth of July celebration at the White House two weekends ago, so I decided to tag along with her to the local nursery. She wasn't wrong to be concerned, work was a madhouse. I'd complete one task and three more would sprout up like weeds.

I was working all day and spending most of my evenings with Teddy. This one and done had turned into a consistent affair that I couldn't find my way out of. Truth be told, I wasn't trying very hard to end things. I was too busy enjoying our late-night romps and breaking all the rules, like spending the night. Eventually, I would have to distance myself from him, but that was easier said than done when he made my body come alive.

Reaching for a small bag of soil, I walked up and down the plant aisle looking for the right one.

"If you're serious about getting a plant, might I suggest a cactus or a succulent," my mom said.

"A succulent?"

"Yes, they are hard to kill and don't require as much care. So, you can neglect it like you've been neglecting me."

My eyes flattened. She was milking this cow for every last drop. I had already treated her to lunch and now I was in Blooms Abundant looking at plants when I had a ton of work that I needed to get done. I headed to the succulent section to pick out my new plant baby when my phone chimed.

Teddy: Where are you?

I did my best to conceal my smile when his name flashed across my screen. Walking further away from my mother, I texted back.

Me: Did I miss something?

Teddy: Yeah, you're missing the opportunity to get ate out like a buffet.

Dropping the phone to my side, I looked around. My mother was busy talking to one of the store clerks. My face, neck, and ears grew incredibly hot. Lifting the phone, I responded.

Me: I'm otherwise detained. I'm with my mother.

Teddy: Tell Ms. Sylvia hello from her future son-in-law.

Me: No and eww.

Teddy: Eww? To what part?

Me: You know exactly what part.

Teddy: Most women would love to hear stuff like that.

Me: I'm not most women.

Teddy: I've noticed.

These last few weeks with Teddy had been fun, but he kept hinting that he wanted more. It was preposterous, how would that even work? He was the President and I was a senior staffer, it would be headline fodder if anyone found out.

Me: Did you need something?

Teddy: I need a lot of things, but I will settle on seeing you tonight.

Me: I can't. I have a ton of work to do.

Teddy: I could come to you. We could cuddle up and watch a movie.

Me: NO!!!! Teddy, are you trying to get caught?

Teddy: No, I'm trying to see you. But clearly you don't appreciate the effort.

Me: It's not that.

Teddy: Nah, it's cool. Have a good day.

I stared at my phone in disbelief. Was he seriously pissed at me for taking a rain check so I could work, work that benefits him and his administration?

My mother approached with a purple succulent in hand. "The nursery guy said that this plant is best; it only needs sunlight, water, and the occasional dusting." She handed me the plant. "Do you think you can handle that?"

"Ahh ... yeah ... thanks."

"What's wrong?" she asked, wiping the dirt from her fingers.

"Nothing. Just work stuff."

"Hmph, the next time you see the President, tell him to stop working you so hard."

"It's not Ted... the President. Everyone works hard, even him."

Walking back toward our stranded cart, my mother said, "I saw him on the news last night. All smiles and handshakes. I even think he kissed a baby." She shook her head.

"It's part of his job. He has to be relatable and likable."

Teddy had made a visit to a Metro DC veterans hospital, talking with some of the veterans and faculty. He was photographed having an extended conversation with a soldier who'd recently returned home after suffering a bomb explosion that left him without a leg. When the press asked Airman Hicks what he and the President had discussed, Hicks said the President was offering some friendly trash talk about his football team's chances of making it to the Superbowl.

"He's likable alright. And single, maybe you could spend less time working and a little more time batting your eyelashes," she half teased.

"Mommy, he's my boss." I added the succulent to the cart.

"He's still a man." She huffed. "I saw the way he looked at you at the White House event."

"How did he look at me?" I crossed my arms, genuinely intrigued.

My mom laughed. "Like you don't know. He looked at you like a grown man looks at a woman." She kissed her teeth. "If I have to explain that then we have bigger fish to fry."

"We're just friends, Mommy." I half lied. We were friends. I was just allowing said friend to blow my back out on a constant basis.

"Well, maybe he wants more."

"Are we done? Are we done here?"

My mom raised her hand to her chest. "Am I keeping you?"

"Yes, actually. I have a crap ton of work to do."

"Clover, I did not teach you to be the girl who works but never plays."

"I play. I just like to make sure that my work's done before I do." I pushed the cart toward checkout.

"Do you hear that sound?" My mother stopped, grabbing my arm with an intense look on her face.

"No, what sound?" I stood perfectly still trying to hear it.

"The sound of your eggs cracking." She shook her head, placing items on the conveyor belt.

"OK, we have time for one more question. Parker, how about you?" I pointed to a young reporter from *The Washington Post*.

Glancing at my watch, it wasn't even noon. This day was dragging, maybe because it was my birthday and instead of laying out on a beach, I was standing at a podium fielding gotcha questions. Normally I didn't work on my birthday, but working in the White House was a whole other ballgame.

Vacation, down time, that was unheard of. You could rest

when you were dead or when you were no longer a part of the Elmsworth administration, which was kind of like the same thing. Besides, it was my thirty-sixth birthday, which wasn't a major milestone. So here I was answering Parker's question regarding the President's recent trip to Vegas on the taxpayers' dime to celebrate a friend's engagement.

"Parker, thank you for your question. The President took a trip to Las Vegas to visit friends, and while in Vegas he had a meeting with the casino union, he visited Nellis Air Force Base and met with some of our brave soldiers, and he was in the front row at Sunday service at a local Baptist church. This trip was far from a vacation."

As I continued to speak, I noticed the reporters in the room shift their attention from me to something in the corner. Immediately followed by frantic shouts.

"Mr. President. Mr. President," the reporters called out in unison along with a mix of questions.

I turned to find Teddy approaching the podium. I stood in wonderment. This was a surprise visit. I hated surprises. My chest began to tighten as I chewed at the inside of my cheek.

"Good morning, everyone." Teddy flashed one of his dazzling smiles.

"Good morning, Mr. President," the reporters chimed in harmony.

Stepping back from the podium, I gave Teddy the floor.

"I don't want to keep you. I know Clover was wrapping things up, but I was hoping you guys would help me." Teddy turned, waving me forward.

Tentatively, I complied, advancing forward and standing next to the President, his arm brushing against mine. My knee-jerk reaction was to yanked my arm away quickly. Hopefully no one noticed just how disconcerting his presence was for me. Giving up control and allowing Teddy to speak freely sans well-crafted talking points was unsettling. His appearance was making the already taut atmosphere frantic. Determined to direct all my nervous energy to one spot, I drove my nails into the palms of my hands.

Teddy continued addressing the crowd. "Today is Clover's birthday and I was hoping we could sing happy birthday to her."

"No," I said, far more sternly than I intended. "I mean… they don't have to do that." I waved his suggestion off.

Totally ignoring my wishes, as he had grown accustomed to doing, he continued. "On the count of three. One, two, three."

As the President and the press core sang to me, I bit down on my lip. This twenty-second song seemed to last an eternity. Halfway through, Brittany appeared cake in hand with a sparkler and a single candle on top. Only Teddy would do something so brazen, like celebrate his mistress's birthday in front of a room full of inquisitive journalists. He knew good and well that any one of these nosy bastards could start asking questions and we would be royally screwed.

"Happy birthday, Clover," Brittany beamed after the singing stopped.

I turned to walk away, but Teddy reached for my hand, his touch sparking shockwaves inside me.

"Not so fast, you still need to make a wish," he chided me.

Teddy's smile was wide and toothy like a sadistic clown. He knew me well enough to know I was hating every minute of this.

Yes, I was used to speaking to large groups of people or talking about our plans for building strong allies in the West on *Meet the Press*, but this was different. In my role as the Press Secretary, I was representing the President and his administration, but this impromptu celebration was all about me. Unnecessary attention was something I could do without.

"Yes, if you don't make a wish it's bad luck," Brittany said.

She seemed all too happy to be near the podium and next to the President of the United States. Power was intoxicating, and if you stood next to it for too long you often lost your sensibilities. I was living proof.

"Go on, make a wish," Teddy said, as Brittany brought the

chocolate-on-chocolate cake with flowers and macarons decorating the top closer.

I decided there was no use in protesting. Closing my eyes, I made a wish and blew.

"What did you wish for?" one of the reporters in the room inquired.

"That's bad luck," Teddy and I said in unison, causing my face to grow hot.

I turned to the reporters. "OK, that was nice and also awkward as hell. Thank you all. Same time tomorrow." I plastered a passable smile on my face, and we made our way out of the briefing room. "I am going to kill you," I whispered under my breath so only Teddy could hear. "You embarrassed the hell out of me."

"I was going for making you feel special and loved."

I flashed him a look. Hearing the 'L' word made my skin crawl and my heart throb at the same damn time.

"Come on back and have cake with us. There's plenty to go around," Teddy announced as we exited.

A crowd gathered in the small suite adjacent to the briefing room. Apparently, the rumors of cake and fresh coffee had lured the overworked staffers from the dark regions of the West Wing and beyond. I tossed my binder on a table and prepared myself for awkward small talk.

Lisa smiled at me from across the room; she was standing next to Gibbs. I wondered what the two were whispering about. The reporters from the briefing trickled into the room, making space in the tiny suite a commodity. I made my way over to my team in one of the less crowded corners.

"For the birthday girl," Brittany said, handing me a generous slice of cake.

"Wow, this is insane. For Gibbs's birthday last month, the President forgot to sign his card and there was no cake," Abby said, walking up to us.

"I think the President only did this because he knew I would hate it," I said, shoving a piece of chocolate cake in my mouth.

I hoped no one else in the room was having the same thoughts about the President's out of character celebratory mood.

"You didn't tell me it was your birthday," Brittany chided me.

"I didn't tell anyone it was my birthday."

"I can't believe you showed up to work. If it were me, I'd be three sheets to the wind right now," Topher joked.

"Isn't your birthday in a few months?" I raised an eyebrow. "Note to self, hire a barbershop quartet for Topher's big day," I teased.

Topher pointed at me with a smile. "Oh, you better not."

"Do they even still do that type of thing?" Abby asked.

"I don't know but if they do, Brittany will find them," I said.

Looking around the room, I located Teddy surrounded by reporters who were all looking to get him on the record. His eyes met mine, and I frowned to let him know that despite the delicious cake, I was not amused. Teddy, in turn, raised an eyebrow as the corners of his perfect mouth pulled into a brilliant smile.

AFTER THE CAKE AND COFFEE, my day was filled with meetings. Returning to my office a little after three, I was determined to leave this place at a respectable hour today. As I proofread my speech for an upcoming event, I found it hard to concentrate. Maybe I was still on a sugar high, but I had to admit that it felt nice knowing Teddy made an effort to make me feel special today. I never told him about my approaching birthday and not once did he mention it while I was wrapped in his arms after sex. He wanted to catch me slipping. Reaching for my phone, I sent him a quick text.

Me: Are you busy?

He must've had his phone in his hand because within seconds, he was texting me back.

Teddy: Yes, I'm the President of the United States. Of course, I'm busy.

I rolled my eyes.

Teddy: What do you need?

That was a loaded question. I was tempted to respond back with an eggplant and tongue emoji, but we had recently agreed that we needed to avoid discoverable evidence. We probably should have thought of that sooner, because there were several message threads with racy content and incriminating photographic evidence. It's harder to deny an affair when the proof was in black and white.

Me: I just wanted to stop by.

Me: Briefly.

Teddy: Can you wait 15 mins?

Me: Yes.

Ugh, I hoped I didn't sound too eager. After touching up my makeup, I headed to the Oval. Abby was at her desk guarding his office per usual.

"Hey, birthday girl," Abby said, with a shimmy of her shoulders.

"Hey, the President's expecting me." I smiled, pointing to his open door.

Abby clicked her mouse several times before saying, "You're not on the calendar."

"Yeah." I scratched my arm. "It was kind of a last-minute thing."

I guess Teddy's ears were burning because he appeared at the door with a smile. "Clover is my four o'clock appointment," Teddy said, pointing at me.

Abby furrowed her brow with a frown. "She isn't on the calendar."

It almost sounded like she was reprimanding him.

"I know, you're right, and I will do better," Teddy said, tapping on her desk with his knuckles.

"Uh-hmm," Abby murmured before smiling at me brightly. "You can go in now."

"Thanks, Abby," I said, sliding past Teddy.

The door to the Oval hadn't even fully latched and Teddy was all over me, kissing my lips before I could protest. He knew the effect his tongue had on me, and he took pleasure in watching me overheat. I tugged at his suit jacket, pulling him closer, indulging in his sweet kiss. After all, it was my birthday and I deserved it.

"Teddy?" I whispered, pushing him away.

If I didn't stop now I would end up face down on the Resolute Desk.

Teddy was reluctant to remove his hands from my backside, but he did. Crossing the room, he stood on the other side of his desk like he needed space between us if he was going to behave.

"I just wanted to say thank you for the cake and the fuss."

"Did you really think I was gonna let your born day pass and not acknowledge it?"

I shrugged. I mean, I kinda did.

"So, what do you have planned for tonight?" he asked, looking down at the papers spread across his desk.

A frown shadowed my face. "Nothing, it's a work night."

Teddy creased his brow, opening his mouth to object, but I stopped him.

"I'm taking Saturday off and having a spa day with my mom and Daysha. A belated birthday celebration," I said, playing with the tassels on one of the pillows on the couch.

"That's whack."

"Rude," I objected.

"No, not the spa day. That sounds relaxing. What I meant was, *today* is your birthday. You shouldn't just go home to an empty fridge and the glow of the TV."

"It's cool. Everyone is busy and I have a ton of documents to review."

Teddy swung his head in a swift arch. "No, that just won't do. I'm not gonna let my girl—"

"I am not your girl." I pointed my finger at him.

I did not want to get into another disagreement about titles. He knew as well as I did what this was, and I wasn't interested in getting caught up in some romanticized version of us.

To my surprise, he didn't object. "Today should be about making memories," Teddy said, coming from behind his desk as he reached for my hand. "Let's make a memory together."

I looked up at him. Who did this guy think he was, Jacques Cousteau?

"That was kinda corny, but I'm intrigued," I said, allowing a smile to soften my face.

Who was I kidding? Going home to an empty bed was not my idea of a good time. If Teddy was offering a better option, who was I to turn it down.

"Great, be ready by eight forty-five. I'll have a car pick you up."

CHAPTER SEVENTEEN

Sifting through my closet, I looked for something to wear. Teddy said to keep it casual so I opted for jeans and a long, red, ribbed duster with buttons, leaving the top button undone so there was a hint of my black lace bra underneath. My hair hung loose in soft wand curls.

I couldn't help but laugh at myself when I realized I was getting all dressed up just to have Teddy take it all off the minute he saw me. The cheery melody that was my ringtone filled the air. Running from room to room, I searched, the ringing sounded distant. I finally found it under a bunch of clothes on my bed that I had rejected.

"Hello?" I huffed, a bit out of breath.

"Hey, hey, hey. Did you have a good birthday?"

The sound of Day's voice made me smile. "I did."

"Great, because if you didn't, I would have to fight somebody," she teased.

"Now you know you can't fight."

"You're right. I am all bark and not a bit of bite. So, what do you have planned for the rest of the night?"

With a soft cough, I proceeded to lie. "Girl, not a damn thing. I'm in my robe and slippers about to pour me some wine and relax."

Daysha didn't know I was still seeing Teddy. I don't know why I hadn't told her. The thought of having to admit that this one-night stand had turned into a damn near every night affair made my stomach hollow out. Daysha didn't believe men and women could pull off a no-strings-attached relationship. In her opinion, someone always ended up catching feelings. She wasn't wrong. Seth caught feelings and Teddy was coming down with something, although I wasn't yet able to diagnose it.

"Do you want me to come over?"

"No," I shouted. "Girl, it's late and you have a man you can cuddle up under. Do not worry about me."

"OK, just promise me you won't be working tonight."

"That I can promise. Have a good night."

"Talk to you later."

As the doorbell rang, I gave myself one last look in the mirror, grabbing my purse before heading to the door. I was shocked to find Teddy standing on the other side with two plain-clothed Secret Service agents.

"What are you doing here?" I asked, my voice squeaking.

"I told you I'd pick you up," he said coolly.

I wagged my finger at him. "No, you said you'd send a car. How did you shake the press pool?" My eyes darted up and down the hall, hoping one of my neighbors didn't make an appearance.

"A magician never reveals his secrets." Teddy pretended to pull a card from his nonexistent sleeve.

The press pool was like the President's shadow, where he went, they went. They represented various media outlets and photographers. Press pool duty was a mixed bag. While it afforded access to the President, it wasn't the ideal working conditions with constant travel and long hours. But being a part of the team that captured history was priceless.

As we made our way to the curb, Agent Mulvaney opened the door to a vehicle that was not The Beast, the President's typical mode of transportation. We were in a nondescript Lincoln Town Car. Teddy was breaking all the rules.

"Tell me you didn't sneak out of the White House?" I asked, shaking my head as we pulled off.

"No. I just told the press pool I was in for the night and then ... I snuck out of the White House." Teddy slapped his knee, letting out a hearty laugh.

"Theodore Elmsworth, this is negligent." I narrowed my eyes.

"I was going to say brilliant."

"You can't just run away from your responsibilities."

"When did spending time with you become one of my presidential responsibilities? Look, I just wanted a normal night out. No reporters, no cameras, just you and me."

"What if something happens to you? The scandal that followed would be cataclysmic."

The President wasn't some celebrity; he was a public servant and his safety and security were paramount. God forbid he suffered a medical emergency. How would we explain why he was out and about when he claimed to be safely in the confines of the residence?

Teddy leaned closer to me. "Well then, you better protect me," he said, before kissing my lips.

When his lips touched mine, all the fight I possessed evaporated. Ditching the press pool was bad but at this moment, with his tongue exploring my mouth and his hand cupping my breast, I didn't really care.

Pulling away far quicker than I would have liked, Teddy licked his lips. "I was thinking we could go to a dive bar a buddy of mine owns in Le Droit Park. Is that cool?"

"Yes, sounds fun."

Internally, I was wondering how this was going to work. Did Teddy think he could just walk into a space unnoticed? Sure, he was casually dress in jeans and a T-shirt and a random observer might not make the connection, so used to seeing him in a suit and tie. But Teddy was a well-built, handsome man. The type of brother that caused women to do a double take. If one of these women stared long enough, Teddy would go from damn, he's fine, to he favors someone, I just can put my finger on it, to holy hell, that's the President of the United States.

Teddy nudged his shoulder into mine. "You'll like Lloyd, he's good people." He squeezed my knee with his large hand.

The town car pulled up to a brightly colored storefront with a vivid candy display in the window. Before exiting the car, Teddy put on a fitted baseball cap, probably hoping that would help conceal his identity, like Clark Kent and his glasses. As we approached the store, with its rainbow awning and bright lights, Teddy held the door open for me. The store was empty, just the clerk, Teddy, and myself, and, of course, the ever-present protection detail. The sound of Foxy Brown's "Candy" filled the air.

"Here we are," he said.

"It's a candy store." I ran my hand over a large rainbow lollipop.

"It is. Do you want anything?" he asked.

Inspecting the gumball art work on the wall, I said, "Nah, I'm good."

At the counter, Teddy smiled at the pretty store clerk with lavender hair. She smiled back, twirling a strand between her fingers. I couldn't determine if she knew who he was or if she was just flirting with the fine ass brother in front of her.

Teddy leaned in and said, "The Joker, the Riddler, and the Penguin."

"What?" I asked, approaching the counter.

"Show me your hands," the clerk said.

I held my hands up, Teddy held his out and was rewarded with an invisible stamp for being able to follow directions. I quickly followed suit, extending my hand and receiving a stamp. The clerk pressed a button under the candy-filled counter, and a door opened behind us revealing a steep stairway.

Teddy reached for my hand. "Shall we trip down the rabbit hole?" he asked.

"Definitely." I gave him a sly smile.

As we descended the stairs, I clutched Teddy's hand tight. The staircase was dimly lit and the last thing I wanted was to tumble head over feet in my red bottom heels. We were sandwiched between Teddy's two-man detail, with one agent leading the way while the other followed me, bringing up the rear. At the bottom of the stairs, my eyes began to adjust and my jaw nearly dropped as we entered a large space with a bar, dance floor, and lounge seating.

"You said this was a dive bar. This is a speakeasy and there is nothing shady about it."

"Have you been to a speakeasy before?" Teddy elevated his voice so I could hear him over the R&B music.

"Yes, a few. But I've never been here. I've probably walked down this block dozens of times and never knew this place existed," I said, checking out the bulbous light fixtures dangling from the wall.

"Let's start this birthday celebration off with a drink."

With his hand on my back, he led me to the bar that glowed in alternating blue and purple lights. I scoped the crowd while Teddy ordered our drinks. There was a nice mix of young Black professionals in their thirties and forties. A place for grownups who wanted to chill, grab a drink after work, and dance to music that made you feel something. I swayed from side to side as Aaliyah sang about her four-page letter.

"Yo, it's the man himself," a loud booming voice came from behind me.

I turned to find Teddy and a short bald man hug while patting one another on the back.

"How have you been, Lloyd?"

"Shit, not as good as you. All over my damn television set." Lloyd cackled, falling silent when his eyes found me. "Who's that?" he asked, cocking his head in my direction.

"Oh, my bad." Teddy turned to me. "Lloyd, this is Clover. Clover, this is my crazy ass friend, Lloyd."

"Nice to meet you," I said, extending my hand.

Lloyd examined my body lecherously. "Damn, young blood, this you?" Lloyd asked.

"Umm, kinda," Teddy said, not looking at me.

I didn't protest, I could be his for the night.

"Sorry, young lady, I don't shake hands. I'm more of a hugger."

Lloyd descended on me, pulling me into a tight hug. He smelled like weed and Marlboro Lights.

"I got a table in the corner set aside for you two. Real private and secure." Lloyd led the way to an oversized wrap around booth with a reserved sign on the table. "If you need anything, you holler."

As we slid into the booth with our drinks, I said, "He seems like a character."

"Yeah, he is. I met Lloyd at Harvard."

I blinked my eyes. "Lloyd went to Harvard?"

"Yes, he did, as a custodian." Teddy took a sip of his bourbon. "Harvard being Harvard, there weren't many black faces, so I just kinda got into the habit of saying hello every morning. Lloyd would grunt in reply until one day, he said, 'What you here studying, young blood?'" Teddy did a pretty good impression of Lloyd's high-pitched voice, making me laugh. "He and I have been cool ever since."

"Wait, so you've known him for over twenty years?"

"Yep. I'm like herpes, hard to get rid of."

"That's gross." I made a fake vomit sound, making us both laugh.

"So, tell me this, birthday girl. What are you looking forward to as you begin your thirty-sixth rotation around the sun?"

I took a long drink from my strawberry martini, smacking my lips. "I wanna travel more. I only left the country once last year. It's my goal to travel to at least one new place each year and revisit old favorites. The world is big and I wanna see all of it."

"Maybe we could do that together." Teddy smiled.

"G-20 summits don't exactly count as travel when we have to work the entire time." I crinkled my nose.

"What if it's not work related?" Teddy asked, stretching his arms across the booth until his left arm found my shoulder.

"So, you evade the press pool once and you think you're ready for an international time heist."

"I'm not the first President to ditch the press. How do you think JFK was banging Marilyn? Or Obama was sneaking off to puff, puff, pass?"

"Just because you can do it doesn't mean you should."

"OK, Miss Goody Two Shoes." Teddy squeezed my shoulder.

I smirked. "You know as well as anyone I'm far from a goody two shoes," I said, shifting my hand to his lap, moving it back and forth.

Teddy breathed a sigh of pleasure, tightening his grip on the back of my neck. I studied his face closely, taking delight in driving him apeshit crazy in a room full of people. I looked around the bar, it was loud and dark and I was feeling frisky. Undoing his jeans, I slipped my hand inside, stroking him up and down.

Teddy leaned into me, gently biting my shoulder. With my free hand I knocked back the rest of my drink, almost choking when Teddy moaned my name in my ear. I removed my hand, giving it a discreet lick before sliding over his shaft once again.

"Lucky, if you don't stop you're gonna find yourself spread eagle on this table." Teddy's voice was low and stuttery as he seeped in air.

Reluctantly, I released my hold, agreeing I wanted to kick the tires but I wasn't ready to drive the car off the lot. That would have to wait until we got back to my apartment.

"I'm gonna go to the restroom."

Teddy brushed his finger across my cheek. "Do you want another drink?"

"Yes, but make it a peach martini this time," I said, sliding out of the booth, and headed to the ladies room.

When I returned, we had company. Lloyd was leaning over our table and he brought a lady friend.

"Ahh, there she is. You good, Miss Lady?" Lloyd asked.

"Great." I smiled, sliding back into the booth next to Teddy.

"Clover, I want you to meet my old lady, Charmaine."

Charmaine extended her hand and her nails were three times as long as mine, all bedazzled with jewels and stones. She smiled to reveal a gold tooth at the side of her mouth. She reminded me of the women who lived in my neighborhood growing up.

I'd watch them on the public bus while on my way to school in the morning in their scrubs or office attire. Long nails, intricate hairstyles, and sensible shoes. Then at night, from the living room window, I would watch those same women all decked out in the latest fashions getting into fancy cars, their sensible shoes replaced with heels so high it was a miracle they didn't bust their ass on the sidewalk.

Charmaine slid in beside me, admiring my necklace.

"So, how do you know Theodore?" Charmaine's voice was raspy like a pack a day smoker.

"From wor..." I stopped myself. I thought it best not to provide specifics. "We go way back," I said, praying she didn't ask any follow-up questions.

After Lloyd told us a very interesting story about Teddy and his fear of birds, he and Charmaine returned to the bar.

"Pigeons, huh?" I turned to Teddy and asked.

"Look, you can tease me all you want, but I will die on this hill. Pigeons are just rats with wings."

I tried my best to choke back my laughter. I looked at the dance floor, which as we approached midnight was packed with people looking to release some tension.

Turning to Teddy, I asked, "Do you wanna dance?"

"Let's do it."

As we headed toward the dance floor Teddy rubbed my shoulders. I let the baseline and drums take over, swinging my hips to the beat as Rhianna's "Work" began to play. Teddy pulled me close to him so that his body could grind against mine in time with the beat. I leaned in, kissing his lips, his mouth sweet and spicy from the bourbon.

He grabbed my face, returning my kisses, still swaying side to side never missing a beat. Wrapping my arms around his neck, I let out a heavy sigh. I wanted to devour him right here on the dance floor. If Teddy wasn't the President, I would be willing to take a lewd and lascivious charge if it meant feeling his hands all over me.

I don't know if it was the liquor or the birthday high, but I turned around grinding my backside into his crotch. Teddy's hand wrapped around, resting on my breastplate. After months of sneaking around, I'm not gonna lie; this moment, with us dancing together just two lovers in a crowd of unfamiliar faces, was liberating.

After an hour of nonstop dancing, Teddy pulled away, breathless from the obscene amount of kissing. "I should get you home."

"Please," I whispered, nibbling his earlobe.

———

BACK AT MY place I checked my phone, heading to the bathroom to pee. It was eight minutes past two. I needed to be up by five, six if I skipped my workout. I couldn't remember the last time I had this much fun with a man outside of the bedroom. Teddy was smart and whether we were talking about sports, politics, or the atrocious wigs in all of Tyler Perry's movies, he kept me on my toes.

This was without a doubt one of the best birthdays I'd had, which wasn't saying much because for me the birthday bar was pretty low. While it was just drinks, conversation, and dancing, it was still a breath of fresh air compared to the effort men from my past had made. And the night wasn't over yet. Teddy was waiting for me right now and I was ready for some after-hour shenanigans.

Back in the living room, I found Teddy examining my bookshelf. Pointing to a framed picture, he asked, "Is this your dad?"

"Mm-hm."

"You look like him." He leaned in, taking a closer look. "I never hear you talk about him."

"Not really much to say. He wasn't really around."

"Yeah, but there must still be love there. Enough for you to display a picture."

When I was little, I was the definition of a daddy's girl. When my parents split I was seven and everything changed. His visits became less frequent and he made promises that he was never able to keep. At twelve he remarried and became a step-daddy to some other little girl.

"I mean, yeah. You can love someone and be disappointed in them at the same time."

Teddy plopped down in my armchair, waiting for me to continue.

"I just decided life was too short to hold grudges. I wanted my father to be someone he clearly never was. I just finally made peace with the fact that if I wanted any type of relationship with him, I was going to have to meet him where he's at."

"And where's that?"

"On the intersection of I know I made some mistakes and to hell with your feelings."

"It sucks when the child has to be the bigger person." His lips were staunch with sadness.

"We all go through stuff, even our parents. Sometimes you have to extend a little grace."

A mirthless chuckle escaped from his mouth. "Hmm, I do not share that philosophy."

"Do you mean with your mother?"

My relationship with my dad was difficult, but Teddy's relationship with his mother was fractured and he wasn't interested in putting it back together.

"Yeah, my dad dipped before I even knew him, but that woman stayed and used every opportunity to make me wish she hadn't." He pinned his arms across his chest.

"Addiction makes people do things they wouldn't otherwise do."

"Or it just heightens what is already innate within you."

It was no secret that Teddy and his mother had a rocky relationship. When he was running for President she granted an interview to ANBS in which she said Teddy had ignored her heartfelt attempts at a reconciliation. She also made some explosive claims after his grandmother's funeral.

"So, you're not even slightly interested in what she has to say?"

"Nope." Teddy stood, making his way over to me, his face softening. "Enough about our f'ed up childhoods." He leaned down, hovering inches from my face. "What do you wanna do now?" Teddy asked, licking his lips.

He knew exactly what I wanted to do but in hopes of clearing up any confusion, I jumped into his arms, wrapping my legs around his waist.

"Stay," I moaned as I licked the side of his neck.

"I thought I was a derelict President who was shirking his responsibilities," Teddy teased.

"Shut up and take your clothes off."

"Yes ma'am."

TEDDY SLAPPED my ass before giving it a satisfied kiss, falling onto the bed. I rolled toward him, leaning my head on his chest.

"Did you have a good birthday?"

I let out a devilish laugh. "Yes," I croaked, my voice still dry and hoarse from screaming his name and calling on the Lord.

There was a window of time right after good sex when I would agree to anything. If Teddy asked me to shave my head right now, I would eagerly comply. I bit my lip, staring up at him with heart eyes, resisting a deep urge to flood his face with kisses. Teddy ran his fingers down my spine, making my body fire like electrons. His touch making it hard to focus.

"I'm gonna get us some water." I rolled off the bed and headed to the kitchen.

If I laid next to him any longer, I was bound to say something I would regret.

Opening the door, I stared inside the nearly empty fridge. I was sorely neglecting responsibilities around the house. The fridge housed three water bottles, coffee creamer, a bottle of expired milk, and a glass container filled with condiment packets from various take-out spots. I needed to look into Instacart or some other grocery delivery service, because this was pathetic.

As I bent into the fridge growing goosebumps on my bare skin, I asked myself, *What the hell am I doing? I need to end this ... whatever it is Teddy and I have fallen into. What do I think, we are going to ride off into the sunset together? I'm sure his ex-wife Mariah thought they'd be together forever, and where is she?*

She was married to some hedge fund manager and living in Connecticut. I may have Googled her then Instagram stalked her one night when I'd had a few too many glasses of red wine. I was a big girl and I understood that this could only end in a handful of ways. I needed to end this relationship before I was forced to end it or worse, not given the choice.

"Did you get lost?" Teddy called from the bedroom, pulling me from my thoughts.

Grabbing two bottles of water, I shut the fridge door. Back in the bedroom, I placed his water on the nightstand. Teddy never took his eyes off me as he examined my naked body via the moonlight from my open window.

"Do you miss being married?" I asked, falling into bed. The alcohol not only made me a slut but it made me inquisitive.

"The marriage, nah. The connection and companionship with someone, yes." Teddy reached out for me, pulling me close. "I like to hold on to people. Unfortunately, I tend to hold on for too long. The writing was clearly on the wall with Mariah, I guess I was just too blind to see it."

"That's weird. I'm the opposite. I tend to let people go before they can let me go. It's safer that way." I rested my head on his chest.

"Safer, maybe. But life only really gets interesting when we venture out of our warm and comfy place."

"Not everybody *wants* interesting."

"Bullshit, everyone wants interesting, they're just too scared so they settle for safe and pretend that it's good enough."

"What do you want?"

After the words escaped my lips, I felt immediate regret, not sure I wanted to hear his answer. What if he said he wanted me? What then? What if he wanted something or someone else? Also, what then?

"Have you ever been in love?" Teddy asked.

I felt my body tense, bracing myself for the direction of this conversation. "Of course, I have."

"So, you remember how that felt? I want that."

"It felt nauseating," I countered. "I never felt secure or certain of anything. I didn't like it. Zero stars, would not recommend."

Teddy laughed, hooking his thumb under my chin, tilting my head until our eyes met. "Sounds like you were doing it wrong. You should probably give it another go." Teddy kissed my lips gently before removing his hand from my chin.

I didn't respond. Why would I expose myself to that again? My last relationship with Julius, a DC area architect, was toxic. For all the degrees between us we were both plum stupid. Our two-year-plus relationship was like Monica's "So Gone" and

Ashanti's "Baby" all rolled up into one. I hated who I was when I was with him. Insecure, suspicious, and argumentative, all over a man. Love was a young woman's game. I had too many scars to keep fighting that fight.

Laying on Teddy's chest, I listened to the beat of his heart like a lullaby in my ear. I slowly rubbed my fingers across his beard. As I drifted off to sleep, I whispered, "Thank you for making me feel special."

"If you let me, every day could feel like this," he whispered back.

"Mmm, maybe," I mumbled, before falling to sleep.

CHAPTER EIGHTEEN

Lisa knocked on my opened door with a concerned look on her face. "We have a bit of a crisis, we need to head to the Oval, ASAP," Lisa said, raking her hand through her ash blonde hair.

Without hesitation I jumped from my chair, notepad and pen in tow. In most work settings when someone claimed there was a crisis, it was usually something that was easily fixable and the staff was just running around needlessly like chickens with their heads freshly cut off. However, when the word crisis was uttered in the White House, we could be facing a hostage situation, soldiers killed or missing in the line of duty, or a political opponent talking reckless.

At the Oval door Lisa entered without knocking, which was practically unheard of; this crisis must be a doozy. In the office I found Teddy and Gibbs staring at Gibbs's tablet on the Resolute Desk.

"What's going on?" I asked, my curiosity fully piqued.

Gibbs waved me over. Making room, he allowed me to view the shaky video playing. Leaning in to get a better look, I could make out a man who was clearly Teddy; I would know his frame anywhere. There was also a woman naked from the top up gyrating on his lap.

"What is this?" I asked, trying to disguise my rising anger and shock.

Gibbs began to answer, "It's a video—"

"It's from that bachelor party I went to last month in Vegas. It's just a lap dance," Teddy said, staring at me with pleading eyes. He was trying to communicate far more than his words implied.

Lisa chimed in, "It's all over the internet. Lapgate is trending number one on Twitter."

"Lapgate?" I whispered, with a mirthless chuckle.

These internet trolls were so unoriginal. Knots coiled in my belly. This was not how I wanted to start my Tuesday morning. Seeing Teddy on that video was activating my crazy girlfriend mode, even though I constantly reminded him that he was nothing more to me but a good lay. It hurt to see the man who had woken me up this morning with his face between my ass cheeks running his hands across another woman's body.

"We need to decide how we're going to address this," Gibbs said, stopping the video. "We have to get ahead of this before it runs us over."

"I think we should have the President apologize for his behavior which is uncharacteristic of the values he holds as commander in chief," Lisa offered, pursing her lips, judgment dripping from every word.

Teddy's eyes were boring a hole into the side of my face, but I refused to meet his gaze. He owed me nothing, and I was prepared to provide him the same because we were nothing.

"He is definitely going to have to do a whole mea culpa," Gibbs agreed, removing his glasses to rub his eyes.

I'd been with the administration for a little over six months now, and Gibbs was aging like milk that had been left in the trunk of a car on a hot DC summer day. It was common knowledge that working in any presidential administration aged you, and Gibbs was living proof.

"Maybe an interview with Robin Roberts?" Lisa suggested.

"No," I said, dropping my notepad and pen on the desk.

"What?" Gibbs asked.

Taking a deep breath, I continued. "No, we aren't going to do any of those things. We are going to ignore this, deprive it of oxygen, and watch it die. The President is forty-one years old. He is beyond grown, and he is single, and as such he is free to get lap dances from strippers or hook up with random women at the Bunny Ranch in Nevada."

Teddy leaned back on his desk.

Lisa looked like she wanted to rip out her hair. "You can't seriously be considering—"

"Go on," Teddy interrupted. "I want to hear how you plan to pull this off."

Clearing my throat, I laid out my plan, "It's simple, really. The President keeps a low profile until my briefing tomorrow. At that briefing the reporters start shooting off questions about the President and the stripper. I will inform them that as Press Secretary I don't comment on the President's personal life. I will also reiterate that President Elmsworth is single and as such he is allowed to enjoy the freedom that being single provides. I will let them know that there are far bigger issues than how the President spends his downtime."

The room was silent with all eyes on me. Lisa's eyes bulged like I had lost my mind. Halfway through my explanation, Gibbs had taken a seat and was breathing heavily. Teddy was staring off into the distance. I knew him well enough to know that he was calculating the odds in his head.

"This is a non-story and we should treat it as such," I added.

"I think we should move forward with Clover's plan," Teddy said, rubbing his beard.

"Really?" Gibbs stood, placing a hand on his hip.

"You disagree?" Teddy asked, cocking his head to the side.

"Damn right, I disagree. The press isn't going to take a no comment and move on," Gibbs objected.

"The press will take what we give them," I insisted. "They can ask the questions until they're blue in the face, but the answer will always remain the same. Eventually they will get tired and start chasing a different tail."

"And if they don't?" Lisa asked, still not convinced.

"In a week there will be some new crisis, a celebrity breakup, the death of a prominent figure, unrest overseas. We just need to wait it out."

"I'm with Clover, I expect you two to support her as we execute this plan." Teddy sounded relieved that everything appeared to be under control.

After additional strategizing, the meeting ended. Grabbing our things, Gibbs, Lisa, and I headed for the door.

"Clover, can I talk to you for a minute?" Teddy called.

"No," I said, not slowing my stride, closing his door behind me.

I SCANNED the crowded restaurant looking for Daysha. I had asked her to meet me for drinks. I needed to let off some steam after the craptastic day I'd had.

"Clover," Daysha yelled across the restaurant, waving her hands to grab my attention.

Lowering my head, I made my way toward the table. I had only been here for a minute and Day had already found a way to embarrass me.

Day stood, giving me a warm hug. It felt good and acted as a much-needed balm for my bruised pride. I held on far longer than normal.

"Uh oh, what up?" Day asked, as we took our seats at the small square table.

"Nothing's up because it's all currently crashing down,

smashing against the ground," I said. "I need a drink."

Daysha summoned the waiter and had a pomegranate martini in front of me in no time flat.

"I saw your press conference today. Is that really the President in that video?"

"Yep, he was stupid and let his guard down."

"Well, you did a great job deflecting those nosy ass questions," Day said, looking at the menu.

I sipped at my drink. "Thanks."

"So, why so glum, chum?"

I crinkled my face, bracing myself to be cussed out by Day. "I kinda never stopped seeing Teddy," I said, my lip trembling.

Closing her eyes, Daysha shook her head. "I knew it. You were always so short whenever I asked you about him." Daysha's jaw dropped as her eyes lit up. "So, you've been messing with him for—"

"Months," I said, finishing her statement.

"Is it serious?"

I shrugged. "I don't know. We don't have any titles if that's what you mean."

"Is he seeing other people?"

I frowned, shrugging hopelessly again. Why was she asking me all these tough questions?

"Clover, so you just gonna be blind, deaf, and dumb." Daysha smiled up at the waiter who had returned to the table for our order. After the waiter left, Daysha continued, "If you wanna have this experimental coupling, you have to have the tough conversations. And I think knowing if the guy you're sleeping with is sleeping with other people would be a good start."

"It never came up."

"I'm sure it didn't because you were too busy making other things come up," Daysha chastised. For the most part Daysha was a good time girl, but when she was serious it was like a stern talking to from a mother. "What did he say about the video?"

I took another slow sip of my martini, knowing Daysha

wasn't going to like my answer. "I haven't talked to him about it, exactly."

"So, you're just totally ignoring the elephant in the room?"

"No, I'm not ignoring the elephant, because I have completely removed myself from the room."

Day rolled her eyes.

"Look, it's over and quite honestly, he doesn't owe me an explanation. I knew what it was when it started. If I allowed myself to believe for one second that I could have a serious relationship with that man, I was only fooling myself."

"So, you told him it's over?"

"Not so much in those words, but—"

"You are so messy, Clover," Daysha said, rubbing her forehead. "For someone who fields difficult questions every day, you sure avoid asking any in your own life."

"Look, actions speak louder than words. I'm avoiding him at work and I haven't returned any of his calls or text messages. He's a smart man, he'll get the hint."

Daysha remained silent but her face, which always gave away her true feelings, was calling me a damn fool.

It was Friday, four days since lapgate, and Gibbs, Lisa, and I were meeting with the President in a conference room to debrief. It had also been four days since Teddy and I had last spoken.

"How many questions did you get about the video this morning at your briefing?" Gibbs asked.

"Three," I said.

Gibbs shook his head. "They are never going to let up. We need to change course before it's too late."

"I strongly disagree, the plan is working. It's only been a few days, you have to be patient," I said, glaring at Gibbs.

"Patience is something I'm running short on," the President

said, pushing his chair away from the table. "What the fuck?" Teddy stared at me with cold eyes. "I thought you had this under control?"

Teddy had me all the way messed up if he thought I was going to allow him or anyone to talk to me like that.

"I did what you asked me to do," I said, trying my best to keep my tone respectful.

"If that's true, why am I standing underneath a pile of crap right now?"

I looked at Gibbs and Lisa, but neither of them would meet my eyes. They both sensed there was blood in the water and neither was willing to stick their necks out for fear of getting bit. It was fine, I was more than capable of defending myself.

"Well, sir, maybe if you didn't take to Twitter and contradict everything I said, we wouldn't have this problem."

Last night, Teddy must have been feeling restless because when I woke up I had Twitter alerts that he had retweeted several funny memes making light of his current situation.

Teddy narrowed his eyes. "Oh, so it's my fault?"

"Yep, how's that shoe fitting for you?" I threw back.

Gibbs and Lisa's heads were turning back and forth like they were watching a tennis match.

"No, I gave you a task that you clearly can't handle."

Now I was standing and had difficulty keeping my voice down. "There aren't any tasks that I can't handle. I've been cleaning up your messes for the past six months now."

"My messes," Teddy laughed.

"Yes, Russia, a mess, troop withdrawal, mess. The embassy in Pakistan, a big steaming pile of mess."

Teddy looked at me like I'd just sprouted a second arm. "Are you insane? Have you bumped your damn head?"

"I have a clean bill of health, but maybe we should get the doctor in here to check on your wellbeing."

"Clear the room," Teddy ordered.

With a choking cough, Gibbs said, "But sir, I—"

"Clear the fucking room," Teddy yelled, never taking his laser-focused eyes off of me.

Gibbs and Lisa gathered their things and left the conference room with no further objections, leaving Teddy and me alone.

"What the hell are you doing?" Teddy asked.

"My question exactly. What are you doing?" I threw his question back in his face.

"Holding you accountable."

"You can hold someone accountable without making them feel like shit."

"Well, maybe if you answered my calls or text messages, I wouldn't have to confront you in front of other people."

It was a fair point. I had made myself unavailable for conversation on both my personal and work cell phones. But still, questioning my ability to do my job was out of line.

I released some of the tension I was storing in my shoulders and softened my tone. "I trust the plan, but you have to give it time to work. And you need to stay off Twitter," I said, stuffing my laptop and notepad back into my tote bag.

Teddy nodded his head. I had a feeling this was more about me ignoring him than my lapgate strategy. "Can you let me explain?" His eyes were soft, his shoulders slumped.

It took all my willpower not to reach for him, allowing his arms to envelope me.

"No. This is my job, Teddy. I don't want to talk about the past."

"Is that what we are? In the past."

Swinging my tote bag over my shoulder, I headed for the door. "Have a good day, Mr. President."

CLOSE TO THE end of the day there was a knock on my door.

"Come in," I yelled.

Lisa opened the door, entering my office. "Did you know Brittany isn't out front?" she asked.

"Oh, I'm sorry, I forgot to chain her back to her desk after lunch. Won't happen again," I teased.

Lisa and I had forged a friendship these past few months and while we didn't always agree and she failed to have my back in the meeting earlier, I liked that she enjoyed talking about politics as much as I did.

Lisa took a seat in one of the chairs in front of my desk. "I don't think I have ever seen anyone talk to the President like that."

I shrugged. "Ugh, I know I was out of line. I was just frustrated. After you left, I apologized to him for losing my cool."

This was a lie, but I didn't want Lisa getting the impression that Teddy and I had more than a boss and staffer relationship.

"If I'm being honest..." Lisa looked back to make sure my office door was closed. "It was kind of nice to watch someone go toe to toe with him." She smiled.

"This has been a week, huh," I said, rolling my eyes. I was tired of talking about Teddy. "Any exciting plans for the weekend?"

"Frank's mother is in town so I'll be tooling around the house with a full glass of wine at all times." We both chuckled. "What about you?"

"Nothing special, but I plan to work as little as possible. I need a self-care weekend," I said, rolling my shoulders that were sore and tense.

"I think you should. You've been working nonstop since day one. Work-life balance is important, even in the White House where stuff like that is hard to come by." Lisa stood, heading for the door. "Don't worry about the President, he'll be mad about something else by Monday." Lisa smiled. "Have a great weekend."

"You too. See you Monday."

I'D ALLOWED myself to sleep in on Saturday morning, waking up at nine. After a quick shower and a cup of coffee, I decided I was going to spend the morning cleaning my apartment. All the clothes that should be in my closet were piled high on a chair in my bedroom. After cleaning I would make a Whole Foods run and stock up on some essentials, like juice and grab-and-go snack foods. In my bedroom I tackled the pile first, sorting through clothes and making a pile for the dry cleaners.

My progress was interrupted by a knock on the front door. It was probably my sweet next-door neighbor, an older gentleman who I would check on, making sure he didn't need anything when I was out running errands. Opening the door, the man that stood before me was neither sweet or elderly.

"What are you doing here?" I scanned the hall before pulling Teddy into my apartment, closing the door.

I didn't want the other tenants thinking the President paid me special visits. I knew the two agents posted outside my front door would surely raise some eyebrows.

"I was in the neighborhood," Teddy said, stepping into my living room.

"I call BS," I said, pulling the sash on my silk robe tighter.

Teddy walked to my window, pushing the curtain to the side observing the block below. He looked good in a green t-shirt and gym shorts that showed off his strong calf muscles.

"I'm sorry to come over unannounced," Teddy said.

That was a lie; he didn't care that his visit was inconvenient.

"I listened to the morning news during my workout and they are still talking about the video." Teddy ran his fingers across a purple crystal I used as a paper weight. "You really think your plan is gonna work?"

I let out a sigh. "You came all the way over here to ask me that?"

"I'm concerned." His jaw muscles firmed into a rigid line.

"You need to trust the process. It's the Anjeni method."

Teddy put down a statue I'd gotten in Cairo and stared at me. "The what? Please don't tell me you're hooking my political future on some pop star."

"No. Not exactly." I stepped closer so I could explain. "Look, remember when Zoe beat Slim Black's ass in the elevator while Anjeni watched?"

"Vaguely?"

"Exactly, because Anjeni never acknowledged the incident. Not once. She let the rumors fly but she didn't comment on it or release any statement. Eventually the vultures stopped circling and moved on to the next dead body."

I knew it sounded crazy, but it worked. Anjeni was the hottest R&B singer on the planet right now. I'd used this method before, all with positive results.

Teddy nodded his head, appearing to accept my explanation. He took a seat on my sofa like he planned to stay awhile. "I bumped into one of your neighbors on my way up."

I stiffened my gaze; it was a mistake for him to come here.

"She had this little yappy dog with her and she talked my ear off about the subpar conditions of the roads throughout the city."

My face brightened with recognition. "Sounds like you met Mrs. Valdez.

Teddy bounced his knee up and down, unable to control his nervous energy. "Lucky, it was a bachelor party. Nothing more."

"So you say," I replied, with a stubborn fold of my arms.

Teddy threw his head back. "What is this about? Really?"

"I don't know what you mean."

"I mean you've stopped taking my calls." He was now leaning forward, his muscular legs spread wide.

"I've stopped entertaining your bullshit."

I knew Teddy was a player, so I shouldn't have been surprised when I got played, but here I was in utter shock.

Standing, he looked at me with fire in his eyes. "My bullshit?

For months I've listened to you tell me this isn't a relationship, Teddy. Don't get too comfortable, Teddy. But now you wanna act butt hurt and disappointed. Last time I checked, I wasn't your boyfriend. So why do you care?"

"Because it's disrespectful," I yelled. "We may not be a couple, but I'm only sleeping with you."

"OK, and I'm only sleeping with you. So now what?" His face was inches from mine.

A bitter laugh escaped my mouth. "The way that stripper was grinding on you, I'm not so sure."

"It was a lap dance." Teddy's voice boomed, echoing against my apartment walls. "What was she supposed to do?"

"If you wanted a lap dance you should have come home to me," I snapped back.

"But you're not trying to be my home. I tell you I think I'm falling in love with you and you laughed in my face. I tell you I feel connected with you and at peace with you, and you tell me it'll pass. You can't have it both ways, Clover. I can't be your man and not be your man."

"I don't want or expect anything from you," I said, rubbing my hand together to symbolize that I was through.

"But here I am trying to give you all of me." He grabbed my face, forcing me to look him in the eyes. "Listen, Clover, I know that you don't wanna hear it, but I need to say it. I love you."

The words turned my heart into a yoyo, soaring and then sinking over and over again. I shook my head, trying to stop the emotions from welling up in my eyes. "Stop. Stop. This is not... this is not part of the plan." I tried my best to wriggle free, but his hold was too strong.

"We agreed to go with the flow, and the flow led me here."

These past few months with Teddy had been sublime. At first I thought it was the thrill of being with someone who was off limits. But as time passed, it was less about breaking rules and more about breaking down walls. We could talk for hours about nothing, just vibing off one another's energy.

He was familiar to me, reminding me of the men in my family who I'd grown up with. The men who protected me and encouraged my greatness, providing the blueprint of what real men should be. The longer Teddy and I were together, the connection I felt with him outside of the bedroom grew deeper. I loved Teddy. I just didn't know how to say it.

"I'm scared," I whispered, my heart beating rapidly, causing pains in my chest.

"I know it's scary, the vulnerable part. I'm scared too. But just because we're scared doesn't mean we shouldn't try. I love you, Clover." His eyes gleamed with conviction. "You don't have to say it back right now. I'll wait."

Teddy pulled me in, pressing his lips against my mouth. His kisses were emergent like being connected to me was the most important item on his agenda. Taking deep breaths, I gorged myself on the rustic scent of him until it invaded my senses. Barefooted, I reached for him on my tip toes, letting his tongue play with mine. It had been less than a week but I missed him desperately, every part of my body jonesing to be one with his.

He buried his face into my neck, kissing and biting at my flesh which caused my core to thrum with an aching so pronounced, one that I knew only his touch, his lips, his entire existence could fix. Untying the sash of my robe, he slid the silk fabric back, letting it drop to the floor exposing my bare skin. In return I practically ripped his T-shirt as I tried to pull it over his head. I was so needy with the desire to be close to him. My erect nipples brushed against his hard chest giving me a high, sparking the reward center in my brain.

The warmth of his hands fondling my thighs and ass forced me to restrict my breathing to short pants for air. Stumbling to the couch I took a seat while Teddy sunk to his knees, his hands stimulating my breast as he planted soft, wet kisses on my inner thigh. I rubbed the top of his head as I waited with anxious anticipation for his tongue to sweep across my clit. As his mouth inched closer it became difficult to control my breathing at all, my chest heaving, longing for the heat of his mouth as it hovered over my soft spot. When his tongue touched down it slid in and over my folds before latching onto my bud. I cried out, my entire body tensing unable to handle the intense rush.

My legs clamped shut practically boxing Teddy in but he didn't stop, using his large strong hands to separate my legs, never once disconnecting his tongue from me. Sinking into the couch cushions, I fucked his face, my hips floating back and forth helping him to hit my spot. The sound of Teddy feasting on me drove me wild, his long slurps, followed by satisfied moans before dipping his tongue in and out. He knew exactly what he was doing, his hands kneading my breast before falling to my waist pressing my hips against his mouth as my juices wet his face.

Like me, Teddy was an overachiever and that work ethic wasn't just reserved to the White House. He licked, sucked, and fingered me like it was his job and the rent was past due. Even when a body shaking orgasm rocked my core, Teddy continued to taste me looking for extra credit. I had to climb to the arm rest of the couch to get away from him.

Teddy stood with a laugh; you know the type. An arrogant low snicker because he knew he had me right where he wanted me ... prepared to grovel at his feet. And grovel I did, now the one dropping to my knees I placed soft kisses up and down his shaft before rolling my tongue over his balls. I wanted a lot of things, world peace, quiet upstairs neighbors, a green Telfar bag, but I didn't want anything more than what I craved in this moment ... Teddy, every last drop of him.

I was unable to keep my hands off of him or myself. Completely aroused and Teddy's dick otherwise occupied, I had to take care of business on my own, plunging my hands in between my thighs. Relaxing my mouth, I moved my head back and forth occasionally looking up at Teddy who was standing over me with adulation in his eyes. I was all for being an independent self-reliant woman but sometimes being on your knees was the most powerful thing you could do.

Teddy pulled out backing away.

"You OK?" I asked, standing.

"I'm great. You on the other hand are about to be in a world of hurt."

I licked my lips, a thrilling ribbon sensation tugging at my core, because I knew Teddy was a man who kept his promises and I was ready to be hurt in the best way.

He retrieved a condom from the wallet in his shorts which I'd tossed across the room when removing them earlier. Condom in place, Teddy moved forward, causing me to back up until I was against a wall. His strong hand encircled my waist, lifting me from the hardwood floor. Grabbing my legs, Teddy used the wall to support us and went to work. The first thrust had my head spinning. The second thrust made me call him by his government name.

"Theodore."

The third thrust left me speechless and gasping for air.

CHAPTER NINETEEN

"WHAT'S THE WEATHER GOING TO BE LIKE?" DAYSHA CALLED from inside my closet.

"I checked and it said it was going to be unseasonably warm for September, like in the nineties," I yelled back, tucking bras and panties in my undergarment bag.

Day appeared from the closet. "Well, Camp David is just like going to a lake house, so pack for that."

It had been a month since lapgate, which as I predicted was no longer a topic of discussion. It had also been a month since Teddy and I made our relationship official. As official as a relationship could be with the President of the United States. We were still pretty much sneaking around and trying our best to keep the goo goo eyes to a minimum.

"So, it's just going to be the two of you? Daysha asked, spritzing her wrist with one of my floral-scented body sprays.

"Yep, well, us and the Secret Service and the Camp David staff."

I made a dash for the bathroom, grabbing my toiletry bag. The car would be here to pick me up any minute now and I was still packing. I'd spent the previous night working. When I looked up from my binder and notes it was almost one in the morning, and all I wanted to do was crawl into bed and rest my weary eyes.

"So, can I call him your boyfriend now?" Day asked, plopping on my bed.

"No ... I don't know," I said, stuffing a few additional outfits in my weekender bag so I had options.

Yes, he was my boyfriend, but it was still difficult for me to say. Teddy was still waiting for me to tell him I loved him back, so calling him my boyfriend was the least of my worries.

"Well, I'm proud of you for finally taking the leap." She handed me my jewelry case. "You've been single for almost as long as I've known you, and it wasn't from a lack of offers."

I shook my head. Day was right. I had been single for a long time, but I always managed to find an attractive man to help keep the left side of my bed warm.

The doorbell rang. "Ugh, can you get the door and tell the driver I'll be right down?" I asked, running to the bathroom to pee and apply my lipstick.

The last time I'd gone away with a significant other we got into a huge fight because his phone wouldn't stop buzzing and chiming in the middle of the night. I accused him of cheating, he called me crazy, which was a huge mistake because he ended up room-less and wandering the beach all night. I was hoping this trip would be different.

"Ahh, Clover, your presence is required," Daysha called from the entryway.

Heading toward the door, I stopped in my tracks at the sight of Teddy and Daysha chit chatting.

"Day, are you gonna let him in or does he need to answer all of your questions first?"

Stepping aside, Daysha allowed Teddy to enter my apartment, closing the door behind him.

"I didn't know you were picking me up."

"I moved some stuff around so we could go down together." Teddy bent down to lightly kiss my lips. "It's nice to finally meet you, Daysha. Lucky's told me so much about you."

Daysha flashed a bright smile. "She's told me some things about you as well."

"Hopefully only the good stuff." Teddy winked at me, squeezing my waist.

"Now what fun would that be?" I teased.

"You ready?"

"Almost, I just need like five more minutes." I cringed apologetically.

He checked his watch. "Well, hurry up, we ditched the press pool but they're getting smarter."

Running back to the bedroom to gather the last of my things, I overheard Teddy and Day's conversation.

"You're a lawyer, right?" Teddy asked.

"Yeah, family law."

"Where'd you go to law school?

"McGeorge in California," Daysha said.

"That's a good school."

"Not as good as Harvard Law."

"No, you're right about that." I could hear Teddy laugh. "But at the end of the day it's all relative. Harvard, McGeorge, the checks clear just the same."

As I tossed the last remaining items into my bag, a smile spread across my face. It was nice to have my best friend and my boyfri—the man I was dating get along. That was an important test and Teddy was passing with flying colors. I don't know why I was surprised. Everyone loved Theodore Elmsworth, even his political opponents had to admit that he was a likable guy.

The chit chat in the other room continued. "So, this is the point in the conversation where I tell you that if you break my girl's heart I will break your nose. Respectfully, of course."

"Yep, I get it. But honestly, I think it's far more likely that my heart gets broken before hers."

"Yeah, she is kinda hardcore."

"I know right. Like Stone Cold Steve Austin and The Undertaker all rolled into one."

"Right ..."

"You don't have a clue who either of those people are?"

"No."

Entering the room, I dragged my weekender and small roller suitcase behind me. "I'm ready."

Teddy grabbed my bags, heading for the door. "It was nice talking with you, Daysha. Maybe we can all get together for brunch sometime. I'd love to meet your husband Nate."

"That sounds like a plan. Nice meeting you too, Mr. President," Daysha said with a giddy chuckle, as Teddy headed down the stairs.

I smiled at her like a proud mother whose child had just recited the "I Have a Dream" speech at the school assembly.

"Wow," Daysha said.

"I know right."

"Girl, he is fine. Like, he's handsome on TV but in real life, that man is fine."

I bit my lip. "You have no idea."

"I like him."

"Me too."

Camp David was tucked away in Catoctin Mountain Park and offered a level of privacy that could not be found in DC. Teddy and I would have four hundred fifty acres of solitude without paparazzi or press nosing around. The press pool was staying nearby just in case the President called a press briefing or was interested in a photo op, but they were far enough away that their presence would go unnoticed.

Agent Tally opened my car door, and outside of the car the air was crisp and cool. Drinking it in, I let the sun kiss my skin. Being a city girl, the wilderness wasn't really my jam. I couldn't recall the last time I allowed myself to be one with nature. Don't get me wrong, nature was beautiful and majestic but so was room service and spa treatments.

Rounding the car, Teddy smiled, looking up at the modest-looking home surrounded by trees. "You hear that?" he asked.

"What?" My head was on a swivel, taking in the large trees with their orange and red leaves that threatened to drift to the ground with the slightest gust of wind.

"The silence," Teddy screamed, throwing his arms back. "I may be a city boy, but there is something to be said about open land and not being stacked on top of your neighbors." As the retreat staff unloaded our car, Teddy slowly inched closer to the house. "In the city it's always go, go, go, sometimes it's nice to slow down and appreciate all that God has created." Smiling, I jogged to catch up to him. "Maybe after all the politics is over we can get us a farm, raise some chickens and cows and make artisan cheese."

"Whoa, slow down there. We've been here five minutes and you are already talking about putting down your executive pen and picking up a shovel."

He would often mention our plans for the future, which, if I was being honest, weirded me out a bit. Yes, I'd agreed to an exclusive relationship, but I certainly wasn't picking out brides-maid dresses.

Inside the house was exactly what I expected: it was rustic with wood paneling and beams. The decor was a bit outdated with the plaid armchairs and clashing floral curtains. I followed behind as we walked through the living room, library, den, formal dining room, sun room, family room, and back to the living room.

"It's not the Waldorf Astoria but it'll do," Teddy said with a content grin on his face.

"Four days and three fun-filled nights, I think we can make it work." Inspecting the large stone-covered, wood-burning fireplace, I made a mental note to clock some sexy time in front of it. "What do you wanna do first?"

He rounded the couch, taking a place in front of me. Wrapping his hand around my neck, he leaned forward. My body tensed as I gave him a stiff arm against his chest.

"Teddy?" I shook my head, glancing around the room.

There were uniformed staff all around us. Two women in the open-concept kitchen were cutting up fruit, there was a young man watering the lush greenery on the wraparound deck. Another gentleman was headed up the stairs with an arm full of fresh towels.

"What?" He eyed me narrowly.

"We're not exactly alone."

"Oh, they don't care. They are here to serve me." We both grimaced at the sound of his last words. "I mean, they've all been hired because of their discretion. They wouldn't care if I filmed a video for Only Fans with ball gags and whips."

I wasn't so sure. Working my mouth into a dubious wad, I backed away. My experience was when you got too comfortable, Karma or the God of Mischief had a way of smacking you across the face like Rick James.

Sensing that I was still uneasy, Teddy turned his attention to the women in the kitchen.

"Excuse me, what's your name?"

The older woman looked up from her cutting board and pointed a sharp knife toward her chest. "Me?"

Teddy nodded.

"Louise, Mr. President."

"Ms. Louise, over the next four days I am going to have copious amounts of sex. In the living room, the bedroom, the pool, shoot, probably that kitchen counter, and it's gonna be loud because, this one..." Teddy pointed in my direction, paying no mind to my jaw that was brushing the ground. "Well, she's a screamer. Are you gonna be OK with that?"

Without missing a beat, Louise replied, "Your house, your rules, Mr. President."

Teddy turned back to me, arms open wide. "Up here, no one cares, Lucky. We don't have to sneak around. I don't have to stop myself from reaching for your hand or suppress the uncontrollable desire to kiss your lips." He leaned forward, whispering in my ear, "Both of them."

My face bore a goofy ass smile as my stomach trilled with excitement.

"We can do whatever we want because it's just you and me. No staffers, no Gibbs watching our every move." He placed a soft kiss on my collar bone, working his way up my neck. In one fell swoop, Teddy lifted me off my feet. "Now let's check out the bedroom." He took to the stairs two at a time, my laughter trailing behind us.

AFTER A MIND MELTING love-making session in which Teddy took his time relishing every crease, dimple, and freckle on my body, we headed downstairs for dinner. This little getaway was just what I needed. Being at the White House was exhilarating and exhausting at the same time. You're always on pins and needles, and although I had the President's ear, among other things, in the Oval I wasn't spared his ire.

The length of the dining table was decorated with a fresh-cut flower arrangement in glass vases and candles scattered among them. You would think we were hosting a dinner party instead of a party for two. On the menu were Cornish hens and cheese polenta with kale greens.

I forgot my manners as I licked my fork clean. Everything was perfect: the meal, the ambience, the man. Glancing over at Teddy, I flashed him a round-eyed expression. This was not the same man I'd worked for years ago.

"What's that look for?" he asked, wiping the corners of his mouth with his napkin.

"Did I give you a look?"

"Yes, a very distinct look."

Raising an eyebrow, I teased, "What did it say?"

"It looked like you were trying to decide if I was full of it or not."

I almost spit out my wine. "My little look said all that, huh?"

His eyebrows were fitted in a skeptical line. "I don't think you realize how bad your poker face is."

"Well, I wasn't thinking that. I already know you're full of it." Amusement flushed my face as I shed a laugh. "I was thinking about how different you are from the man I remember."

"Different how?"

"From when you were senator."

"Newsflash, man evolves over eight years."

"OK, you know what? Never mind." I pouted when I didn't get the reaction I wanted.

"Is that why you weren't checking for me back then? Because I was *different*."

"What are you talking about?"

"You know I tried back then to get to know you but you weren't having it. I've always had a thing for you."

"Bullshit, you've always wanted to sleep with me."

Teddy was a huge flirt back in the day but he wasn't looking to settle down. And I was dating the surgeon who thought he was a psychiatrist because he was always trying to diagnose me.

"No, I had a crush on you for the longest."

Tilting my head to the side, I gave him a crooked grin. "Then why didn't you say anything?"

"Because you were all men ain't shit and claimed we could easily be replaced by robots."

My face illuminated as my memory was jogged. "I'd forgotten about that."

There was a time when I supported the idea of fully funding

the science behind animatronic male robots, with limited speech capabilities but detachable dicks. So you could customize your experience. The attachments would be sold separately. So, you could go with sports mode, which would provide concentrated thrust that got you to the corner of orgasm and ecstasy lickity split, or the feel it in your chest attachment that rearranged your organs.

"Also, we worked together, so ..."

"We work together now." I blinked my eyes, flinging my hands in the air.

"Yes, we do. But, I wasn't going to let you get away twice."

I didn't know if that made him charming or stupid.

Flashing me a smile, he stood. "Let's wind down in the hot tub."

"OK, let me change into my swimsuit."

Shaking his head, he said, "I don't think you'll need it." Teddy extended his hand and I slipped mine in his firm hold, allowing him to lead me to the bubbling water.

The jacuzzi was steamy, mostly because Teddy's hands were beneath the surface pleasuring my body. With my leg hooked over his, Teddy's fingers slid deep inside. My head lulled from side to side as my core became taut in anticipation of a release that built in intensity before washing over me. Everything faded into the background as my body shook uncontrollably.

Teddy whispered in my ear, encouraging me to let go. He took great joy in working me into a tizzy. "That's it, baby. Don't fight it."

Ecstasy slowly fading, my body relaxed, practically slipping under the water because I felt so Zen.

"I love you, Lucky," Teddy whispered over my mouth.

The vertebrae in my spine stretched to full length as I pulled away, moving to the other side of the tub in need of air. Reaching for a bottle of water, I chugged the entire thing in one gulp.

"You good? You having trouble keeping up?" Teddy asked, with an impatient snort.

I shook my head, causing my messy bun to tumble. "No, I'm great. I just need to rehydrate for round ..." I'd lost count at this point.

Teddy strangled out a laugh, splashing water across his even-toned skin. I could stare at that face for hours. His rich brown eyes that wrinkled at the corners when he laughed deeply. His mouth that he used to persuade Americans to vote for him and urged me to call out his name. His beard, with a few flecks of gray hair that I would run my fingers across as I lay in his arms. His chest that was broad and strong and yet still provided my head a soft place to rest.

"Clover?"

"Hmm," I mumbled, still lost in my thoughts.

"You make me nervous."

His words snapped me back to reality. Why would I make the most powerful man in the world nervous?

"I doubt that." I rolled my eyes.

"No, you do." His tone turned serious. "Because I need you and I don't think you need me."

How did I ever think this man was a playboy? He was literally wearing his heart on his sleeve. When he was a senator, he seemed like the type of guy who liked the chase but quickly lost interest once he got what he wanted. At least that's what I'd always assumed. *Where did I pick that idea up from?*

Teddy continued, "I know what love feels like."

Swallowing hard, I braced myself. Love wasn't something I'd experienced in recent years. In fact, I avoided it like gum on the sidewalk, or a cheap wig. It was possible love was like a muscle and if you didn't use it regularly that muscle would atrophy, making it harder to give and receive it.

Shrugging, I offered, "Well, maybe my love feels different."

"If by different you mean cold, then yeah."

I felt myself overheating as sweat dripped down my face. This was not a conversation I was interested in having. I just wanted to fool around in the jacuzzi and collapse into bed.

"I need to protect myself."

I could tell from the way he screwed his face that was not the correct answer.

"From me?"

Taking a shallow breath, I scurried out of the water, my chest tightening as my eyes threatened to fill with tears. I wrapped a towel around my body. What didn't he get? I needed to protect myself from him, from myself, and these feelings that were popping up like weeds telling me that this could be my fairy tale.

The lies that whispered in my ear claiming that this time it could be different. The thoughts that occupied my mind saying that if I allowed myself to love again, truly love, that this man would return my energy tenfold. I'd believed all these falsehoods in the past only to end up embarrassed and depleted.

"Lucky, wait." Teddy climbed out of the water.

Raising a hand to silence him, I walked away, leaving him dripping wet and naked. Finding a guest room, I crawled into bed alone.

CHAPTER TWENTY

THE BIRDS CHIRPING OUTSIDE MY WINDOW SIGNALED THE start of a new day. "What the hell are y'all so chipper about?" I grumbled aloud toward the window. Pulling the covers over my head, I focused all my energy on disappearing. Maybe if I tried really hard I could spontaneously combust and then all that would be left of me was ash and smoke.

I lay still for several minutes, and all I could feel was my stomach growling. Tossing the cover aside, I headed to the bathroom. The counters were bare because all my things were in the room I should be sharing with Teddy. I caught my reflection in the mirror. My makeup was smudged and without my satin scarf my hair looked like a tumbleweed.

You have got to be the stupidest bitch ever. You have a man who loves you.

Claims to love me.

That man has to love you to continue to deal with your baggage. If you don't unpack that mess and shove the empty suitcases under your bed already.

You act like it's just that easy.

Because it is. You're the one holding on to this bone like a rabid dog. Damn, so a few men hurt you and you just close yourself off.

A few?

A couple.

Do you need me to run down the list? I can start with Rodney from high school who claimed to love me but cheated on me with Cheryl James 'cause she put out.

Fuck Rodney, he graduated with a 2.9 GPA. Are you really going to let a brother who couldn't identify Nairobi on a map block your blessings?

I rolled a thick shoulder, I was making valid points. Rodney was always an underachiever.

So, what do you suggest I do since you know every damn thing?

Apologize. Tell Teddy you were tripping. Suck his dick until he forgets your toxic.

I'm gonna pretend it never happened. Maybe he wants to forget too.

Whatever you do, don't do that.

I splashed water over my face and used one of the towels to remove the leftover makeup.

I'll go back to the room and just fake it till I make things right again.

Clover! Bitch, don't walk away from me.

Back in the master suite, the bed was made and the room empty. Releasing the breath I was holding as I walked the halls, I headed to the bathroom and took a hot shower. Throwing on some yoga pants and a crop top, I brushed my hair back into a slick bun. If this was the end of us, at least I'd look cute when he broke my heart into teeny tiny pieces.

Downstairs I found Teddy on the couch in the den, laptop open, concern written all over his face. Gibbs's high-pitched voice, which only happened when he was stressed out, rang out from the other end of the landline.

"Gibbs, hold on a sec." Teddy pressed a button, muting the call. "Good morning," he said, addressing me now.

"Morning." Unable to meet his eyes, I just examined my poorly laced running shoes.

"Where are you headed?"

"For a run." That was a lie, I don't run. I was going to walk slowly but it didn't sound as cool.

Pointing in the direction of the kitchen, Teddy added, "There's breakfast."

"I'm good." I headed toward the front door and ran toward the trail until I was certain I was out of view.

A stitch in my side formed as I stopped to catch my breath. Emil, my trainer, would be so disappointed. I continued down the path, this time walking slowly taking in the nature so many others raved about. Reaching for my phone, I decided to call Daysha. I needed advice from someone I trusted.

"Why are you calling me when you should be laid up under your man right now?" Day's voice asked.

"He's on a work call so I decided to get all one with nature and go for a walk."

"Wait, you're walking outside?"

"I walk all the time."

"Yes, to brunch, to the bar. You do not walk aimlessly along a path."

"Yeah, well, I need to clear my head."

"Uh oh, what happened?"

"Do you think I'm crazy?"

I heard Daysha gasp on the other end. "Did that asshole call you crazy?"

"No ... he called me out."

"For what?"

"I don't know, for not making him feel loved." The silence on the other end was deafening. "Daysha," I yelled.

"Yeah?"

"You ain't got nothing to say?" She always had something to say.

"Clover, if a man says he doesn't feel loved, that's major."

I nodded my head even though she couldn't see me. "What should I do?"

"Make him feel loved."

"OK ... OK. How do I do that?"

"Clover!"

Was I the only one who sucked at this relationship crap? Daysha was acting like this was common sense. I can assure you love and all that it entails is not elementary.

"You could tell him." Day's tone sounded like she was perturbed by my lack of comprehension.

I would rather eat boiled nails than say those three words. "I think he's mad at me."

"Why do you think that?"

I didn't want to tell Daysha that I had walked away from a naked Teddy because I was unable to handle adult emotions.

"I'm probably being dramatic, it was just a minor disagreement."

"You had a disagreement your first night there?"

"No, it was more like a miscommunication, but it's all good."

I didn't know why I was backpedaling. I felt dumb. If I was being evaluated on my dating and relationships skills, I would be on academic probation. Damnit, that's a lie too. I would've been expelled and forced to pack my things and return home.

"It doesn't sound all good."

"I want this to work," I said more to myself than her.

"Then find a way to meet his needs while still remaining true to yourself."

I wanted to ask her how I did that, but it was my mess and I needed to act like Mr. Clean and mop it up.

BACK AT THE CABIN, Teddy was exactly where I'd left him with a stack of papers and what looked like a Google aerial map.

"What's going on?"

"Ahh, North Korea pulled some dumb stunt and now I have to decide if we're gonna let it slide or clap back. How was your *run*?"

"Very enlightening." I inched forward, taking a seat next to him on the couch. "Tell me about North Korea."

Taking a deep breath, he leaned back on the couch. "I have to make a decision about possible sanctions. They launched some test missiles. The generals want to send a strong message because the behavior is habitual. I'm all for sending a message, but I don't wanna start a war."

"And the generals are recommending force?"

"Yes." Teddy cleared his throat and imitated one of his top generals with a thick Southern drawl. "Mister President, you don't want people thinking 'Merica's weak. And that you're soft on North Korea."

I raised my brows. It was a valid point. "What are you going to do?"

"I'm gonna hit them in their pocketbooks. It will send the message 'don't mess with us or we will make things difficult for you' while also saying we don't have an appetite for a conflict."

"That's smart." I knew he didn't need my seal of approval, but I wanted him to know I supported his decision.

The phone rang and Teddy answered. It was a conference call with Gibbs, the Secretary of Defense, and several top key officials providing a status report. I sat next to him, silently rubbing his neck and back. The call ended with a game plan in place.

Teddy turned to me, his eyes tired and stressed. Placing a hand on my knee, he said, "So, about last night ..."

"I'm sorry," I blurted out. "I was tripping, I'm sorry."

"If this is gonna work, we can't just walk away from difficult conversations."

Nodding my head, I took the scolding. He was one hundred percent right. I was acting like a child.

He continued, "I need you to be all in, because I can't be the only one falling."

"I am," I assured him.

Teddy's face was doubtful of my words. I wasn't falling, it was more like I'd been pushed and I was alternating between screaming in fear and laughing from excitement.

Grabbing hold of his face, I kissed his lips frantically; I couldn't lose this man. "I am all in. I'm just scared. If you knew the things I've been through. There's ..." I stopped short.

I didn't want to bring life to the ghost of relationships past. But I'd been lied to, cheated on, gaslit, I'd been told I'm the problem. I'd been told I didn't deserve the love I wanted. I was told I was selfish and would end up alone. When you get told that stuff for years you start to believe it. So, it's hard to let that all go and believe that Teddy's intentions were sincere. I didn't know if I could survive another heartbreak.

Reaching for me, Teddy pulled me on his lap. "I had to sleep alone last night. I don't like it when you're not next to me." He was running his hands over my thighs and ass.

"Let me see if I can make it up to you."

***

IF YESTERDAY my day started with a bust, this morning my day was definitely beginning with a bang. Like the illegal fireworks that lit up the sky so bright and spread sparks blocks over threatening to set everything on fire. I grabbed at the shower door in vain as Teddy tag teamed me with an assist from the pulsating showerhead. After breakfast we headed out to the lake, setting the canoe on the water.

"I have a confession to make," I said. "I have never been canoeing."

"Me either, I'm from the hood. You ain't noticed I've been paddling in circles for the last ten minutes?"

My laughter rang out clear across the lake.

"Nah, for real, though, we may need to call for help." Teddy looked toward the cabin as we floated aimlessly in the middle of the tranquil waters.

I knew he was dead serious, but his words only made me

laugh harder. Opening my phone, I took a picture of the cabin followed by a picture of Teddy and I making goofy faces. I did my best to ignore the email and text message notifications that popped up on my phone. Just because I was on vacation didn't mean the work stopped. There were several missed calls and over ninety-one unread emails, even though I had whittled that number to twenty-six before we headed out in the boat.

"Do you miss the frantic energy of the White House?"

"No," Teddy responded without hesitation. "What, do you?"

I hitched my shoulders. "Yeah, a little."

Maybe because for so long work was the only consistent and stable thing in my life.

"That's because you're a workaholic."

I pouted. "I'm good at my job and I like being relied on."

"Well, once we get married and have our first kid, all that will change." My face must have borne an expression of horror, because he quickly added, "I'm kidding, Lucky."

"Yeah, no, I knew that." But his statement prompted another question.

"You wanna get married again?"

"Don't you?"

The look in his eyes revealed a vulnerability I didn't often see. It was clear he was desperate for me to want a trip down the aisle.

"It's never really been an option."

"What if it was?"

It was my turn to feel desperate. The last thing I needed was false hope. If we weren't surrounded by water I would be eyeing the exits.

Shaking my head, I whispered, "I don't wanna talk about this."

"Why not?"

"Because it's cruel. Stop trying to sell me this fairy tale and just give me right now."

"What if I want to give you both?"

Reaching for the paddle, I plunged the blade into the murky water in an attempt to guide us back to shore, but Teddy wrestled the paddle out of my hand, resulting in a tug of war that ended with the paddle falling from our battling grip into the water.

"Clover," he shouted. We sat in the boat watching the paddle float away. "What was that about?"

Why did I always overreact at the hint of a future. Isn't that what I wanted? Hell, wasn't that what I deserved?

"I just don't need you making promises. What I want is this right now with you." I leaned in. "This moment, that look, this feeling." I pressed my hand to his cheek, running it down his neck until my hand came to rest on his chest.

The corners of his mouth tugged upward. "This moment?"

Teddy shifted my hand lower, causing me to blush, but I was in no rush to remove my hold. Leaning in to kiss him, the canoe wobbled, but I managed to find his lips that anxiously received mine.

"We are gonna die on this lake," I mumbled against his lips.

Before I could stop him, Teddy removed his shoes and jumped into the water, swimming to retrieve the paddle. I watched as he performed effortless strokes, scooping the paddle in his hand and raising it over head with a warrior scream. Within seconds, the Secret Service detail pulled up in a motorized boat.

"Are you OK, Mr. President?" Agent Tally asked, reaching for Teddy's arm.

"What the hell are you doing?" Teddy asked.

"We saw you fall from the boat, sir," Agent Mulvaney said.

Just a reminder that someone is always watching even when you think you're all alone.

Back at our boat, Teddy chucked the paddle in before climbing back in. Which caused me to clutch a death grip on the edge of the boat for fear it would tip over.

Wiping his face, Teddy looked to Agent Tally. "I think we're gonna need an assist back to shore."

Tally tossed a rope, which Teddy secured to the bench rail so we could be dragged back to land.

AFTER DINNER I suggested we have a nightcap in front of the fireplace that I was determined would see me on all fours with my back arched before the night was through. Teddy handed me a glass of wine before settling in next to me.

"This is nice. I'm still very much a city girl, but I could see myself returning to nature once in a while."

"I like the sounds of life all around us during the day. And then the silence at night," Teddy said.

"See, I find the eerie silence a bit creepy. Maybe I've watched one too many scary movies, but bad things happen at secluded cabins in the woods."

"I don't watch scary movies so I wouldn't know." Teddy lifted his beer bottle to his mouth.

"Wait, what do you mean you don't watch scary movies?"

"I don't like them. I remember my uncles letting me watch *Nightmare on Elm Street* with them when I was a kid and I had trouble sleeping for weeks."

"I didn't peg you for a scaredy cat," I teased.

"Very funny. Life is scary enough. I don't need to watch a man hack teenagers in half."

"So, what is your viewing preference?"

"Documentaries. I like learning new things." Teddy pointed to my frowning expression. "What's that face for?"

"I just forget sometimes that I'm dating a nerd."

"Newsflash, nerds run the world. And you need to stop pretending like you don't have a VIP ticket on the nerd train. Ms. 4.5 GPA, who in her free time works on jigsaw puzzles while shouting at CSPAN on the television."

"Ouch, If I'm on the nerd train you better believe it's a window seat. But I'm far from running anything, especially the world." I took a long sip from my wine glass.

"Well, it's all about perspective. You run the hell outta that press briefing room every day."

With a bump of my shoulder, I said, "I guess so."

Teddy was thoughtful for a minute, stroking his chin before asking, "What ever happened with your business idea for a PR firm?"

My lashes flipped wide open, genuinely surprised he still remembered my ultimate career goal of running my own boutique public relations firm.

"I don't know, life happened. It's not easy stepping out on faith."

Teddy leaned forward, the gold rope chain around his neck peeking over his T-shirt. There were three things I was a sucker for: a man who could cook, for obvious reasons. Second, a man that didn't rush the foreplay and enjoyed kissing. I could linger on first base for hours just kissing and enjoying one another's vibe. Lastly, it was a brother in a gold chain. Not the gaudy rapper chains but the subtle hint of gold. Cuban, herringbone, beaded ... ugh, that just did me in.

Teddy rubbed my knee with a squeeze. "You're a sure thing. That's a bet I would take any day of the week."

My lids hardened as I processed his serious expression. Everything was always so simple to him. I guess when you get elected President and are responsible for over three hundred million people everything else seems easy in comparison.

"A business needs startup money, an office building, staff, and clientele." I rubbed my eyes, overwhelmed by the list of to do's I just ticked off. "I have some money saved but not nearly enough."

"How much are we talking about?"

"Like one hundred thousand dollars." I chuckled at the absurd amount.

His face crinkled as he blew out air.

Nodding in agreement, I added, "I know right, a lot."

"You just need some investors."

Of course, why didn't I think of that. I'll just ask my grand-papi for a small starter loan and everything will be all gravy. Yes, I was making good money, but that money was paying for rent on two homes, mine and my mother's. That money was putting my cousin, Mya, through college. That money was occasionally being lent to my father, even though each time I vowed it would be the last. Six figures doesn't stretch as far as you'd think when you're supporting your entire family.

"I don't feel comfortable begging people for money," I said.

"Why? White people do it all the time. Shoot, I'd invest."

"I'm not asking you to."

"And that's your problem right there." He wagged his long, perfectly manicured finger in my face. "Baby, a closed mouth ain't gonna get fed. I believe in you, but you have to believe in you too."

"I do." My voice barely a whisper, I couldn't even convince myself. Bennett Communication had been a dream for so long that the possibility of it becoming a reality scared me.

"No, you don't. Because if you did you'd have a hundred-thousand-dollar check in your hands right now signed by me." He stood, strolling to the kitchen to grab another beer.

I popped up from our comfy pillow fort and lifted my glass so he could top off my half-empty glass of wine. "Are you trying to get rid of me?" I teased, hoping to dim the glare from this particular line of questioning.

"No." Setting the bottle on the kitchen counter, he smiled, running his hand down my shoulder. "I just remember how passionate you were when you talked about that firm and I remember thinking, I don't want anything as much as this woman does. So, what happened?"

I searched the room for answers. He was right. I used to be a spitfire, working all day and then come home and work on my ideas for the firm. The last thing I wanted was to spend the rest of my life making other people millions.

"I guess I got scared and comfortable," I said, surprised by my confession.

"Them six-figure paychecks will do it. Have you wearing out your welcome in the comfort zone."

He wasn't lying. When I told my mother about my plan, she told me I would be crazy to walk away from a reliable paycheck.

"Do you really think I could do it?"

His eyes grew wide. "You can do anything. You can captivate a room. Leave heads of state speechless. You can comfort a distraught mother who just lost her child. You can play dominos with my uncles and win. Clover Bennett, when the hell did you forget who you are?"

Tears escaped from my eyes. Oh my God, I was crying in front of the President of the United States. I tried to escape but he grabbed a tight hold, not letting me go. My hands balled into tight fists. I tried to mentally will the sob session to end. Teddy wrapped his strong arms around me, his embrace like a security blanket. My body unknotted, melting into him.

Teddy's reassuring caress prompted my eyes to reload with fresh tears. Emotions I had pushed deep inside long ago were all bubbling to the surface. There wasn't time for tears in politics. All these years in DC I had learned to harden the soft spots. When you have tough skin it's harder to suffer a mortal wound.

I can't remember the last time I cried. I was used to disappointment in my personal life, so I rarely spilled tears over a failed relationship. Maybe I'd cried while watching a sappy movie on the Hallmark channel. But these tears were different. These tears were old, from slings and arrows from the past that connected but which I thought had never drawn blood. These tears were a mixture of sadness, disappointment, and paralyzing fear that no matter how hard I tried, I could never be good enough.

Teddy applied pressure against my back, running his hand up

and down. I breathed him in; he smelled like lake water, sunshine, and shea butter. My stomach tensed. For the most part the tears had dried up, but now I was sitting in a well of embarrassment, my tears splashing around my toes. Lifting my head slightly to gauge the temperature in the room, I caught Teddy's gaze looking down at me, a soft smile across his kissable mouth. In an attempt to speak I parted my lips, but my throat was dry and all I could manage was a croak.

I couldn't find the words, but I wanted to show him how much this meant to me. On my tip toes, our lips found one another. My body shivered from the electricity that flowed between us. Teddy pushed me back until we stumbled into our toasty pillow fort. His hands crept up my thighs, and I moaned as he gently dragged his fingers across the side of my leg. Resting my butt on the soft cushion, I lifted my arms and let him pull the sundress over my head.

One of his hands was playing with my nipple like a knob on a video game controller, the other hand was pulling down his swim trunks. I raised my hips so he could easily slide my thong past my thick thighs. Sinking into the pillows scattered around us, his hands parted my legs before grabbing hold of my waist, pulling me closer to him. My breath hitched before releasing a loud gasp as he entwined his body with mine. I clawed at the grooves in the hardwood floor as our bodies moved in syncopated time together.

I could feel words bubbling up in my throat as I tried to push them down to stop them from forming. Teddy grabbed my neck, pulling me up so we were looking into each other's eyes. His gaze trained on me said more than words ever could. I wrapped my arms around him, wanting to be closer. Kissing his mouth, I moaned as he gripped my thighs.

I could no longer contain the words, and I whispered breathlessly, "I love you, so much." My eyes filled with tears and they threatened to tumble down my face once again.

"Say it again."

"I love you." My legs shook, my face now awash in tears, my body on fire, every corner of me yearning for him.

Teddy kissed me gently, probably realizing I couldn't handle much more; he provided four final strokes that sent me shooting into orbit. Was this what an out-of-body experience felt like? Because I could see myself crashing to the pillows, shivering and writhing, but I also felt like I was outside of my body as Teddy wiped my tears and wrapped his arms around me, encircling me in his embrace.

"Damn, it took you long enough to say it. Say it one more time so I know you weren't just dickmatized."

"I love you, Theodore Elmsworth."

CHAPTER TWENTY-ONE

"Thank you so much for coming over early," I grunted as Alan and I tugged on my dining table trying to separate it so we could insert the leaf that would turn my four-person table to one that could comfortably seat ten.

"No problem. Besides, you're cooking, the least I can do is help you set up."

After one last good pull, the table parted, allowing me to return to the kitchen to check on the curry chicken pot pie. A Caribbean twist on the old classic that I'd learned from my mother. I loved to cook I just never had any time, but tonight was an exception. It was my turn to host the monthly get-together with my friends. There would be food, copious amounts of alcohol, and good laughs.

Grabbing the plates and silverware, Alan helped me set the table. "There was another reason I wanted you to come over early."

Alan raised his brow.

"I wanted to gauge your temperature on something."

"Sure, shoot." He flashed a cautious gaze in my direction.

"OK, what I'm about to say is top secret and highly confidential."

He dropped my one-hundred-dollar plate from Williams Sonoma on the table. "See, now you have my full attention."

"I've been thinking about what I'm going to do after the White House."

"Girl, you ain't even been there a year."

"You know me, always two steps ahead. Anyway, if I opened a PR firm, would you be interested in working for me?"

Alan placed his well-moisturized hand, with several rings on each finger, on his hip. "In what capacity?"

"Hmm, maybe you could head up the social media team?"

"Bitch, don't play with me." He swatted at me with the linen napkin.

I let out a chuckle. "It's just a thought and probably a few years off, but something to think about. Hopefully when the time comes, I can woo you away from McCaskill."

"Man, funk that job."

"Funk?"

"Yeah, I'm trying to slow down on the cussing."

I eyed him suspiciously. Alan peppered his speech with four-letter words like it was glitter.

He rolled his neck. "I'm a work in progress. Trying to be a refined bitch ... like you."

"Oh God, I've missed your stupid ass," I said, pulling him into a tight hug.

ALAN HAD DONE me a solid allowing me to get dressed while he entertained the others. I threw on a brown crocheted dress and piled my hair into a deliberate messy bun before joining my friends mingling in the living room.

"There you are," my best friend from college, JoJo, said, giving me a hug, glass in hand.

JoJo was a natural beauty with thick blonde hair that cascaded perfectly over her shoulders. She was married to

Russell, a sports agent. They had several homes and a couple of kids.

"What are you drinking?" I observed the fruity punch in her glass.

"Mateo bought sangria."

"Yes." I pointed at Mateo, who, fun fact, also happened to be an ex-lover. Luckily, we learned we were better as friends before it was too late.

"I'll pour you a glass," he offered, heading over to my kitchen.

"Hey, Clover?" Daysha shouted over the mellow vibes of Masego. "I think someone's at the door."

Heading to the entry hall, I prepared to curse out that one neighbor who always complained I was too loud. Swinging the door open, I said, "I will not turn down the music."

"Whoa, that's some dress." Teddy scanned the length of my body, inhaling me with his eyes.

He was in sweats and my eyes honed in as well, lingering on the noticeable bulge in his gray sweatpants. If I was alone, the things I would do to this man.

I looked back toward my living space. "What are you doing here?"

His head bobbed left then right, trying to get a good look inside. "I tried calling but it kept going to voicemail, so I decided to stop by. Are you having a party?"

"Oh my God," Alan squealed from behind me.

"No, don't do that ... please, don't," I said, anxiety wrapping itself around me like a worn-in blanket.

"OH MY GOD. YOU'RE THE PRESIDENT." Alan was jumping up and down, screaming like he was Oprah handing out free cars.

"Please, you can call me Theodore."

"No, he cannot. Please do not call him that." I released a nervous chuckle.

"You have to come in." Alan grabbed Teddy's arm, pulling

him inside, ignoring Agents Tally and Mulvaney shooting daggers in his direction.

"Sure." Teddy breezed past me. "Damn, it smells good in here. Is that curry?

"Tedd ... wait."

At this point, there was nothing I could do. I closed the door as the voices in the living room escalated to a fever pitch. Taking a deep breath, I assured myself I could fix this.

"OK, calm down, guys. My boss, the President of the United States, needs to talk to me about a work thing."

"I do?" Teddy said, accepting a glass of sangria from Mateo.

Turning to Teddy with a glare, I said, "Why else would you be at my place after hours?"

"I did try to call. But you didn't answer and I *need* you." His voice was deep and throaty at the last part of his sentence.

Teddy was inches away from me, looking intensely into my eyes. He was not helping in making this look less suspicious.

I chuckled. "To help you with work, right." I nodded, willing him to mimic my head motion.

"I definitely had a job for you."

Was this a joke to him? Because I wasn't finding any of this funny.

Teddy continued, "I see you have company, so it can wait until tomorrow." He finally stopped staring at me.

"Well, thank you, sir, I appreciate that."

"You should stay," Nate, Daysha's husband, said.

Spinning around, I shot Nate a halfcocked glare. I knew good and damn well that Daysha had informed him of my situation with the commander in chief. Men were so messy.

"He can't stay because he has presidential stuff to do."

"Like what?" Daysha asked.

Et tu, Brutus?

"Like ... working on that bill ... that's been sitting on Capitol Hill ... waiting to become a law."

"That's really Congress's job," Teddy chimed in.

"Yes, but you need to be there when that hopeful little bill comes humming through the White House." Turning to face Teddy, I pursed my lips.

"Nah, it's good, I could stay for a bit. I'm starving." Giving my shoulder a squeeze, he took a long sip from his glass as the others made room for him at the table.

"It's nice to meet you, Mr. President," Russell said.

"Call me Theodore."

"So, what do you do for fun, Theodore?" JoJo asked.

"Same thing as everyone else, I guess. Spend time with friends and family."

"I couldn't even imagine living in that kind of fish bowl," Alan said. "I'm Tik Tok famous. Nothing like you, but I have over a hundred thousand followers."

"Whoa, that's impressive." Teddy nodded.

"Thanks. I mostly do funny videos, outfits of the day. My handle is big black —"

"Absolutely not," I said.

"But—" Alan protested.

"No. I told you that username was problematic, and now you want to tell the President of these United States that your Tik Tok handle is big black cock."

The table broke into scattered laughter.

Alan chided me. "Chill, Clover, we are all grown here, and Theodore doesn't look like a prude."

"OK, this is my boss. And you guys are embarrassing the hell out of me right now. I hate you all," I only half joked.

"It's OK, Lucky, I'm thoroughly enjoying this conversation."

He squeezed my knee under the table, causing my pulse to race as a wave of pleasure thrummed deep within my core.

"Lucky?" Mateo repeated.

"Ahh." Teddy glanced over at me. "It's just a nickname that kinda stuck."

JoJo leaned forward with a big smile on her face. "Can I just say I voted for you, despite everyone who said you would turn this country into a socialist state."

"No, not the I voted for you card." Daysha chuckled.

Teddy nodded his head. "Thank you for your vote. Hope you don't regret it."

JoJo cleared her throat. "Uhm, well it would be great if you'd do a bit more to protect women's reproductive rights and—"

"That sounds like buyer's remorse," Nate teased.

"At the very least it appears the new car smell has worn off." Teddy joined in on the ribbing.

I tapped the table. "Now, no ... we can leave the politics talk alone for the night."

I heard Alan whisper to Jo, "Don't get on the President's bad side, he'll have you and your colonizer family shipped back to Europe."

"Ugh, I'd kill for a trip to Europe right now. Venice, Florence, Rome and all the carbs you can eat."

"OK, dessert ... yes." I jumped up, heading to the kitchen to gather the dessert plates.

Daysha followed behind. "Need help?"

"Yeah, could you start some coffee?" I handed her a bag of my favorite blonde roast.

"I think this is going well," she offered.

"Oh yeah, it's just peachy, you all treating Teddy like he's a regular degular dude."

"I think he appreciates it. Isn't that what you want, to have a normal relationship with the man you love?"

My mouth curled at her last words. Of course, she was right, normal would be nice right now, but that wasn't our reality.

"Where are you going?" I snapped my fingers at Teddy, who was headed to the back of my apartment.

"Bathroom." He stopped in his tracks at my overaggressive tone.

"OK, I can show you where that is because you've never been here, so how would you know where to go." I scurried from behind the kitchen counter.

"You'd think he'd just look for the room with a toilet," Alan suggested from the table.

"Follow me." I walked briskly, making my way to the bathroom Teddy had frequented so many times before. Grabbing my arm, he pulled me inside, closing the door behind us.

"I thought you thrived under pressure," he teased.

"Work pressure, sure. Having to lie to all my friends about our relationship, not so much."

"Then don't lie." Teddy advanced, boxing me in against the wall. So now I was anxious and aroused at the same time.

I laughed at the audacity of his statement, but his face remained like stone. "Are you suggesting I tell people we're dating?" I blinked rapidly, unsure of where this was going.

"They'll have to find out eventually." He ran his fingers across my face like he was tracing it by memory.

I sucked on my bottom lip. I was in no rush to make public declarations of forever. In the past, that had gotten me burned. The minute I started talking about a guy I was really into or genuinely cared for with my friends, the relationship would go to pot.

"I gotta say, I'm disappointed in you, Lucky." His gaze was pensive, the usual twinkle in his eyes absent.

"What?"

"I guess my invitation got lost in the mail?"

"This isn't a party. It's just a get-together." I threw my hands in the air, feeling deflated.

"With your friends."

"Yeah."

"*Yeah.*" His beautiful brown eyes grew wide.

"What did you want me to do?" I twisted the chunky silver

ring on my finger. "Say something like, hey, do you want to come to this stupid dinner at my place?"

Teddy scowled. "Or maybe, hey, I'm having a casual dinner with friends at my place and I would love for you to meet them."

I shrugged. Clearly, I couldn't do anything right.

Teddy backed away, and I was relieved and disappointed in the same moment.

"I don't know, it just shows intention and effort to make me part of your life." He picked up a prescription bottle from the bathroom counter and examined it.

Snatching the antibiotics for my ear infection from his hand, I shouted, "HIPAA."

Teddy held his hands up, showing his palms.

"You are a part of my life. But I'm trying to respect your privacy, and throwing you in the middle of a dinner party with my nosey friends is a lot."

Teddy nodded, pulling his member out of his sweatpants to pee. "OK."

As he drained the main vein for what seemed like an eternity, I stood there with my eyes pointed upward to the ceiling. "Are you mad at me?"

"Nope," he said with a shake.

He was mad. He walked to the sink, lathering up his hands.

"I'm new to this whole couple thing. But I'm really trying to figure it out." Running my hand over his muscular back, I continued, "I didn't mean to exclude you. I just didn't want to waste your time. You have so many priorities."

Drying his hands on the towel, Teddy whipped around to face me. "You're my priority. We make time for the things that are important to us. If you wanted me here, I would have found the time."

"It's not like you don't have tons of events I'm not invited to," I countered.

"Work events. If you want to be invited to a meeting with

the prime minister of Haiti to discuss disaster relief, just let me know."

I actually had some interesting ideas on strengthening relations with Haiti and the way the United States could be a good steward who helped in times of need but also looked toward building back infrastructure with innovative technology.

"OK, I'll invite you to all future dinner parties. I promise."

The last thing I wanted to do was argue, the omission was not intentional. Now that I knew things like this were important to him, I would do my best to make him feel like a fixture in my life.

"Thank you."

"Are we good?" I asked, holding my breath as I waited for confirmation.

"We were never bad."

Leaning in, his lips enclosed on mine. Gentle yet powerful at the same time, I couldn't stop my body from melting against his. The warmth of his body contorting mine like putty in his arms. He stopped kissing me far too soon, smiling against my lips.

Bellies full with curried meat and sweet treats, we lounged in the living room exchanging funny stories. Refilling my glass of wine, I took a seat on the sofa next to Teddy. Leaning back, I allowed the side of my body to rest against his. He was right about so many things. If this man wanted to love me, who was I to smother that desire? Teddy's hand instinctively found me as he absentmindedly stroked the back of my neck. I held my breath, the room growing silent as my bestest friends processed what was happening.

Alan cocked his head to the side. "Damn, I did not have Clover and the President on my bingo card."

The room erupted in laughter. Looking into Teddy's eyes, I exhaled and allowed myself to fall.

CHAPTER TWENTY-TWO

Releasing a long yawn, I glanced at my phone, it read 10:47 p.m., and it looked like I would not be seeing my bed anytime soon. Teddy, Gibbs, and I were in the Oval practicing for the interview with American News Broadcasting Station scheduled for tomorrow. It was important that Teddy be mindful of his words. The last thing we wanted was for him to say something that gave Seth an opportunity to pounce.

"OK, Mr. President, how do you plan to address the growing tensions in the Middle East?" I was playing the role of the interviewer asking the questions.

Teddy let out a long sigh, rubbing his eyes. "I don't know, robots? Maybe robots."

"Mr. President, you need to focus," Gibbs said.

"I was focused three hours ago. Now I'm tired and cranky. This is redundant."

"It's better to be prepared than surprised," I offer.

Gibbs removed his glasses from the top of his head. "Maybe we should take a break."

"Yes, I like that idea. Fifteen-minute break." Teddy stood with a stretch.

I frowned. "Or we could just power through for thirty more minutes and then call it a night."

It was too late, I had lost them, both men scrolling their phones.

Gibbs stood, placing his laptop in his seat. "I'll be back. I've needed to piss for the last hour."

With Gibbs gone, I tried to reason with Teddy. "You need to take this seriously."

"I am. I have." He chugged a bottle of water.

"Seth is a good interviewer."

"And I'm a great interviewee." He took a seat next to me. "Don't worry, I got this." Teddy gave my knee a quick squeeze. "What do I do best?"

A blush tickled up the back of my neck. "You do a lot of things well."

"This is true." He nudged me with his shoulder. "But I was thinking about talking. I'm a verbal assassin and no one is going to box me into a corner. Especially not your ex-boyfriend."

My chin jerked back. "Seth was never my boyfriend."

"Yeah, well he was campaigning hard for the job."

My shoulders flinched with disinterest.

"There is such a thing as being overprepared. This needs to be organic."

He was right. Yes, I was a bit of a worry wart, but it was my job to be prepared for the unexpected. Seth was a good journalist and he would come with hard-hitting questions, and it was our responsibility to defend this administration's decisions. Something Teddy would have no problem doing because he believed deeply in his agenda and the policies we were pushing forth.

When Gibbs returned, I agreed it was time to call it a night. I didn't have to tell him twice. From the bags under his eyes, it was clear he was exhausted.

He collected his belongings and was heading to the door, throwing a curt, "See you in eight hours."

"I'm right behind you," I said, as I slowly placed files, notes, and pens into my tote bag.

This was all a lie because the only place I was headed was to Teddy's bed.

THE EAST ROOM was staged with two large American flags that flanked Teddy. He was dressed in a black suit and red tie. A safe fashion choice, unlike the time he wore a hunter green suit. Don't get me wrong, he looked fine as hell, but the elites in DC were all up in arms, calling his outfit choice disrespectful to the office. We chose a black suit to eliminate any distraction from the message. How could anyone complain about a nondescript black suit?

The interview was well underway with Gimble and I standing in the corner of the room as Teddy hit all his prepared talking points with ease. Even when Seth pushed back, Teddy would double down or pivot the conversation to a place he felt more comfortable. I felt silly for having worried so much. Teddy was an orator and he loved the sound of his own voice.

"Seth, the thing is, this country needs to work for everybody. Not just the richest one percent, or the upper middle-class family. Every child should have a shot. But for far too many the starting line is staggered."

"Sounds like you're talking about handouts. Studies have shown that handouts only encourage people to look for more. These people can work but they just don't want to."

"Well, I'd like to see the studies you're referring to, because my information tells a different story. When you provide assistance, it actually improves people's chances of getting and maintaining a job, which allows them to transition off assistance and move out of poverty."

The interview was drawing to a close and Teddy had maintained his composure, never taking the bait Seth was trying to lay for him. When he and I were alone tonight I was going to show him how proud I was of him.

Seth checked his notes, flipping through some documents. "I wanted to ask you about something that was brought to my attention the other day." Seth referred back to his stack of documents and pulled out a paper, handing it to Teddy.

Gimble whispered next to me, "What is he doing? We didn't authorize any handouts."

Knowing Seth and ANBS, it was probably one last attempt to throw Teddy off his game so they could use his reaction to call him unfit and unprepared for the job like they did every day on that channel.

Teddy's jaw clenched as he reviewed the document. His eyes jetted toward me briefly before returning to Seth.

"What is this?" Teddy asked.

"I was hoping you could tell me. It looks like you and your Press Secretary, Clover Bennett. You two appear pretty close."

Gimble looked over at me, eyes wide. My heart was beating triple time. We had been careful, we didn't go places together, we did our best never to be photographed next to each other. Yes, we'd snuck out of the protection of the White House a few times, which was sloppy on our part, but there was no way there were photos of us doing anything untoward. Gimble made a move like he was going to object, but I grabbed his arm. This interview was live, we couldn't save him, he was on his own.

"If by close you mean that we are standing next to one another, then I guess."

Seth handed him another photo. "How about this one with your arm around her?"

Teddy considered the picture for a long time, too long. "If this was a picture of me and my Secretary of Defense, would you be asking me these same questions?"

"With all due respect, sir, Ms. Bennett is far more attractive than General Ratcliffe."

"I'll give you that. But what you have shown me is innocuous, and trying to paint some nefarious story behind it is poor journalism."

"You and Ms. Bennett left together in the same vehicle."

Teddy shrugged, furrowing his brow. "So what? I'm not allowed to carpool?"

"I guess that would depend on what happened when you got to her place."

Teddy flashed Seth an icy gaze, his jaw set and his hands balled into tight fist.

"So should I take that as no comment?"

"You can take it for whatever you want." Teddy removed his mic, pulling out the cord.

"Sir, we still have a few minutes remaining, so if you could—"

"Oh no, we're done. After that stunt you just pulled, we are done." Tossing the mic pack on the chair, Teddy left the room in a huff with Gibbs close on his heels.

This was the clip they would play ad nauseum for the next few days at American News, maybe weeks. Seth had burned me. He could have at least had the courtesy to give me a heads up before he threw me in front of a moving bus. I watched as he signed off, throwing back to the anchor in the studio. Once I knew the feed was dead, I advanced toward him.

"What the hell was that?" I yelled as the camera crew broke down the equipment.

"What are you talking about?" Seth said innocently, removing the ear piece from his ear.

"You know damn well what I'm talking about." I was inches away from his face and ready for a verbal slug match.

"Seems to me your President can't answer simple questions."

I scoffed. "Simple? You blindsided him with some pictures of us standing together."

He pulled the pictures from his portfolio. "You two were doing more than just standing together."

I snatched the photographs from his hand, flipping through them. They were from the night we went to the speakeasy. We were standing outside the store talking with Lloyd. In the first picture, Teddy and I were standing close but nothing to raise eyebrows. The second picture Teddy's arm is resting over my shoulder as I look up at him. The last few photos show us getting into the waiting car. Seth was grasping at straws, but I needed to tread lightly because there could be additional photos, and I didn't want this thing blowing up in my face.

"These photos are not telling the story you think they are. I really wish you'd have come to me first with this instead of trying to be salacious for your gullible viewers." I had a death grip on my cell phone, which was vibrating incessantly, no doubt from people who had seen the interview.

"Clover, I know you. You and the President are both adults, free to do what you want."

"I know you, too, and you're better than this. This isn't the story you think it is."

"Well, I guess the public will decide." Seth tossed his items into his messenger bag and turned toward me for one final word. "Keep the photos. I have plenty of copies."

With that, he and the ANBS crew were gone. And I was left with photographic proof of my affair with the President in my trembling hand.

IGNORING the several text messages and calls blowing up my work and personal cell phones, I made my way to the Oval Office.

"Is he in there?" I asked Abby.

"Yep, he seems pretty pissed."

"Thanks." I knocked on the door, not waiting for a response before I entered the room.

Gimble was pacing back and forth, staring at his phone. I handed him the photographs. Teddy was seated behind his desk, hands clasped with a sour expression on his face. Chewing on the inside of my cheek, I opened my mouth to speak, but Teddy interjected.

"That was bad."

"No, it wasn't all bad," I offered.

Teddy jumped from his chair. "Really, Clover, which fucking part!"

He was mad at me and his anger was warranted. I had pushed for this interview and it had blown up in his face. But this was not time to assign blame, it was time for solutions.

"I think you made some really strong points about the Middle East, and that piece about education and teachers was heartfelt and will resonate with lots of people."

"All that was lost the minute he pulled out those photos," Teddy said, shaking his head.

Gibbs chimed in from the corner of the room. "Where did he get these pictures from?"

Teddy's shoulder lurched. "I don't know."

Gibbs looked from Teddy to me, incredulous. "I don't really know how to say this, so I'm just gonna. Mr. President, are you and Clover sleeping together?"

Without missing a beat, Teddy responded, "No, we're not. Next question."

Gibbs adjusted his horn-rimmed glasses. "Then why were you two together?"

"I don't know, Gibbs. I'm not tethered to this desk twenty-four-seven. Sometimes I do go out. I guess I was out and she was out and we bumped into each other."

Gibbs narrowed his eyes in my direction. "Is that how you remember it, Clover?"

Clearing my throat, I nodded. "Umm, yeah, I think so. And we were both like, funny meeting you here."

Teddy glared at me to let me know I wasn't helping.

"Mr. President, as your chief of staff, I need to know the full story. I'm not looking to judge, but I can't fix this if I don't know the truth."

"The truth is I just bombed an American News interview. Seth is an asshole with his gotcha bullshit. But there's nothing to tell, so we should just stick to the Anjeni method like we have in the past."

Teddy wasn't wrong, normally the Anjeni method would be appropriate, but this situation was different. I wasn't some random woman, I was the Press Secretary. We could be looking at sexual misconduct, sexual harassment, abuse of authority, and favoritism if anyone started causing a fuss. This was not a story we wanted to ignore.

"Gibbs is right, we have to control the narrative. Make it appear as a nothing burger." My brain went to work trying to spin a plausible story. "The President and the Press Secretary are friends. She worked on his first political campaign. DC is small and people are bound to run in the same circles. Those photos show nothing more than a friendly exchange, and any attempt to make it into something more is insulting."

I could feel Gibbs's eyes on me, but I couldn't meet his gaze. If this was a PR client, I would force them to tell me the truth. It's harder to clean up messes if you don't know what else could potentially slither from the tall grass to bite you.

Gibbs resumed pacing back and forth across the presidential seal. "We could say you two were at a mutual friend's event. That you came separately but the President gave you a ride home. I'm going to need the name of a friend that can vouch for you."

Teddy pointed at Gibbs. "Yep, see, that's exactly what happened. I was at my friend Lloyd's spot, and Clover knows Lloyd and was also there."

"And Lloyd will support this statement?"

"He will tell you exactly what happened that night. It was a good time. Lloyd throws one hell of a party."

Gimble lifted his glasses, rubbing his weary eyes. "What about after the party, when you took Clover home?"

Once again, Gimble's eyes were on me, but I had nothing to add. Apparently I wasn't as good of a liar as Teddy was.

"I walked her to her door and then went back to the car and met up with a friend."

"And would that friend remember this?"

"Yes, she would."

I raised my eyebrow. He had me questioning what actually happened that night and I was there.

"Clover?" Gibbs stared at me, waiting for me to confirm the President's story.

I swallowed hard. "Yeah, it sounds about right. I mean, I don't know what he did after he dropped me off, but I can attest to everything else."

"OK, looks like we have a story." Checking his watch, he added, "Let me go make some calls and get ahead of this mess." Heading to the door, he stopped to provide one last instruction. "Don't talk to anybody." With that, he was gone, closing the door behind him.

AFTER TEDDY TRIED to reassure me that everything was going to be OK, I made my way back to my office. I wasn't as confident as he was.

"Hey Brittany, any calls?"

"Yes." Brittany fumbled through Post-It notes. "You have several messages from CNN, MSNBC, ABC, CBS, CSPAN, TMZ."

Holding out my hand, I collected the messages and trudged into my office, closing the door behind me. This was bad and reporters were like sharks; with blood in the water, they would all circle with snarling teeth. There had to be a way out of this. I just needed a minute to think things through, to remove the fact that it was my scandal and pretend I was advising a client. We needed to be careful with the messaging on this. If we went on record, professing we weren't a couple and then more damning photographs leaked, it would be ruinous.

Dropping my head in my hands, my mind flashed back to the night of my birthday. We danced. We kissed ... a lot. I'd given Teddy a Handy Mandy under the table. A sudden coldness hit my core. If there were pictures from inside the speakeasy ... it would be difficult to spin the narrative with pictures of Teddy's tongue down my throat and hands cupping my ass.

My office phone buzzed. Lifting my head from the desk, I pushed the button. "Yes."

"Chief of Staff Gimble is here to see you," Brittney said from the other side.

I pinched the bridge of my nose, tightly squeezing my eyes. "Send him in."

I stood as Gibbs entered my office. "Hey Gibbs, shouldn't you be extinguishing fires right about now?" I hoped my tone conveyed that I was unbothered.

"Yeah ... I was hoping we could run through your side of the story."

"I thought we already went over this."

"One more time. For me." Gibbs placed his hand over his heart.

"OK, I was invited to the Candy Shop Speakeasy by my friend, Lloyd."

"How do you know Lloyd?" Gibbs settled in at the circular conference table.

I pulled my face, turning to the window. I was an expert liar for others ... myself, not so much. "I don't really remember how we met. It was some years ago."

"So, Lloyd invited you to what, a birthday party?"

I couldn't play along with this party story line. It was an easily verifiable fact. From what I could tell, it was a normal night. When the press started poking around, they would quickly discover that claims of a party were a lie.

"There wasn't a party. I decided to go and get drinks because it was my birthday and I wanted to celebrate." I leaned on my desk, preferring to keep my distance.

"Who did you arrive with?"

"I went alone."

"So, you wanted to celebrate alone?"

I shrugged. "It was a spur of the moment decision."

"Did you take an Uber there?"

Checkable fact. "No, I took the Metro."

Gibbs closed his notepad and exhaled a swash of air. I was doing my best to sell this story, but it was pretty clear Gibbs wasn't buying it.

"I like you, Clover, you're smart and damn good at your job. I need you to step outside of the situation. If this were one of your clients, what would be the first thing you would tell them?"

"I'd tell them if they want me to help, I need to know the whole truth. Every lie, every secret, every sin."

Gibbs nodded his head and rubbed his chin. "So, I'm asking that of you now. I can't help if I don't know the full story."

I was tempted to break and info dump the sordid details right into Gibbs's lap. But my brain wouldn't let me form the words. Denial was an ignore now, pay later type of deal. I desperately wanted to ignore the mess that Teddy and I found ourselves in, even though I knew the bill would come due, if not now, eventually.

"The President already gave you marching orders. It's not my place to second-guess him."

"You're not a stupid woman, I don't have to tell you that this could ruin your career."

He was right, he didn't have to tell me because I'd been reminding myself of that fact for the past few months.

"I trust that you'll do everything in your power to prevent that. I mean, the last thing this administration needs is another scandal."

DC was a funny place, you never really know where you stood. A friend can turn into a foe in the blink of an eye. I respected Gibbs and I believed that he had the President's best interest at heart. But I also understood that if he had to, he would sell me down the river and not lose any sleep. His loyalty was to Teddy not me. I was the only one concerned about my future.

I added, "You think you know what's going on between the President and I, but you don't."

"Listen, you don't need to explain anything to me. You're an attractive woman and that's Theodore Elmsworth's kryptonite."

I didn't offer a response. I just stared back at Gibbs, his thinning hair raked through, shirt rumpled, and glasses askew.

"You know he told me to hire you, against my better judgment." He pursed his lips. Standing, he walked toward one of the two windows in my office, looking out onto the White House grounds.

Furrowing my brow, I corrected him. "No, he said Lisa chose me for the job."

"Lisa loved you too, but the President made the final decision. He suggested your name and then subtly insisted that we interview you."

My eyes narrowed, and if I focused hard enough, I could probably cast laser beams onto Gibbs's blue tie. My temperature rose as my blood boiled to a simmer.

Gibbs recognized the look of bewilderment on my face. "He lied to you. Welcome to the club."

I set my jaw, doing my best to push down my raging emotions.

Gibbs headed toward the door. Resting his hand on the doorknob, he turned to face me. "I just want to find a solution that works for everyone. Oftentimes, Elmsworth can't see beyond his own vantage point. You know that as well as anyone. I'm trying to be a friend here, Clover."

With that, he left me in my office with much to think about. Was this Teddy's plan all along to get within close proximity to me once again and wear down my defenses? Was it all just some lark to him? My life, my career, my future left to a big game of chance?

It was difficult to think as my head reeled with competing thoughts. *I need to get out of this building and clear my head.* Hastily collecting my laptop and purse, I headed for the exit only stopping to ask Brittany to clear my calendar of in-person appearances for the rest of the week before leaving the White House, not sure if I would ever come back.

CHAPTER TWENTY-THREE

It was Saturday and the ANBS interview was all anyone could talk about. I'd worked from home on Friday and planned to remain locked inside of my apartment until Monday morning, hoping that some distance would help the story lose steam. Of course, I couldn't hide out in my apartment forever, but I just needed some time to collect my bearings. Teddy reluctantly agreed it was best to lay low for the next few days.

Gimble's words on Thursday evening were still wiggling around in my brain. I planned to mention it to Teddy, but that conversation was best had face to face, so I could see every twitch, darting eye, and chin tug. Teddy claimed I'd gotten the job based on my own talent and I still wanted to believe that. But Gibbs had made everything murky and it was hard to discern what was true. This was not how I wanted my White House career to end and eventually, I would pull my big girl panties on and try to fix this mess I'd gotten myself into, but right now I wanted to sulk and watch sappy Hallmark movies.

I was currently rewatching the one where the city girl invests in a flower shop and moves to a small town to escape the humiliation of getting fired from her dream job. This rewatch was more for research purposes than anything else. While I didn't have a green thumb, maybe I could move to Virginia and open a stationery store.

A knock on the door interrupted the meet-cute scene where the handsome landscaper walks into her shop. Hitting the pause button, I peeled myself from the spot on the couch that had been my safe space for the last few hours. Before opening the door, I checked the peephole to make sure it wasn't a reporter looking to get a comment. Last night I was accosted by a reporter after opening my door expecting a pimple-faced teenager to be holding Thai food on the other end. It was a tabloid reporter and I quickly slammed the door in his face.

"I can see your eyeball. Open the damn door," Daysha yelled from the other side.

I unclasped the chain and clicked the lock, stepping aside to let Day in.

She was carrying a reusable bag filled with groceries. "Girl, them damn reporters are staked outside blocking the entrance." Removing her shoes, she shuffled toward the kitchen. "I got you a few things. Because I know all you ever have in this house is coffee and vodka. I got you a rotisserie chicken and some couscous and grilled veggies from the premade food counter. There's also two bottles of that wine you like and three pints of ice cream."

My eyes watered at her thoughtfulness. Daysha always had my back.

"Bitch, are you fittin to cry?"

"No," I said with a sniffle.

Daysha looked around the living room with the food containers and various cups. I wish I could say this stuff had just accumulated but truthfully, I was never home, spending most nights with Teddy, and cleaning had never been my forte. Daysha collected the glasses, mugs, and plastic cups and headed back to the kitchen, running the water.

"So, what do you have planned for the day?" The disapproving tone in her voice was undeniable.

"You're looking at it." I plopped back down onto my well-worn spot on the couch.

"So, you're going to lay on this couch all day?"

"No, I plan to head to the kitchen in a little bit."

"When are you planning to head to the shower?" She wrinkled her nose.

Frowning, I smelled my T-shirt. I didn't stink, I smelled like peanut butter and jelly.

"A shower is on my list of to do's, but first I need to make progress on this jigsaw puzzle."

I ran my hand over the 500-piece puzzle I'd purchased weeks ago, only now opening the box this morning, hoping to occupy my time and distract my mind, which kept playing out doomsday scenarios to my dismay.

I could feel Daysha's eyes examining my pitiful situation. With a huff, she asked, "Clover, what's your plan exactly?"

"My plan is to do absolutely nothing for the next few days."

This was a lie. When I wasn't rooting for the untenable love story between a grumpy male and sun shiny bright female in the latest Hallmark movie, I was flipping through the twenty-four-hour news cycles. There was a lot going on in the world, but every day they found time to talk about the President and his Press Secretary. *Was this all just a coincidence like the White House claimed? Is the President having an affair with a staffer? Who is Clover Bennett?*

"So, the kitchen starts to get hot and you run?"

I released a mirthless chuckle. "The kitchen isn't hot, it is literally on fire. Sometimes running is the safest option."

Day took a seat next to me, tossing the dish towel over her shoulder. "I've never known you to give up so easily."

"I'm not giving up. I'm resetting. Staying under the radar and away from the White House is best for everyone right now."

"Last time I checked, Theodore Elmsworth was single. Why is who he dates anyone's business?"

Hoisting a shoulder, I said, "I don't know, maybe because he's the leader of the free world."

He was also the most eligible bachelor on the planet. Who he was and wasn't dating was big business and dissected on the gossip-driven daytime talk shows and many legitimate news outlets.

Day exhaled. "What does Theodore say?"

"He was pissed at first, but now I don't think he's taking it very seriously." I popped a stale tortilla chip in my mouth. "Remember that stuff with the stripper?"

Day nodded her head.

"Well, he seems to think I can make this magically disappear like I did with that."

"He's not wrong, that's kinda what you do. You clean up messes."

"Yeah, other people's messes. I've never been good at keeping my stuff tidy."

"Damn, Seth is a first-class asshole. He could've at least given you a heads up."

Rolling my eyes, I didn't offer a response. Seth was doing his job; he didn't owe me anything. Maybe if my eyes weren't filled with hearts, I would've seen this coming. I had no one to blame but myself.

"What can I do to help?" Day asked.

"You brought me food and wine. You've done more than enough."

Daysha pointed to the window. "If you want, I can call the police on those reporters. I can pretend to be an angry neighbor." Day cleared her throat and held her hand to her head, pretending to make a call. "Yes, hello, 911, I would like to report a group of aggressive individuals outside of my building.

"They are loud and yelling at the tenants as they come and go. Not exactly the kind of element we're used to seeing in Logan Circle. I don't pay a bajillion dollars in taxes to feel unsafe. Oh, you're going to send ten patrol cars right away?

Excellent. Make sure your officers have enough mace and taser beams for everyone. Byyyeeee." Day ended her pretend call. "Did I do that right? Isn't that how they do it?"

"I think you forgot to use the word thug."

Day snapped her fingers, pretending to be disappointed. "Yes, thug, how could I forget that one."

We both laughed. The first real laugh I'd had since this all hit the fan.

When Daysha left a few hours later, my house was spotless and my spirits lifted. Reaching for a handful of hair, I pulled the dry strands to my nose. My hair smelled like the curry from last night's dinner. Daysha was right, I was in need of a shower. I decided to spend an hour or two washing my hair and lathering my parched skin with oils.

In the bedroom, I turned on the television, which was a huge mistake. As I pulled out my shampoo, conditioner, and body scrub from under the bathroom sink, I heard the all too familiar baritone of Theodore Elmsworth. On his way to Air Force One, he stopped to take a few questions from reporters. Teddy looked good in a tan suit, which I knew he was going to get roasted for. My body tingled and grew hot at the sight of him. The questions were pretty standard, asking him about his infrastructure plan and the growing tensions with Russia.

As Teddy turned away, a reporter with ABC News yelled out, "Are you and Clover Bennett dating?"

I tried to speak to him telepathically through the air waves, whispering "keep walking" under my breath. The message was not received, he didn't continue to walk away; he turned on his heels.

"I don't talk about my personal life. But I will say this, Clover Bennett is an important part of this administration, and I for one can't wait until she returns on Monday so you guys can stop with the conspiracy theories."

Teddy flashed his all-American smile, which sent my entire body into a rolling shiver, before heading for the plane. It was stupid of him to comment. But one thing about Theodore Elmsworth: he was always going to follow his gut.

After a hot shower, shampoo, and facial, I felt much better. With a pint of mint chocolate ice cream from the freezer, I curled up in bed with a book. I wasn't three pages in before my phone chimed, notifying me of an incoming video call. The display lit up with the words El Presidente across the screen. I tossed my book aside, immediately accepting the call. My face beamed at the sight of his. This man wasn't fine, he was scrum-diddlyumptious.

"Hey, you." Teddy smiled back at me. He was still in his tan suit, but the jacket was gone and his shirt sleeves were rolled up with his tie hanging loosely from his neck.

"How's San Diego?"

"I think I get why people love California so much. This weather can't be beat."

"Busy day?"

"Always, I met with some local residents to discuss what our infrastructure bill would mean for their community. One thing about voters, despite party lines, everyone wants smooth roads and reduced traffic."

"Sounds like this trip was successful."

"You sound surprised. You know I wasn't just elected because of my rugged good looks." He pulled off his tie and began to unbutton his shirt, as if on cue.

"I know you're a man of substance."

"You know better than anyone just how substantial I can be."

I gulped down a wad of spit.

"How was your day?" he asked.

I was thankful for the change of subject. "Ahh, you know, kinda like being on house arrest without the itchy ankle monitor."

Teddy set the phone down on the bathroom counter, positioning it so we could still see each other. "I hate that those reporters are still out there pestering you." He removed his shirt, tossing it aside.

"This too shall pass," I said, trying to sound unbothered.

Teddy leaned in closer, narrowing his eyes while examining my face. "You're not letting them get to you, are you?"

My shoulders bumped a shrug.

In DC, your reputation was a form of currency, offering you access to people and opportunities. Once that reputation took a tumble, it was difficult to rebuild. I'd spent years crafting the Clover Bennett brand. When people heard my name, they thought of words like reliable, trustworthy, fixer. Any romantic association with Teddy would place an asterisk over everything I'd worked to achieve.

Teddy sucked his teeth. "Fuck them, haters will always do what they do best ... hate. And let me add, we aren't doing anything wrong. We're both single adults, you're not some intern. Honestly, I don't even get why this is a big deal."

"It's a big deal because optics matter."

"Optics Smoptics."

I chuckled at his childish use of words. He didn't have anything to lose so, of course, everything was a joke to him. His head disappeared as he rinsed soap from his face. This man was a wonder. It wasn't just his looks, although that was worth its weight in gold, it was the confident grown man swagger.

He wasn't into childish games or power plays. In the past, men would throw out the 'L' word to control me or get me to stay, but when Teddy said he loved me, I genuinely believed it. It had only been two nights but I missed him and wished I was in that bathroom, in his arms, in his bed right now.

With a clean, dry face, Teddy looked into the phone with a smile. "I miss you," he said.

I blushed, it felt good to know I wasn't the only one with these stupid feelings.

"Are you alone?" he asked.

"Yes, but that ten-person orgy I ordered should be here any minute now."

"Really, where'd you go to order that?"

"Umm ... DoorDick."

We shared a laugh as I watched lecherously as he rubbed his hand across his chest.

"Do you think you could spare some time for me?" he asked.

"What did you have in mind?" I bit my lower lip.

"Go get that toy I got you."

When I tell you I dropped that phone and nearly broke my neck trying to get out of that bed and to the lingerie drawer where I stored my unmentionables. I hopped back on the bed to find Teddy sitting on the couch in his hotel suite completely naked.

"Looks like I have some catching up to do." I pulled my silk sleep dress over my head, dropping it to the floor.

CHAPTER TWENTY-FOUR

On Monday morning I was back at the White House podium taking questions from the rabid press, with a big smile and bright orange pencil skirt. Orange was a power color that conveyed confidence, and I needed all the help I could get. The first question of the briefing was about, you guessed it, those pictures of me and Teddy.

An ash blonde reporter from *The Washington Post* stood and asked, "Thanks Clover, are you at all concerned about the perception the recently surfaced images of you and the President may pose?"

Without missing a beat, I responded, "Perception and reality are two very different things. My job here at the White House is to accurately convey this administration's agenda and policies. A little stint in the rumor mill isn't going to distract me from that."

From the faces of the fifty or so reporters glaring back at me, it was clear they were not ready to buy the brand of BS I was selling. I received a few more questions about the nature of my relationship with Teddy, all of which I deflected. Eventually the reporters took the hint and turned their attention to more substantive questions.

After the briefing I headed to Lisa's office. I was hoping to pick her brain for a bit.

"Knock, knock." I tapped on the open door, walking inside her spacious office, closing the door behind me for privacy.

It oftentimes felt like the White House walls had ears. Several staffers had their offices swept for possible eavesdropping devices, including yours truly.

"I hope this isn't a bad time, I just wanted to check in," I said.

"No, come on in." Lisa waved me toward a love seat near the windows. She grabbed two bottles of water from her mini fridge before crossing the room, taking a seat beside me. "I caught your presser, it was good."

I offered a bright smile, twisting the cap off the bottle.

"I see there are still some lingering questions about those photos," she added.

"Yep, there were."

"Not gonna lie, I have a few questions of my own."

I clasped my hands around the cold water bottle to quell the uncontrollable fidgeting I was experiencing. "I'm more than willing to answer any questions you have, just ask."

Lisa pulled her red glasses from her face, placing them on top of her head. "You're a smart woman, Clover, I just hope you know what you're doing. No judgment, the President is a hottie."

My eyes grew wide hearing that word come out of Lisa Prince's mouth.

"Do the young people still use that term?" she asked.

With a clipped nod, I said, "Yes, hottie is still an acceptable term."

"Glad to know I'm still in the loop. My daughters think I'm a relic from the past because I don't understand any of the new social media language."

"I'm right there with you. The other day I had to Google what TBH meant."

We shared a laugh. After eight months in the White House,

I considered Lisa a friend. But there were levels to friendship, and she and I were not at, nor would we ever be on, the sharing deepest darkest secrets level. So, any real conversation about Teddy and my relationship was essentially dead in the water.

"Anyway, I just truly would hate for you to find yourself in a hole you're unable to dig yourself out of." She rested her soft hand over mine, giving it a pat, her blue eyes showing genuine concern.

"I appreciate it, I do. But my momma didn't raise a fool."

No, Ms. Sylvia had raised me to be an independent, confident woman who never had to rely on anyone for anything. My foolishness wasn't taught, it was something that I had learned gradually over time.

"I'm a mother, worrying is part of my DNA."

"I can assure you the only thing you have to worry about is the infrastructure bill and what we're going to say if it doesn't pass."

Lisa rolled her eyes. "Don't remind me."

After a fifteen-minute conversation about the best way to apply lipstick to the pig that was our infrastructure bill, I worked up the courage to ask Lisa the question that had really brought me to her office.

"Can I ask a random question?" I chewed on the inside of my cheek.

"Sure, shoot."

Taking a deep breath, I asked the question that had been nagging at me most of the weekend. "Who made the final decision about offering me the Press Secretary position?"

"It was a group vote. Gibbs was against it. Between you and me I think he was a bit intimidated by you. The President and I both wanted you for the position."

"And what the President wants, the President gets," I murmured under my breath.

"Why'd you ask?"

"No reason, really. I was just curious about the process."

I quickly changed the subject to the citizenship event scheduled in the Rose Garden this Thursday. Lisa's response confirmed Gibbs's words. Teddy had played a role in my being here. Even though he made it appear that he was just an observer to the process. Why lie about that? What was his ulterior motive?

"Please stop cheating," I yelled, grabbing the play Monopoly money from Teddy's hand.

Teddy let out a laugh. "I'm not cheating, you just really suck at this game."

"Because Monopoly is boring."

We'd been playing this board game for over an hour, and the most exciting thing that had occurred was the warm peach cobbler that I was slowly savoring.

Since the ANBS interview, we had to be extra careful. Right now, the confines of the White House residence was the safest place on earth. As Teddy moved his top hat seven spaces, I couldn't help but stare in a daze. I sure knew how to pick them. I always gravitated toward powerful men, a surgeon, a military officer, a mathematician who graduated from college when he was thirteen. And all these high-value men were just as dysfunctional and insecure as the postal worker and aspiring rapper I also once dated.

Teddy landed on Park Place, which I had converted into a tourist destination with my two hotels.

"Pay me," I squealed. Standing, I got to twerking in celebration.

Teddy made the three thousand dollars in rainbow-colored cash rain over me, tucking a loose orange hundred-dollar bill into the cup of my bra. I fell back to my knees, planting a kiss on his lips. I was done with this game, and was ready to have a different type of fun.

Teddy grabbed hold of me, pulling me onto his lap. With his face in my hands, I ran my manicured nails clad in OPI's Wanted Red or Alive across his beard. Our lips once again connected as I rolled my hips over his lap. The last few days had been stressful and I just wanted to lose myself in him. I wanted to pretend that I could have it all, the powerhouse job and the man that filled my cup, rooted for me to win, and gave me mind-numbing orgasms each night.

From the way Teddy kissed my breasts and sucked my nipples, it appeared he also wanted to wander from the beaten path until we were both so lost that even bread crumbs couldn't help us find our way back. I tried really hard to ignore the voices in my head that at the start of the night were a whisper but were now yelling at me.

So, you're just gonna ignore the fact that he lied to you? This is how it starts, one small lie snowballs into an avalanche of lies. If you don't call him out, how can you ever believe anything he says? Do you remember what happened the last time you ignored your gut? When the wife of the secretly married man you were dating rear ended your car with you still in it.

I reached for my neck. It was still messed up, and the monthly chiropractor visits and acupuncture weren't helping. Teddy stood quickly, scooping me up in his arms, leading me to the bedroom. I wrapped my legs around his torso and he walked slowly toward the master suite, stopping every few steps to kiss my lips.

"How did I end up getting the Press Secretary interview?" I blurted out.

Teddy's husky voice tickled my ear. "What?" He stopped in his tracks.

"Did you suggest that Lisa and Gibbs extend an interview to me?"

His face was a veil of confusion.

I'm sure, to him this question was straight out of left field but for me, this had been tumbling around in my head for the past four days. If my many failed relationships had taught me anything, it was that honesty was an integral component to a successful relationship. When I told Teddy I was all in, I meant it. But I wasn't an idiot, and I wasn't just going to allow my heart to get the rest of me hurt.

He removed his hands from my ass, allowing me to release my legs from his waist and plant my feet on the floor. "Where is this coming from?"

"It's a valid question."

"It's irrelevant, you have the job. Why does it matter how you got it?"

I'm pretty sure my eyes grew to the size of saucers. "Of course, it matters."

"Lucky, you got the job on your own merits. So what if I put in a good word?" His tone was defensive, his naturally deep voice a few octaves higher.

"So, you did say something."

He shrugged, stroking his beard. "I don't remember. I may have mentioned your name. In fact, I think Lisa brought you up and I just cosigned your experience."

I closed my eyes, trying my best not to lose it. I didn't want to show that I was holding a handful of jokers.

"So, you lied." My voice was shaky as I tried not to yell.

"When did I lie?"

"You said Lisa chose me." I searched his face, waiting for some type of recognition that his story didn't track. "So, what is it? Was it Lisa or was it you?"

"Lisa chose you. I agreed."

"Did you agree or did you strongly recommend?"

"Lucky—"

I clapped my hands in time with my words. "Did you agree or recommend?"

Now I was yelling and my body temperature was rising, even though I was standing there in only my panties.

"First, watch your tone." He exhaled deeply. "I wanted

someone I could trust, and the thought of having an individual I had established rapport with as part of the administration was a selling point. I may have said your name, but your experience got you this job."

As he moved closer, my shoulders wilted. Maybe I was being paranoid. I think the American News interview made me question everything. I didn't want people thinking the only reason I was in the White House was because I was sleeping with the President. I knew I was a hard worker and I was deserving of this position.

Teddy hooked his thumb under my chin. "I swear to God, Lisa and Gibbs raved about you after that interview. They wanted to call and hire you on the spot."

I pulled away. Lisa had said the opposite, that Gibbs wasn't a fan. Why was Teddy making it sound like Gimble was Team Clover? If you're willing to lie about the small things, then you won't think twice about lying about the big things.

"It's late, I should go." I circled the living quarters in search of my clothes.

"What did I say now?" Teddy threw his head back.

"Nothing, I'm just tired and I want to sleep in my own bed."

"OK, I'll throw on some sweats and we can head to your place."

"No," I screamed. "I mean, that isn't a good idea. The press is still following me. The last thing we want to do is give them another story to fill the news cycle." I jumped into my fuchsia pants, tucking my blouse inside.

Teddy grabbed my hand and pulled me close. "Are we good?"

A muscle ticked under my eye. "Yeah, of course." I lifted to my tip toes, kissing him on his cheek. Pulling away, I scooped up my heels and tote bag and exited the residence.

CHAPTER TWENTY-FIVE

It was business as usual in the White House press shop, but the undercurrent in other parts of the White House were strained. I'd admit that some of it was due to my hyper imagination and guilty conscience. I'd spot two colleagues chatting in the office kitchen throw furtive glances in my direction as I warmed up my leftover takeout from the night before.

While walking to a meeting, I distinctly heard my name being spoken between two policy wonks before they converted to hushed tones at the sight of me. It wasn't just the blogs and news channels that were eating this up, it would appear that some of my colleagues believed the rumors too. And when I say rumors, I mean the fact that I was one hundred percent sleeping with the President of the United States.

Back in my office, I found an old Black man, in a perfectly creased white short-sleeved shirt and a blue polka dot tie that was entirely too long for his torso, assessing my bare walls.

"Can I help you?"

"How long have you been here?" the grizzled old man asked, never turning his attention from my stark white office walls.

I pointed to my chest. "Me?"

"You're the only one standing there."

OK, fair enough. "Eight months."

"So, you've been here eight months and your walls look like you were just hired or just received your pink slip."

I lifted a blasé shoulder, not really sure what he wanted me to say.

"President Elmsworth was right. You're in desperate need of a splash of color in this office."

"I'm sorry, who are you?"

The old man extended his hand. "Herschel from Staff Services."

The light bulb finally illuminated over my head as I shook his hand. Teddy had recommended I call Herschel months ago. I guess he got tired of waiting. Also, since I wasn't talking to him right now he probably sent Herschel to scout for intel.

"You're that press gal everyone's talking about?"

I wrinkled my forehead. "If you knew who I was, why did you ask how long I'd been here?"

"You know I don't believe none of those stories they're spinning on the television."

"You don't?"

I may have found the one person in all of DC who was on my side.

"No, you ain't even Elmsworth's type. Do you remember his ex-wife?" Herschel released a whistle. "Now she was a looker."

Herschel from Staff Services was an asshole. Most old people think just because they'd been on this earth for three-quarter quills they could just say anything.

"Geez, thanks."

"Now don't take no offense, you're pretty too. If you were around back in my day your dance card would stay full."

"I'm really busy but thanks so much for stopping by." I gave him a wrinkle-nosed smile, which was my way of politely telling people to fuck off.

"How much time do you spend in this office?"

Letting out an aspirated sigh, I hitched my shoulders. "I don't know, maybe twelve to sixteen hours a day."

"So, shouldn't your office be your sanctuary from the bullshit of the day? Pardon my French."

He wasn't speaking French but he was talking facts. At my old job my office was decorated with accent pillows, sparkly picture frames, and neutral vases. I'd even enlisted Alan to help me paint the one wall not made of glass. Why had I not done the same here? I had every intention. I glanced over at a banker's box that was filled with cute office trinkets I'd bought in my first weekend on the job and then just pushed further and further into a corner.

"Look, Herschel, I don't think pictures of old white dudes is gonna help make this space a sanctuary."

"Fair enough, but I can help you make this place whatever you want. Just say the word."

Laughter bubbled in my throat. Herschel sounded like a fairy godmother and I was a poor, design-challenged, not-so-young lady in need of a miracle.

"I'll keep that in mind. Thank you." I moved toward my desk taking a seat, hoping he would finally take a hint.

"I'll tell the President you're thinking about it."

"No, anything that needs to be said to the President can be said by me. Have a good day."

"You take care of yourself, ma'am." Herschel left my office shaking his head.

"Of course, they're sleeping together. Have you seen her?" Tara with White House social events said.

I stopped short of entering the staff kitchen, deciding to hang back so I could overhear the conversation.

"I've asked her out for drinks a few times. I was starting to think it was me, but looks like she was already dropping to her knees for the big guy," Jared from the management and budget office agreed.

"Allegedly, we don't even know if it's true," Ashton corrected him.

"If it is, that would explain a lot."

"Oh yeah, like what, Jared?" I appeared from the other side of the wall.

Mouths dropped as the gaggle of gossipers wrung their hands and tried to moonwalk their way out of it.

"No offense, Clover, we were just talking," Ashton said.

"Yeah, talking smack."

"No one believes those silly rumors." Tara planted an apologetic smile on her face.

"Apparently, you all do."

I wasn't completely paranoid. People were talking and most of the talk wasn't favorable.

Jared slid his hands in the pockets of his tailored thousand-dollar suit. "What do you expect, you got too close to the boss. Shit like that comes back and people wonder."

"Wonder what exactly?"

Jared rolled a bony shoulder. "Wonder how you got this job. At first I thought you were a diversity hire, but now I guess—"

Tara interrupted him. "Nope, I never thought that. I don't want anything to do with this conversation." She rubbed her hands together to indicate she was done with this topic. "I'm going back to my office." Tara scampered out of the kitchen with Ashton close on her heels, leaving Jared and I alone.

"So, you think I got this job because I what?" I furrowed my brow.

"Don't make me say it."

I moved closer, narrowing my eyes. "No, please do."

"You got the job because you were boning the President or intimated that you would."

This was nothing new; I had always been underestimated. People looked at my flowing hair, bright clothes, and firm ass and assumed I was sleeping with someone to be where I was. I made sure they learned quick, fast, and in a hurry that I wasn't just a good lay, but an expert in my field. When that up-and-coming congressman got caught in a hotel room butt ass naked with illicit drugs and male prostitutes, he called Clover Bennett to write his mea culpa speech.

"Isn't your father Senator Abernathy?"

Jared nodded with a shrug.

"And your grandfather is Judge Abernathy?"

He flashed a proud smile. "I come from a long line of highly educated, hard-working alphas."

"Yeah, and you graduated from Columbia with what, a 2.6 GPA? Don't get me wrong, college can be hard, especially when you spend most of it hungover and banging your political science professor."

His mouth formed a straight bloodless line. I performed a simple Google search after he asked me out for drinks months ago. My research had informed me that while he was handsome with sandy blond hair, brown eyes, and a toned physique, he was the type that expected his last name to carry him through life. And for the most part it had. In fact, the Abernathy name had gotten him his job at the White House after his daddy had begged Teddy to hire his son as part of the administration. Teddy had agreed, nepotism at its finest.

"You wouldn't know what hard work was if it sat on your face and jiggled. So, I would suggest that you keep my motherfucking name out of your mouth." Walking to the fridge, I grabbed a bottle of iced coffee and left the kitchen.

IN YET ANOTHER MEETING, I listened as Teddy asked the group how we were going to whip the votes to get senators to vote for this infrastructure bill. Passing policy was a team effort from the politicians on Capitol Hill to the pundits on the nightly news programs. For my part I was helping with the messaging, including a scheduled Town Hall in which the President would take questions from John Q public.

Working closely with his speech writing team, we were crafting talking points that would resonate with the American people. After the meeting I collected my things and exited the conference room. In the hall, Teddy was lingering, waiting for me to appear. His face lit up at the sight of me. Did his eyes grow wide and his smile overtake his face like that every time he saw me? I wondered if my face had also forsaken me.

"Are we all ready for the Town Hall next week?" Teddy said loudly. Too loudly, like he wanted anyone in earshot to know we were talking about work.

"Yes, Mr. President, I've been in talks with Franklin Carter from CNN and he is prepared to moderate." I made my way down the long hall with the President following beside me.

"Great, this was a good idea. A Town Hall is intimate and personal."

I nodded my head, continuing my pace.

Teddy dropped his tone and said barely above a whisper. "Can we talk?"

"I'm really busy."

"Lucky." Teddy stopped, grabbing my arm.

He quickly dropped it as a group of interns rounded the corner. All walking next to the wall of windows to give the President space.

Being in the White House was about getting the opportunity to work alongside the President while being terrified that at any moment you could say or do something so stupid that it would get you fired and the story of your transgression would go down in history as a staffer's urban legend.

When the group passed, Teddy hustled me into a nearby room. I don't know what this room was used for, but it had Pepto Bismol pink wallpaper with gaudy decor and window curtains with tassels. I was all for preserving history, but some of these rooms were in desperate need of a refresh. Most of these items looked like they were picked out by First Lady Eisenhower herself.

"What the hell is going on?" Teddy asked in a huff.

"What are you talking about?"

"You're doing that thing you do where you ghost me."

"I can't ghost someone I see every day."

"You can if it's emotional ghosting," he said with a sneer.

I rolled my eyes. What he called emotional ghosting I called protecting myself.

"You're mad at me. I get that much. But what I don't get is why?"

And that, my friends, is the crux of the problem. He doesn't get why I was upset because he doesn't take exception to anything. Not the looks in the halls or the tabloid articles or the fact that *Good Morning America* ran a story about me in which they talked to my college roommate. Thank God we were still on good terms because, the stories she could tell.

"I'm not even mad at you. I'm mad at myself because I knew better and I let this become a thing." I moved my hand in the space between us.

His eyes dropped as he took a step back. "So, you regret us?"

When he said it that way it sounded worse than I intended. I didn't regret falling in love with him, I just wished the timing was better. I felt like Erykah Badu, maybe whatever this was needed to wait for another lifetime.

"I'm not saying that. I just feel like I'm trying to keep my hair from singeing as I watch my career slowly burn around me and you're like that meme with the dog in the burning room saying everything is fine."

"Because it is fine."

"No, Teddy, it's really not." My stomach clenched into a tight fist.

"No one cares about that shit."

"Everyone cares," I yelled. "But because you're the President they don't have the balls to say anything to your face. But they are talking about it. They think you're a playboy and I'm a whore."

He reached for my shoulder, pulling me close. "Who called you a whore? I will fuck them up and then fire them."

"So, you're just gonna fight everyone?" I threw my hands up at the absurdity of his words.

"If I have to." His voice was soft like velvet, his brown eyes brimming with sincerity.

I leaned my head onto his chest. I loved that this man genuinely wanted to slay every dragon for me. He was a man and most men just wanted to fix things, and Teddy was no different. I'm sure he wanted to get back to good, but I was no longer sure we could.

"Call me naïve, but I still believe that love is enough." Teddy lifted my head, planting a kiss on my lips.

I'd been around the block enough to know that love and good intentions were not always a healing salve. I needed to put these rumors to rest but at this point, I wasn't sure I knew how.

"So, when exactly do I get to see my future son-in-law again?" my mother asked, running her hand over a scarf and gloves set.

Irritation hooded my eyes.

"Does he like spicy food?" she continued.

"Momma, please. The President won't be eating your jerk chicken anytime soon."

"Why not, you two are an item now."

"You make it sound so simple."

After the pictures were released, I couldn't lie to my mother any longer. Believe me, I wanted to, but she knew me too well. So, I had to confess that I had been seeing Teddy for months. And do you know what the first words out of her mouth were? "Oh, so that's why you got the job."

My mother said that. It hurt. All my years of education, long work hours, sacrificing relationships, training, and building my resume were reduced to my abilities in the bedroom. I expected that from my peers but not my own flesh and blood. She didn't mean to hurt my feelings but she did, because her words just confirmed what I knew everyone else was thinking.

"Why does it have to be complicated? You like him, he's crazy about you. The hard part is over."

She sounded like Teddy. "Aunt Ed would love these gloves." I held up a pair of purple leather gloves, knowing that Aunt Edwina would rock the hell out of them but also hoping to shift the dialogue.

"You know Michelle was a career woman, so was Jill Biden. I think even Laura Bush had a job as a librarian."

"What is your point?"

"My point is, if you're worried you'll have to give up your career, that's not necessarily true."

I shook my head. "Give up my career for what?"

"To become First Lady."

I ripped out a laugh with a loud snort, causing a clerk at the counter to glance in our direction.

With her hands on her hips, my mother replied, "Is it really that far-fetched? You're dating the President, after all."

"Yes, it's far-fetched. I have a better chance at winning a gold medal at the Olympics in javelin throwing than ever becoming the First Lady."

"Have you and Theodore talked about it?"

I stopped in my tracks, confusion written all over my face. "What is this? What are you doing? I tell you my career may be over and my reputation ruined and you want to book wedding venues?"

"I'm trying to look on the bright side." Her eyebrows mashed together in a frown.

"What bright side?" I said those words far too loud. Taking a breath, I lowered my voice. "I've worked entirely too long to just settle for being some man's wife."

"He's more than just some man. He's the President of the United States. Anyway, at your age marriage should still be a goal."

"No, it's not a goal for me. I want to start my own firm. I want my name to be mentioned when they talk about DC power players."

I could see now that my relationship with Teddy had made me lose sight of what was most important. Myself. My goals, my dreams, my future.

"Maybe you can have both?" My mother's voice was hopeful.

They feed this BS to all of us at a very young age. The fable, with the handsome prince that gallops in and saves you from all of life's problems. The happily ever after always centering around being loved by some man, which in turn makes you worthy and special.

"Mmph, I appreciate your optimism but I live in reality. The truest words ever spoken were when someone opined that you *can't* have it all."

You will always have to choose. There will always be sacrifices. So, no, I don't get the man and the fancy house and the kids. I get this, the career. And I'm going to make sure that no one can ever take that away from me.

CHAPTER TWENTY-SIX

WALKING DOWN THE HALL TO LISA'S OFFICE FELT MORE LIKE the lonely walk to the guillotine. In which your mind turned into a projector replaying all the choices that brought you to this exact moment. My knuckles were taut from clenching the envelope in my hands. At her office door, her assistant instructed me to head in as Lisa was expecting me.

"Clover, come in, come in."

"Hi," I said meekly.

"Sit, do you want tea or coffee?"

"No, I can't stay long, I just wanted to give you this." I thrust the envelope forward with a shaky hand.

"What's this?" Lisa narrowed her eyes.

"My resignation."

Lisa snatched the envelope from my hands, reaching for her reading glasses. I stood in silence as she read through the one-page letter I'd spent all weekend crafting. Trying my best to strike the perfect tone of gratitude and optimism.

"Clover." She said my name the same way my mother would when I disappointed her. "Have you thought this through?"

"Yes, while I have enjoyed my time at the White House and the opportunity to serve the American people, I think that it's time that I focus on professional endeavors that are closer to my heart."

"Have you told the President?"

"No ... actually, I was hoping you—"

Lisa raised her slender hand. "I won't. That is a conversation I'm certain Elmsworth will want to have with you personally."

Nodding, I collected the letter and slid it back inside the envelope. "Working with you was an honor. I appreciate all your guidance and support," I added.

In Washington, you never wanted to burn bridges because you never knew when you'd have to cross them again.

Lisa's expression softened. "I hope you consider me a friend and I'd like it very much if we could keep in touch."

"I would like that." I turned, heading for the door.

"Clover?" Lisa called. "You can still change your mind."

"Honestly, I've been flip flopping on the issue worse than an overeager politician."

"It doesn't count until you tell the big guy. So, maybe you'll flip one last time."

IT WAS late and I was outside the Oval pacing back and forth. I knew my resignation would take him by surprise and he would be angry with me. Yes, I was a communications major, but this was different. No matter what I said he would never understand my decision.

Teddy was the first man I'd allowed past my hard outer shell in so long. He'd patiently and gently maneuvered past my walls, challenging me to accept that I was deserving of love. He never fell back even when I pushed him away. He created a soft place for my heart and I loved him for it. So having to walk away was the hardest thing I'd ever had to do.

Glancing at my watch, I realized I'd been standing outside his office chewing on my bottom lip for fifteen minutes now.

Maybe I should wait until after the holidays. He already had so much on his plate. Who breaks up with someone weeks before Christmas? Shaking the thought from my head, I approached his closed door. This needed to be done. I just couldn't keep wearing a groove in the carpet. I knocked softly but there was no response. Maybe he'd already retired to the residence. Knocking again, I used more force.

"Come in," the sound of Teddy's voice called from the other side.

His face brightened at the sight of me. Removing the earbuds from his ears, he stood, smoothing down his light blue, button-down shirt. His sleeves were rolled up, which sent my lady parts into overdrive. Maybe I didn't need to do this tonight. Maybe I should let him bend me over the Resolute Desk and have him wield his executive powers.

A smile played at the corners of my mouth as his eyes devoured me. One last kiss couldn't hurt anything. As Teddy walked toward me warmth blossomed in my chest, his strong hands overtaking my face causing sparks to ignite as his lips inched closer to mine.

"I'm here to quit," I blurted out.

Dropping his hands from my face, he took several steps back. The muscles around his jaw firmed into a rigid line.

I thrust the envelope I was holding in his direction. Snatching it from my outstretched hand, he ripped the envelope open. Time slowed as his eyes scanned the words of my letter, his features becoming heavy with recognition. Placing the letter on his desk, he stood in silence for a moment just staring at the single sheet of paper, his jaw uncompromisingly rigid. My eyes swept over his face looking for a hint of what he may be thinking. His body was like stone but his face was clouded with anger.

Teddy broke the silence with a question. "And us?"

The cords in my neck protruded. "I think it's probably best if that also comes to an end."

Teddy's body recoiled like I'd pierced his heart with an arrow.

He whipped around, walking toward the windows surrounding the desk. His shoulders sank into a rounded heap, as I continued.

"I just think it's best that we be realistic. We both knew what this was."

Ripping around, his voice was booming. "And what was that, Clover?"

"Fun, convenient, a little naughty," I said, with a weak smile.

"So, this was convenient for you." Teddy moved his hands back and forth in the space between us.

My voice audibly hitched in my throat. "No, that's not what I meant."

"No, I get exactly what you meant. I was something to do. A bit of fun that you can share during brunch with the girls."

"Teddy—"

"Effective?" he interrupted, his anger masked behind a veil of indifference.

"Immediately."

He broke into a mirthless laugh. "You are unbelievable, Lucky."

"I get that it's bad timing but—"

"Bad timing? Fuck you."

"Fuck me? All because I've handed in my resignation?"

"You know damn well this isn't about that stupid piece of paper."

"I just need to do what's best for me."

"So, ending us is best for you?" He tilted his head forward, nostrils flared.

"Let's stop pretending that we could work."

"I wasn't pretending, Lucky. I believed that shit. I believe it still." His eyes were a tornado of emotion with flashes of anger, glimpses of sadness, and a constant swirl of confusion.

I raised a perplexed shoulder. It was clear that every time I spoke it made things worse.

"You know what?" He lengthened his neck and squared his

posture. "You're right, we would have never worked because you're a broken, bitter bitch who's gonna die alone."

Shock unhinged my jaw. What was it with men who thought I needed them in my life to be happy?

"Newsflash, Teddy, my happiness isn't dependent on you. I was fine before we got together and I'm gonna be golden without you."

He gave his head a thoughtful nod. "Anything else?" His eyes clouded with emotion.

"No, I think that's it." I turned toward the door.

"Thank you for your service." His voice was laced with sarcasm.

Pausing at the door, I turned back. I wanted to run into his arms and feel the weight of his warm body pressed tight against mine. I wanted to hear him whisper in my ear that everything was going to be OK.

"Teddy, I ..."

His face softened as he began to walk toward me.

"I'm sorry," I said. My vision blurring with tears, I fled his office.

CHAPTER TWENTY-SEVEN

THE HOLIDAYS PASSED WITH LITTLE FANFARE. I SPENT THE majority of the time with my mother, who was having difficulty accepting that Teddy and I were through. On January second, the White House announced that I was no longer a part of the administration and just like that, I was a footnote in history. All this newfound freedom allowed me to focus full time on Bennett Communication. A boutique public relations firm that would act as brand architects crafting company images that were authentic and innovative.

At the start of the new year, I called a leasing agent so I could secure an office space. Today, I got the keys to a modest fourth floor space in the heart of downtown DC. I walked around the empty area envisioning all that this office could be, a little paint, the right furniture, decor, and lighting fixtures, and this space would be worthy of the Bennett name.

Daysha's loud voice screaming alerted me of her arrival. "Oh, this is nice."

"Do you like it?" I asked.

I'd picked this place all on my own, not wanting to be influenced by others' opinions. But now that I'd added the keys to my keyring, I wanted confirmation that I'd made the right choice.

"I love it," Day gushed. "Clover, these windows are great." She moved through the space, decorating it. "You'll need a big couch for the waiting room and some arm chairs." Stopping at a scuffed blank wall, she continued, "I know just the piece for this wall. A Chicago artist named Evelyn Townsend; her stuff is amazing. The art for this wall is on me." She snapped a picture of the wall with her phone.

"You don't have to do that."

She waved her hand, brushing my concerns aside. "Consider it an office warming gift. I'm so proud of you. Big baller shot caller. Oh, that reminds me." She rummaged through her over-sized tote bag pulling out a bottle of champagne and two plastic cups.

"Champagne? Day, really?"

"It's a celebration, bitch. Ooo, is that gonna be your office?" She pointed to a large room.

I beamed. "Yep."

Day walked toward the office, leaving me holding the champagne bottle. Taking a deep breath, I surveyed the space for the millionth time. It was crazy to think that one month ago I was still at the White House, and now I was starting a new journey.

If Teddy was here, he would be so proud. He was always rooting for me and believed that my reality was only as small as my imagination. There were so many times over the past few weeks when I wanted to call him. To hear his deep reassuring voice tell me everything was going to be OK. On Christmas Eve I'd broken down and called him from a blocked number but when he answered, I couldn't form the words and quickly ended the call.

"So, what's next?" Daysha re-entered the room, interrupting my thoughts.

"Next, I transform this space in time for the grand opening in three months."

Daysha fanned her hands, shaking them over her head with excitement.

"It'll be a crazy tight schedule with contractors and staffing interviews, but I'm confident I can get it done."

"If anyone can do it, you can."

"Plus, it'll be nice to have something to occupy my thoughts."

Daysha took a deep breath before saying, "Have you thought about calling Teddy?"

"And say what?"

My usual vocal friend was biting her tongue. Maybe because I'd bit her head off on more than one occasion over the past month when his name was mentioned.

"I'm just saying, it's obvious you miss him. And I'm sure he misses you too."

All I could do was shake my head for fear that tears would spill from my eyes.

Daysha grabbed my shoulders. "Clo, you deserve the world. I know how you feel about love, but being loved by someone and loving them back is kinda what life is all about. I just don't want you to limit your happiness."

Brushing away a rogue tear, I said, "We should open this champagne before it gets warm."

Taking the bottle from me, Daysha used her keys to break the foil, twisting the bottle until the cork made that delightful popping sound. I let Day pour generous amounts in both cups before handing her one.

Daysha held her cup high. "To Clover Bennett, a woman who has never shied away from a difficult task. A woman who laughs when people tell her it can't be done and then shows them that it can and that she has. To my best friend and role model, I am so very proud of you."

Her toast left me misty eyed. Since leaving Teddy, the waterworks were nonstop. Tapping our cups, we both downed our bubbly.

"OK, let's get some music on so we can christen this place with some twerking."

I quickly obliged by playing Megan Thee Stallion as we gyrated, swiveled, and booty popped to the upbeat tune.

* * *

BACK AT MY APARTMENT, I was sitting in front of the television with a glass of wine and client portfolios. When I reached out to my contacts list and told them I was branching out on my own, the response was overwhelming. I'd already signed on fourteen clients and had meetings with perspective clients in the coming days and weeks. You could call me a natural born saleswoman, especially when the product I was selling was myself.

With my MacBook on my lap, I spent the evening handling client intake and building their files. Right now, I was a one-woman shop. Well, it was me and Alan, but I had interviews set up this week for a much-needed assistant. Once that position was filled, I could focus on recruiting for other vacancies. Reaching for my glass of wine, my eyes flashed to the television and Teddy was on the screen in a tuxedo addressing an audience. I scrambled for the remote, unmuting the sound.

"It's so exciting to be here with all of you tonight. Despite what the reporters say, I don't really get out that much. You go to one strip club and you never hear the end of it."

The audience laughed at his self-deprecating joke. He was at an annual black tie bipartisan charity event. Teddy looked charming in his dark navy-blue tux and perfectly tapered beard. Leaning forward, I hung on his every word, laughing at his jokes despite myself. After a series of quips his tone turned serious, discussing the state of the country and the American people. When he was done the politicians, celebrities, and power players in DC applauded enthusiastically.

Smashing the power button on the remote, I gulped down my wine, pouring another glass taking steady gulps. Normally when you broke up with someone you could block them on social media, delete all the pictures in your phone, throw their toothbrush and sweatpants in the trash and move on. When your ex was the President of the United States, none of those things were options. No matter how hard I tried, he was always there. Kinda hard to heal when the wound was constantly gushing blood.

He looked so happy I wondered if any part of him missed me. Maybe he was relieved that I'd ended it because he was over the relationship and didn't know how to tell me. Every time he appeared on the news channels he was all smiles. On Christmas morning he helped feed the homeless and he was jollier than St. Nick himself.

On New Year's Day a reporter asked him who he kissed at midnight and his response was "A gentleman never kisses and tells" with a sly expression. At the New Year's Eve party Daysha forced me to attend, this random man next to me grabbed my face at the stroke of midnight and planted a wet, drunken kiss on my lips. Much like Teddy, I had no plans of telling anyone else about that sloppy kiss.

This was what my night devolved into most evenings, me obsessing over my decision to leave. Just because I left the White House, it didn't mean I had to leave him too. That was a choice I willingly made. I'd already fallen so deep inside his love; it was warm and soft and pulsating. But even though I was shielded I was always terrified that eventually I'd be ejected from my safe place inside his heart against my will. Reaching for the wine bottle, I planned to pour another glass but the bottle was empty. *Damn, when did that happen?*

Maybe I should just call him and wish him a Happy New Year. We were still kind of friends. With white wine coursing through my veins, I unlocked my phone and dialed his private cell phone number. I'd deleted his numbers from my phone, but that was only because I'd memorized them by heart. The sound of the phone line ringing set off an avalanche of uncontrollable shivers. *What would I even say?* On the third ring, tendrils of fear curled in my stomach. *Hang up, Clover.*

"Hello?" a voice that did not belong to Theodore Elmsworth answered the phone.

I was certain the woman on the other end could hear my ragged breath through the line.

"Hello, are you looking for Theo?" Her voice seemed to bubble and pop with happiness.

I scrambled to end the call, but my shaking hands dropped the phone and it slid under the ottoman.

"There's someone on the other line but they're not saying anything," I could hear the female voice announce.

"Hello? Lucky, are you OK?" Teddy was now on the line, his voice filled with concern.

Damn caller ID.

Finally reaching my phone, I ended the call before slumping on the floor a sweaty mess. The buzzy ring of my cell interrupted my heavy breathing. The number that flashed was Teddy's. I sat perfectly still, shutting my eyes tightly until the ringing ceased. Dropping my head back on the couch cushion, I let out the breath I'd been holding while fanning my sweaty pits. *Well, that was a stupid idea.*

My phone chimed. *Oh my God, he left a message.*

Pacing from room to room, I gnawed on my gel nails. *Why would he leave a message? Who does that?* I had a moment of weakness, no need to make it a whole thing. And who the hell was the woman who answered his phone? Marching back to the living room, I pressed play, placing his message on speaker.

"Lucky, did you just call me? I just got a call from your phone. Maybe it was a butt dial. I'm sorry. When I saw your number I thought maybe something was wrong and started to worry." He breathed heavily. "Anyway, I hope you're doing well. Happy New Year. No need to call me back. Bye."

Sinking into the couch, I buried my face in one of the pillows. *Great, now he probably thinks I'm a stalker.* I needed to let this go. Clearly, he'd moved on. He was probably hugged up with that mystery woman right now. It was time that I move on too. Scrolling through my phone, I called up one of the men who had been riding the bench all these months. How do you get over an old man? With a new one, of course.

CHAPTER TWENTY-EIGHT

"Oh, my goodness, Clover, this place looks great." My mother wrapped her arms around me.

"Your momma's right, this is real nice," my father agreed.

"Thanks guys." I beamed.

You know it had to be a special occasion to get both of my parents in the same room. I think the last time all three of us were together was at my college graduation.

"Is it open bar?" my dad asked, his head swiveling as a pretty woman walked by.

"Yes, Dad, knock yourself out."

As my father ambled toward the bar near the bank of windows, my mother rolled her eyes. "You know he brought his *girlfriend*."

"I noticed that."

"She looks younger than you."

"Well, Daddy's always been a ladies' man."

My father was a struggling artist that often bounced from job to job, but one thing he was good at was finding a woman to take care of him, myself included.

"Mommy, promise me you'll be on your best behavior."

"I don't need to be reminded how to act in public. Save that mess for your cradle-robbing daddy."

Never a dull moment with Ms. Sylvia. "I'm gonna check on the caterers."

In the office breakroom things seemed to be running smoothly. Hors d'oeuvres were making their way around the event. I'd snagged more than a couple of the lobster deviled eggs, quickly devouring them. This grand opening event was already a success, with three new companies signing on to the firm for their branding needs. And we were fielding several other inquiries about retaining my services. My client list was growing fast and we hadn't even officially opened for business. Why I'd waited so long to take the leap, I'd never know.

Peeking out from the breakroom, I observed the crowd of family, friends, and clients. Aunt Ed was in an animated conversation with JoJo and Russell. Alan was moving around the space hobnobbing with potential clients. I spotted Daysha and Miles near the bar sharing a laugh. His hand caressing her neck.

Nights like this made me acutely aware of my singleness. Experiencing all this professional success and having no one to share it with was a dismal feeling. Yes, I had my friends and family to share this night with, but I wanted my person. The person who cheered the loudest because they were there for the sleepless nights and panic attacks. The person who would tell me I was exceptional and capable of anything I set my mind to. The person who would whisper in my ear at the end of the night and tell me they were proud of me.

When you've been single as long as I have, you learn to be self-sufficient. I definitely didn't need a man to give me anything. But after being with Teddy, it was hard to just ignore the longing in the pit of my stomach that ached for more. Unfortunately, Teddy was the one bridge I couldn't revisit. Not after dousing it in kerosene and lighting that bitch on fire.

Back in the main space, I chatted with an assemblywoman who was interested in an image overhaul. Apparently, her reputation had taken a few hits in the past year and her constituents were questioning where her loyalties lied. I provided a few prospective options, keeping it high level. If she wanted the details, she would have to retain our services.

Daysha approached, and after offering apologies to the assemblywoman, she grabbed my waist ushering me to a sparse corner of the room.

"What are you doing?" I wriggled loose.

"OK, don't freak out." Daysha held her palms up.

"What?"

"Theodore is here."

Spinning around instinctually, I scanned the room for his six-foot-four frame. My eyes settled on a crowd of people near the reception area circling around hoping to meet the commander in chief.

"What is he doing here?" I asked in a raspy, secretive hush.

"At first I thought maybe you'd invited him but based on the expression on your face, I'm gonna go with no."

My heart pounded in my throat as my chest grew tight with panic. The lobster deviled eggs and poblano pepper mac and cheese bites I'd consumed solidified, forming a rock in my gut. I was having difficulty breathing. I wasn't ready for this, not tonight. Any air in my lungs evaporated as I gasped in vain for breath.

"Stop it. You stop it right now, Clover Bennett," Daysha reprimanded me. "Take some deep breaths. In and out."

I complied and slowly my chest began to relax, oxygen expanding my lungs.

"What do you want me to do? 'Cause I'll march over there right now and tell him to leave." Daysha was in full momma bear mode.

She understood how hard this break-up had been on me. I believed her when she said she'd escort Teddy from the building.

"No, I don't want a scene." Forcing a smile on my face, I added, "It's fine. I'll be fine."

I shouldn't be surprised that he knew about me starting the firm or the party tonight. We were essentially moving in the same circles. Lucky for me, these past three months never overlapped. But I was foolish if I thought I could avoid Teddy forever. Half my clientele were politicians. It was inevitable that our paths would cross. However, the fact that they were crossing at my private event was a little unsettling.

Moving along the edges of the office space, I did my best to steer clear of Teddy.

"Great event," JoJo said, folding me into a hug.

I think that was the fourth hug she'd given me tonight. She was happy for me and I was grateful for the support.

"I just had the nicest conversation with Theodore. I didn't know he was coming. You sure like your secrets."

"I've been so busy it must have slipped my mind."

"Don't know why I'm surprised, of course he'd want to support his girlfriend."

Other than Daysha and Alan, I hadn't told my other friends about our split. I wasn't interested in the faces people make when they feel sorry for you. *"Poor Clover, I wish she could just find a nice man and settle down. At this point there has to be something wrong with her, she is the common denominator in all her failed relationships."*

The distinctive raspy laughter of a religious smoker traveled through the air. I turned to find my dad patting Teddy on the back like the two were old friends. I was certain my father was trying to convince Teddy to commission him for his presidential portrait.

I allowed my eyes to play across Teddy's frame. He was in a hunter green suit jacket and trousers. Sans tie, the top few buttons on his crisp white shirt allowed for a sliver of his chest to peek through. He must have sensed me staring; the tether of his gaze latched onto mine, ruining the steady current of my pulse. Was that a hint of a smile I saw dancing in his eyes?

AFTER A BIT more socializing and me maneuvering the space so as not to encounter Teddy, it was time for toast. Daysha was the first one to raise her glass and toast my accomplishment. She was followed by colleagues and family and friends who all sang my praises. My face and neck warmed. I was never one who liked being the center of attention.

My father ambled up to center stage created by the crowd of people circling around and wrangled the microphone from my assistant, Shay. I took a deep breath, preparing myself for the worst.

After tapping the mic, he said, "Howdy, my name is Reginald Bennett. And for those of you who don't know me, I'm Clover's father. Clover's always been an overachiever since the day she was born. She came into this world a whole month early because she couldn't wait to start making her mark on this world. Now I ain't always been the best father, but one thing I've always been is a proud one."

He sniffled before continuing. "Proud to be the loud parent letting everyone know that that was my baby winning them spelling bees, or giving that big speech. I don't tell you this often, but you are the best thing I've ever created." My father tossed back his glass, finishing the brown liquor before handing the microphone back to Shay.

My eyes twinkled as I did my best to hold back my tears. Reggie Bennett was really a softy even though he tried to pretend like nothing affected him. I was very much my father's daughter in that way.

"Thank you, Mr. Bennett," Shay said. "Would anyone else like to say a few words?"

"Yeah, I'd like to speak." Teddy walked to the center of the room, standing next to Shay who offered him the microphone, but he declined. "I'll speak loud."

Ducking my head, I took a couple steps back. The desire to

retreat itched at my feet. The last thing I wanted to hear was Teddy saying nice things about me.

"Clover and I go way back. She was my communications director when I ran for senator ten years ago. I knew then Clover was someone special. She was great at what she did and she always made me look good, so I loved working with her."

The guests chuckled at his joke, each hanging on his every word like he was about to reveal the location of the fountain of youth.

"That's why I was so excited to reconnect with her all these years later as my Press Secretary. If you've had the good fortune of working with Clover, then you know that she doesn't play and that she is fiercely protective of her clients. She was like the Dora Milaje the way she fought for my administration every day in that press room. I would say that Clover doesn't know how amazing she is but that would be a lie. She knows her worth and she's gonna make you pay for it."

Daysha laughed along with the other guests. "So true. He knows you so well."

Teddy continued, "But when you bet on Lucky Bennett, you can never lose." He raised his wine glass. "To Lucky, may every year be better than the last."

The guests all raised their glasses in honor of me, causing my face to flush.

"I think that's a perfect segue to have Clover say a few words," Shay said, holding the microphone in my direction.

Smoothing my dress, I stepped forward. "Thank you so much for joining me for this event. I've wanted to start my own firm for a long time, and I have so many people in this room to thank for supporting the dream when it was just a seedling in my brain. To my mother, thank you for being a fierce, powerful woman. Your example was the blueprint for the woman I became. To my father, your creative mind taught me to always think beyond the box and that the only limitations are the ones I set."

I ran through my thank yous to my friends and talked about

the vision and mission of Bennett Communication to a crowd of smiling faces. This was without a doubt the top five best nights of my life. I was living the life I wanted, professionally anyway, and I couldn't be happier. I finished my speech and held out the microphone for Shay, before pulling it back.

"Sorry, I just want to thank one more person. Like most dreams, if we don't nurture them then they can shrink until the dream becomes more like a fable. A few months ago, my dream was in need of some TLC and the words of a very special person breathed new life into me." I snuck a quick glance at Teddy before averting my eyes. "You believed in me and I love you for that. And I just wanted to say thank you." I laughed nervously. "OK, that's it. This alcohol ain't gonna drink itself," I joked before heading toward the bar.

"Hey, boss lady, great speech," Alan said, wrapping his arm around me.

"Thanks."

"I especially like the part when you thanked me."

"Honestly, I couldn't have done this without you."

"Oh damn." Alan dropped his voice.

"What?"

"Theodore is heading this way. Wait, maybe he's going to the restroom." Alan craned his neck, looking over my shoulder. "Nope, he is definitely headed this way."

Before I could pull myself together, he was standing next to us.

"Hi, Alan, good to see you again."

"You too. It's been a minute." Alan fidgeted with his hands, appearing to be at a loss for words, which was an absolute first for him.

"Do you mind if I steal Clover from you?" Teddy asked.

"Please steal her. Abduct her. Throw her in a sketchy white van and go. Ahh, stranger danger."

"Alan..." I said to stop him from rambling.

"Yep, I'ma be over there."

I shuffled my feet as Alan exited stage left.

"Thank you for your kind words. Very nice of you to say all those things," I offered.

"Well, I meant every word. I'm proud of you, Lucky. I hope you've taken the time to process how big this is." He scratched at the back of his neck.

Was he nervous? It was comforting to know I wasn't the only one thrown off kilter being this close after all this time.

"I was hoping we could talk," he said.

And I was hoping a hole would open under my feet dropping me to the ground floor so I could make a quick exit. Daysha was right, for a communications professional I sucked when it came to communicating my own emotions. Looking around the crowded office, I nodded. "Yeah, follow me." We headed to the elevators and made our way to the roof. The last thing I wanted was to end up red eyed and runny nosed for all my clients to see. The Secret Service agents swept the roof, giving us the all clear.

Once they were out of earshot, I asked, "What are you doing here?"

"Your mother invited me. She can be very persuasive when she wants to be."

I nodded, of course, my meddling mother would not pass up a chance to insert her nose into my affairs. I loved her dearly, but boundaries were not her strong point.

"That makes sense. I know you're very busy, so don't feel obligated to stay any longer. I release you from my mother's request."

"Actually, I was glad she reached out. I wanted to be here to support you. I just hope you're not upset I came." He shoved his hands in the pockets of his trousers.

"I'm not upset. Surprised that you'd still want to be here for me."

"I always wanted that. I consider myself the President of the Clover Bennett fan club." A smile shadowed his mouth.

"Look, Teddy, I..."

There was so much I wanted to say. But I didn't know if I had the words to make it right. I'd pushed him away. He wanted to love me and I got scared, and in classic Clover fashion I'd messed everything up.

"I miss us," Teddy said, his brown eyes searching my face.

"I miss us too. I was wrong to shut you out. I warned you I was lousy at this relationship stuff." I threw my arms in the air hopelessly.

"Yeah, I was warned."

"I didn't mean to hurt you. I just got scared. And when I get scared, I run."

"I ain't gonna lie, you leaving cut me deep."

I bobbed my shoulders. "I don't know, you seemed OK every time I saw you on television." I peered at him with an intense lens.

"Acting OK and being OK are two completely different things."

He was right. I knew that from first-hand experience.

"Well, I'm sure your lady friend helped to make things easier for you."

Teddy's eyebrows collided in the center of his nose. "Who?"

"The woman that answered the phone when I called ... when I accidentally butt dialed you that one time."

"Woman? Clover, that was my niece. She was visiting with my uncle and thought it would be funny to answer my phone."

My face lit up with realization. That made sense, he did have nieces and nephews in their twenties. I'm surprised my legs weren't tired from always jumping to conclusions.

"There aren't any other women, Lucky. It's just you, all I've ever wanted was to be with you."

And just like that, my mouth turned into a leaky faucet.

"Teddy, ending things with you was a mistake. I regretted my decision the second the words left my mouth. I just didn't know how to fix things or if you even wanted to fix us. So I threw myself into work."

"I should have called; I should have convinced you to talk to me. But your words just seemed so final."

"This isn't on you. This is me. You deserve an apology. So, first, I apologize. Leaving the White House was necessary. Our relationship was just collateral damage, I guess. I've never been loved the way you love me. The fact that I willingly walked away from all that ... from you is crazy.

"You asked me to try, you asked me to trust you, and I didn't. I was constantly waiting for you to realize that I was unlovable. I wanted to be happy, but inside I was holding my breath because I thought we were too good to be true. Love scares me because every man I've ever loved has disappointed me. Insanity is doing the same thing over and over and expecting the same results. So, trusting in a man, even if that man was you, was insane. I was trying to protect myself and I ended up hurting us both.

"The past months without you have just confirmed what I already knew. I love you, Theodore Elmsworth, and all this is just a dull carbon copy of what life can be. I wanna live out loud. I want everyone to know how much I love you and how much you mean to me." I cleared my throat and shouted, "I am in love with Teddy Elmsworth." My nervous laughter peppered the air, feeling invigorated and silly at the same time.

Teddy's face brightened as he placed his hand over his heart. "Say it again so I know it's real."

"I love you, Teddy. I always have and if you let me, I always will."

Heat rose in my stomach as he moved closer to me. Every cell in my body craved his touch. As he leaned in, my heart stole a few extra beats. The smell of his familiar scent like a dinner bell calling me home. Parting my lips in anticipation, I sighed as he washed over me. The warmth of his body acting like a cocoon.

My body tingled as he pulled me in, pressing the weight of his solid frame against mine. His kisses were urgent, as if he was making up for lost time. My knees threatened to surrender.

Grabbing hold of his jacket, I tried to pull him closer still. The cool night air whipped around us but the shiver that crawled up my back wasn't from the brisk breeze; it was all because of Teddy's touch. He pulled away, far too soon for my liking, placing one last soft kiss on my lips.

"We should get back to your guests," he said.

Fuck them guests, I thought.

Pouting, I had to agree. "To be continued?"

"Definitely."

With my hand securely in his, Teddy led me back to the party. I stood corrected. This was without a doubt the best night of my life.

EPILOGUE

I straightened Teddy's bow tie, his hands resting on my knee. "Very dapper, Mr. President."

"Thanks, Ms. Bennett, you don't look too shabby yourself."

"I look amazing." I ran my hand over the bodice of my yellow evening gown.

As he leaned in for a kiss, I pressed my finger to his thick lips. "We're almost there and I can't let you mess up my makeup."

"I just want one little kiss."

"Hmm, with you one little kiss ends with my dress around my waist and my lipstick smeared across my face."

He backed down, settling for a kiss on my cheek. "After this event is over, I am going to devour you."

"I'm counting on it," I teased, licking the side of his mouth with my tongue.

Since the party for Bennett Communication, we'd made our relationship public. The President and his girlfriend were splashed on the cover of every magazine and a daily hot topic on the news shows. I feared that being romantically connected to the President would ruin my career and it had actually done the opposite. Clients came to meet the woman in the headlines but at the end of our consultation, they were swiping their black cards or writing a check. What can I say, I'm my father's daughter and I knew how to hustle.

Tonight, we were headed to the White House Correspondents Dinner, a high-profile event with journalists, celebrities, and political power players. This was our first official appearance as a couple. I'd be lying if I said I wasn't nervous, but having Teddy by my side eased my nerves because I knew we were in this thing together.

"Have you given any more thought to us moving in together?" Teddy asked.

"You make it sound so simple, like we'll just rent a U-Haul and pull right up to the South portico."

"It can be that simple." Teddy was the eternal optimist of this relationship.

"The American people do not want to see their President shacked up. They want the dream."

His eyes twinkled as he leaned in, pressing his forehead to mine. "Then we can do that too."

"Please tell me that is not your idea of a proposal?" Backing up, I narrowed my lashes.

"I'm sick of bouncing from my place to yours each night. I want a place we can share. I wanna wake up to this beautiful face every morning. Fuck what people think, shouldn't this be about what we want? Unless you don't want it?"

"Of course, I do more than anything. But I don't want to cast your administration in a bad light."

"You quit months ago, remember. So, stop talking like my Press Secretary and start talking like my girlfriend."

My fingertips skimmed over his strong jawline. "I adore you."

"I like where this is headed."

Teddy was right. We agreed we were done caring about what others thought, and I'd promised that when it came to us and our relationship I wouldn't listen to outside influences. When I stopped to think about it, by living together we would save the taxpayers money because Teddy wouldn't have to make the fifteen-minute trip to my place every other night. And I'm sure my neighbors would be relieved to be rid of me and the hordes of reporters staked out in front of my building twenty-four-seven. But more importantly, I wanted to stop living out of my gym bag and just be with the man I was so madly in love with.

"I have some conditions."

"Shoot."

"We need to redecorate the residence."

"What, you don't like the plaid curtains and floral couches?"

"No, I do not. And if it's gonna be our space, I want it to feel like home and a place you look forward to resting your head after a long day in the West Wing."

"You're my home. So, if you're there I'm straight. But, I don't disagree that it's outdated. So yes, we can hire an interior designer. What else?"

"I'm not the First Lady." I pointed a finger at him.

"You are to me." His hand found the slit in my dress and was creeping up my thigh.

"That's fine. For you I'll be whatever you need. But I'm not planning state dinners or visiting schools."

Bennett Communication was up and running and my professional attention needed to be directed there.

"Understood. We can revisit that after the wedding."

A girlish giggle filled the cabin of the car. "We're not even engaged."

"If you think I'm not gonna put a ring on your finger before this year's over, you haven't been paying attention to just how much I love you."

I'd been promised forever by men who never intended on spending forever with me. But when Teddy made plans for our future or declared his love and desire to grow old with me, I believed it. Because I trusted him with my whole heart. I couldn't believe I was even saying stuff like that, but it was true.

Planting a soft kiss to his lips, I whispered, "I love you too."

As The Beast pulled up to the venue, I reached for Teddy's hand and he gave mine a soft squeeze. Exiting the car, the screams from the reporters and paparazzi all trying to get our attention were deafening. The flashing lights blinding my view, I relied on Teddy to lead the way.

We stopped at a gaggle of reporters each yelling louder than the other in hopes they'd be called on. "Mr. President, is this date night for you?"

"Every night is date night when I'm with Clover."

Teddy's eyes met mine, sending my heart racing, my blood pumping, and causing my insides to melt all gooey and warm like a chocolate chip cookie.

"Ms. Bennett," a reporter who looked like he should still be in high school called. "I'm sure many women want to know what it's like being the President's girlfriend. Can you offer any insight?"

"Honestly, I don't even think of it in those terms. He's just Teddy to me."

Teddy chimed in. "What you should be asking is what's it like to date public relations guru Clover Bennet. Short answer, I spend a lot of time pinching myself to make sure I'm not dreaming."

The flashing cameras all around us were most definitely capturing me looking up at Teddy with heart eyes, but I couldn't help it. I loved this man and the way he loved me, and if that meant I had to give up some of my privacy to be with him, so be it. I was all in, having pushed every last chip to the center of the table. This time I was betting on our love, and I was feeling lucky.

THANK YOU. LET'S CONNECT.

Thank you so much for reading Figure of Speech. If you liked the book, please help a sister out and leave a review or tell a friend. Your feedback is important to me and will help other readers decide whether to read my book too.

Feel free to connect with me virtually. I would love to engage with you.

instagram.com/authorkashathompson

twitter.com/thomkat29

facebook.com/authorkathompson

ALSO BY KASHA THOMPSON

WORKING THROUGH IT

Makayla and Travis are still in love ...

they just haven't figured it out yet.

When Makayla and Travis end up unlikely coworkers tempers flare and sparks reignite. Ex-lovers now enemies must attend to old wounds and revisit feelings both claimed died with the end of their relationship years ago. The two agree the past should remain in the past, but the possibility of a second chance could change everything.

www.ingramcontent.com/pod-product-compliance
Lightning Source LLC
Chambersburg PA
CBHW061218310726
48971CB00007B/1864